THE SISTERS NEXT DOOR

L.H. STACEY

Boldwood

First published in Great Britain in 2021 by Boldwood Books Ltd.

This paperback edition first published in 2022.

1

Copyright © L.H. Stacey, 2021

Cover Design by Aaron Munday

Cover Photography: Shutterstock

The moral right of L.H. Stacey to be identified as the author of this work has been asserted in accordance with the Copyright, Designs and Patents Act 1988.

All rights reserved. No part of this book may be reproduced in any form or by any electronic or mechanical means, including information storage and retrieval systems, without written permission from the author, except for the use of brief quotations in a book review.

This book is a work of fiction and, except in the case of historical fact, any resemblance to actual persons, living or dead, is purely coincidental.

Every effort has been made to obtain the necessary permissions with reference to copyright material, both illustrative and quoted. We apologise for any omissions in this respect and will be pleased to make the appropriate acknowledgements in any future edition.

A CIP catalogue record for this book is available from the British Library.

Paperback ISBN: 978-1-80415-268-3

Ebook ISBN: 978-1-80162-573-9

Kindle ISBN: 978-1-80162-574-6

Audio CD ISBN: 978-1-80162-581-4

Digital audio download ISBN: 978-1-80162-572-2

Large Print ISBN: 978-1-80162-576-0

Boldwood Books Ltd.

23 Bowerdean Street, London, SW6 3TN

www.boldwoodbooks.com

This novel was written during the coronavirus pandemic of 2020.
It was a time of great uncertainty, a time when none of us knew where our future would take us, or even if we had one. And even though I chose not to include the virus in this story, this book is for every key worker who fought so hard to keep our country going and for those who put themselves at risk for the sake of others!
From the bottom of my heart, I'd like to thank each and every one of you x

1

Swinging her car onto the single-track lane, Molly cringed as the suspension gave an instant groan of displeasure, and immediately she wished she'd put more items into the furniture van, rather than filling her trusty old Astra Estate up to the gunnels. Its load was now far too heavy for the car, especially on a potholed lane like this one.

Narrowing her tear-filled eyes, she tried to focus. The darkness was surrounding them quickly, casting long, eerie shadows, and she found herself slowing the vehicle, looking up at the cliffs that towered vertically to one side of the car and felt herself almost cowering away with a fear she couldn't understand as she took in their vast and impeding height. The sight was made even more intimidating by randomly planted trees. Most were old and gnarly, with long overhanging branches, all of which reached out to resemble long, spindly arms that seemed to be grabbing at the car.

To the other side of the lane, the view couldn't have been more different, and Molly gasped, in awe of the vast and rugged North Yorkshire coastline. The long, sweeping beach and the pretty little fishing town of Filey. Her view only slightly obstructed by two small properties, each balanced precariously on the cliff top, with just enough space between the buildings and the cliff edge to save them from falling into the sea. It was a thought that made her shudder; the reality of living in such a remote place had suddenly become real and she blew out a long, slow breath while carefully manoeuvring her car along the lane, through the rainwater that had collected and pooled outward from the edge of the road, and warily she tried her best to avoid the grass verge that had already turned into a furrowed and dangerous quagmire.

Molly slowed the car, leaned forward, sighed. She knew she had to stay calm, had to believe that moving here, to this house, was the right thing to do, and while taking deep, measured breaths, she switched off her car's engine, took a moment to gaze at the view, mesmerised by the way the waves dramatically increased in size. Each one rolling forward, bigger and stronger than the one before. Each commanding its place in the sea, before finally throwing itself violently towards the shore, in one final explosive gesture.

Opening the car window, Molly took in a deep breath of fresh salty sea air, her eyes constantly on the coastline, where clouds scuttled moodily across a sky that was getting darker by the minute. A rumble of thunder echoed somewhere in the distance, a sound that left her with no doubt that an impending storm was heading their way and she wondered how long it would be before the rain came down and, when it did, how torrential it would be. Keeping one eye on the rear-view mirror, she hoped that the removal van would miraculously appear. Yet quickly she realised that getting a van of that size along this lane, during a storm, could prove to be a challenge.

'Hello. Earth to Molly.' Her teenage sister, Beth, waved a hand up and down in front of her face. 'Please tell me that isn't it?' She rolled her eyes and pointed to one of the two cliff top houses. Both were unkempt, but one was dramatically worse than the other. 'I am not living there. Not a chance.' Rummaging in her bag, she dragged her phone from its depths and slumped back in her seat to stare aimlessly at its screen.

Molly bit down on her lip. Hesitated. Picked up a clear plastic folder the solicitor had given her. 'No, this one's ours.' She pointed to the picture. 'From what I remember, it's just a bit further along the lane, round the corner. You'll see it in a minute.' Dropping the folder in the footwell, she waved a hand at the sea. 'I was just taking a moment to look at the bay. That'll be the view we get from the house, it's beautiful, isn't it?'

Beth tutted, curled her lip in disgust, flicked her long, copper hair away from her face, kicked off her shoes and lifted her bare feet to rest against the glove box. 'I suppose so, if you like that sort of thing. Personally I'd rather go back to Dan's. I liked it there. Dan was nice.'

'We couldn't stay at Dan's forever, and...' Molly sucked in her breath. 'Well, it was getting awkward. Wasn't it?' she said through gritted teeth. 'Since me and Dan split up, I've found it... difficult. So, it was time to move on, time to come here and since we had to give Mum's house back, we had nowhere else to go. You do know that, don't you?' Looking down and into the passenger footwell, she focused on her handbag, thought about the letter within, feared for what it meant, what repercussions it would bring and wished for life to be different.

'Right,' Beth spat back. 'So, I'm supposed to be grateful that we inherited a house that stands on the edge of a bloody cliff, am I? Well, sorry if I'm not overjoyed, Molly. But I didn't want to move, not again, and what's more, we shouldn't have had to inherit anything. Our mum, she should be here, and coming here doesn't feel right. Not without her.'

Molly glanced at her sister, felt her pain. 'Hun, we...' She caught her breath, didn't know what to say. 'We couldn't stay at Dan's. When I asked if we could move in, he wasn't as overjoyed as you might think, looked as though he'd been offered a glass of arsenic. And I thought he'd be okay, eventually. But he started acting all cagey...' She carefully thought about her words. 'I think this house, our new home, came through at just the right time.'

'He was only acting "cagey", as you put it, because he wanted you back, he still wants you back.' Beth gave her hopeful eyes. 'He loves us, Moll, I just know he does.'

Molly could feel her sister's heartbreak, she loved Dan like a brother, and it was more than obvious that she felt like the middle sibling of two others. Two others who had quarrelled, and she was doing everything she could in the hope that everyone would shake hands and make friends. Sighing, Molly rolled her eyes. She needed to find a way to pacify her sister, to get her on side, without telling her the truth. Without destroying yet another part of her life. 'Besides, you're fifteen now. You're growing far too fast and that terrifies me. You really need your own space, your own bedroom, not one you share with an older sister.' She smiled, dropped a hand affectionately on Beth's leg. 'And, not to put too fine a point on it... I want my own space, too.'

Beth squirmed in her seat. Wriggled her toes and stared at her feet, which were still balanced on the glove box. 'Did Mum ever sleep here, at the house?'

Molly laid a hand over Beth's. 'Sure she did. She spent time here with Michael, they loved each other. She was finally happy, Beth. She was planning a life. That had to count for something, didn't it?' Closing her eyes, she nodded, thought of how their mother had tried to convince them to move here with her, how they'd both selfishly resisted. Neither had wanted to move, neither had wanted the long commute to school or to work. Neither had wanted yet another father figure in their lives.

Molly might have felt differently if she'd known her own father, but she hadn't. 'He was a childhood sweetheart, a boy I met at school,' her mother had always told her. 'He was a kind young man, with beautiful eyes, that looked just like yours, but he went away to university, we lost touch. He didn't even know you existed and the last I heard – he'd died. It was a tragic, meaningless accident.' She'd always looked wistful when she spoke, as though trying to keep the picture of his face permanently preserved in her mind, making Molly wonder what would have happened if he'd lived and what kind of life they'd have had if he were around and came over to visit.

'Michael dying changed everything for all of us, didn't it?' Beth put her phone down, flicked at the zip on her school bag.

'It did. Our mum hadn't known him long, seemed very happy and when he died, it was as though all her dreams died with him, all her plans.' Blinking away the tears, Molly smiled awkwardly. 'When the solicitor rang Mum and told her that Michael had left her the house, she started planning again. Started looking forward. Making a new life, a new life she wanted us to be a part of, and all of us living here together was what she dreamed of.'

Beth held both hands out, palms up. 'And instead of starting again, she went and got herself murdered, didn't she? And then, somehow – we got to move here without her.' Arrogantly, she held two thumbs up in the air and spat the words. 'So yay, how lucky are we?'

Molly once again took her younger sister's hand. 'Beth, don't be like that. Please, give it a chance.' With a half-smile, she closed her eyes for just a moment, tried to think of the right thing to say, felt totally inept. 'Did I ever tell you that Mum used to bring me here?' She tried to think of a nice story, pointed to the beach. 'We'd spend hours and hours making the biggest sandcastles, with really deep moats. I'd fill them with sea water using my little pink plastic bucket.' She took a deep breath, blew it out and made an attempt to stop the tears from flowing. 'I'd always have a flag, one of those plastic ones that'd been glued onto a long straw and...' she wiped a tear from her eye, 'I used to make Mum stand up and salute the waves, while we placed the flag on the top of the castle.'

Beth looked thoughtful; took her feet down from the glove box, sat forward and stared at the beach. 'Huh, I guess you didn't think too much about the environment back then, did you? You do realise that all those bloody straws will still be out there, don't you? They'll be floating around, killing the wildlife for up to two hundred years.' Her hand suddenly became animated and made a wave like motion in the air. 'They're probably still out there, causing chaos,' she said, accusingly.

Molly went silent. A surge of guilt swept through her conscience. 'You're absolutely right,' she agreed, 'we didn't know any better then.' She shook her head, knew it had been wrong, but couldn't help but wish for the simplicity her life used to have. A time when she'd been a child, young, naïve, happy and her only responsibility had been getting up and going to school.

Leaning back in her seat, Beth flicked the screen of her phone, lifted it to the window and clicked to take a photo. 'You once told me she'd brought me to this beach. Is it true?' she asked wistfully, her eyes never leaving the beach, or the dog that ran playfully in and out of the water.

'Sure it is.' Molly laughed, rolled her eyes to the ever-darkening sky. 'The last time we came, you were a very excited toddler. Around two years old. I'd have been ten or eleven and I remember you escaping Mum's clutches. You set off running across the sand and straight into the sea, where a massive wave tossed you up in the air – and you landed back on the beach with a thud. Mum must have thought you were about to drown because she screamed so loud that my ears literally rang for hours.' Molly furrowed her brow, while trying to remember. Suddenly she saw Charlie's face, the fury he'd shown that day.

'What is it?' Beth questioned.

'I just remembered your dad, Charlie, he went mental with a man who saw you running away from Mum. You were running towards the steps, screaming and he jumped up, scooped you up from the beach and well... I thought Charlie was going to kill him. I'd never seen him so cross, scared me to death.' Her words trailed off as the memory faded.

Huffing, Beth threw her arms in the air. 'So, let me get this straight. We've ended up inheriting a house. That's perched on a cliff. That overlooks the very same beach where I was almost killed and then abducted as a two-year-old.' She shuffled in her seat, tutted. 'Well, thanks...' She paused, looked skyward.

A single tear dropped down Molly's face. The months had taken their toll. Overnight their lives had turned into an unpredictable rollercoaster, one that wouldn't or couldn't stop. And now, as well as everything else, they were moving into a house they didn't want. In a town that was miles away from the life they'd known and taking the first daunting steps into an existence they couldn't possibly understand. For the first time in their lives, they'd be living alone. Just the two of them. Something that Molly had both looked forward to and dreaded in equal measure. And now they were here, she took a deep breath, stared at the sea, at the beach, wished for answers, for the knowledge that whatever happened, she'd be able to keep Beth safe, keep them both safe, and she shook her head, knowing full well that she couldn't promise either.

2

'Seriously, Moll, have you seen the length of this lane?' Beth tutted as Molly turned the car. 'There isn't even a proper path and I can't believe we have to travel up and down it twice a day... just to get me to school and back.'

Molly wrinkled her nose, shook her head and paused, once again her eyes went to her handbag. To the letter. Was it wrong to keep the truth to herself? '*We...*' she emphasised the word before continuing, 'we don't have to drive along here at all. But you, young lady, you do have to walk,' she said apologetically.

'School bus pulls up at the top of the road, right over there.' She pointed to a distant car park that stood along the roadside. 'Eight fifteen, every morning,' she said, keeping up the pretence, but deep down she knew that on most days she'd be doing the driving, the protecting, the making sure Beth got on and off the bus safely.

Blinking repeatedly, Beth huffed in frustration. 'Oh great, that's just great,' she said, jutting out her chin in protest. 'And I'm guessing that you'll provide the bloody welly boots too, will you?' Her hand went through her long hair, flicked it back from her pale freckled face. 'I mean, look, just look...' She pointed her finger around in a wand-like fashion at the lane. 'There's, you know... there's mud. It's everywhere. Moll, my shoes will be ruined...' She threw herself backwards in the seat and gave off a long audible sigh, shuffled impatiently. 'And the nearest shop, it's just got to be a million miles away and what about my friends? How am I going to get to see them? Dan drove me back and forth. I hardly ever had to catch a bus.'

Molly felt her patience wane. 'You need to learn to look after yourself. Dan isn't your taxi service. And neither am I.' She paused, placed her hands back on the steering wheel and squeezed the leather. 'If I'm going to work effectively, I need my sleep. You should try being a dentist, it isn't easy. Some days I just want to go home and lock the door. I don't always want to start getting the car out again and running you all over. Besides, we're miles away from York now and it certainly wouldn't be a quick trip to pop you back and forth to friends.' She thought of the days following her mother's death, all the patients she'd smiled at, when in reality all she'd wanted to do was throw the towel in, stay home and hide under the duvet, not go out for days, but knew that she couldn't.

'Dan liked giving me a lift, he looked out for me,' Beth insisted.

'Well, if I know Dan, he'll be absolutely delighted to get both his car and his house back.' Pressing her lips tightly together, Molly thought of Dan, of how much she'd previously loved him and how, over the last couple of weeks, she'd felt more and more anxious in his company, feeling an immeasurable sense of relief when she'd been allowed to take possession of the house.

Beth threw her arms up in the air. 'I give up and I want to go back to York. I liked living in the city, Moll. My friends are there... and here... I don't know anyone.'

Taking in a deep, measured breath, Molly noted that her sister would have been more suited to attending a drama school, rather than the local comprehensive. 'You'll soon get to know people and the nearest shop is in the next village. It's only a two-minute drive away. And as for the house, we have no control over where it is, so please suck it up, 'cause without it, we're homeless. Mum left it to us and...' Molly added wistfully, 'it's a new start, Beth, we should be grateful.'

'You're ruining my life,' Beth suddenly growled. Her bottom lip wobbled and her hands went up to her head, where she pressed them tightly to each side of her brow.

'I know,' Molly replied thoughtfully. She didn't know how to explain. Couldn't grasp that she was suddenly a parent, wanted to tell her sister the truth, but couldn't. 'But I promised her, Beth. I went to her grave and I promised our mum that I'd look after you, that I'd bring you to live in this house.' She pulled the file out of the footwell, laid it on her knee, with the picture of the house looking back at them. 'It's exactly what she'd have wanted.' Placing a hand on Beth's shoulder, Molly stared directly into her eyes, nodded. 'Don't you see? This house, it's the perfect sanctuary, it could be our final move, a place we'll never have to leave.' She smiled, arched a brow. 'It's our chance to stop running, Beth. Our mum, I think she felt safe here and what's more, I'm absolutely sure she'd have known how far it was to the bus stop, and how annoyed you'd get about that lane.' She gave her sister a slight smile, winked.

Putting the car into gear, Molly carefully squeezed the pedal, manoeuvred slowly along the track. It was getting darker and more eerie by the minute and while struggling to avoid the furrows that defined each side of the lane, she turned the corner, spotted the house, hit the brakes at the last minute and, with a jolt and a thud, she watched as the once white picket fence begin to wobble and fall.

Flinging the car door open in disgust, Beth pushed her shoes back onto her feet and stepped into the breeze that immediately whipped her hair up and around in all directions, making her grab at it with one hand, while slamming the door with the other.

Watching her sister go, Molly followed, took a quick look at the damaged fence and shrugged. 'It was probably about to fall down anyway,' she whispered to herself, then made her way along the cobbled path and towards the front door.

As a child, she'd often sat on the beach below, looked up and commented on how beautiful this very house had looked. But now, as she got closer, she noticed the disrepair, the overwhelming look of being worn and unloved. Even the climbing plant that used to grow around the front door had long since withered and died, along with the many shrubs and plants that were fighting a losing battle among the brambles and bindweed.

'Bloody hell, Moll, are we seriously going to live in that? It looks even more of a dump than I imagined,' Beth grunted as she walked back to the car, peered cautiously over the top, one hand taking pictures with her phone, the other still holding tightly to her hair.

'Hey, language,' Molly chided, gave Beth a look, adjusted her sunglasses that sat neatly on top of her head to create the perfect headband. 'Okay, so I admit it. It's not quite as beautiful as it used to be, or even as good as it looked on the solicitor's paperwork. But with a bit of work, it'll be fine. You'll see,' she said hopefully. She pushed her shoulder firmly against the front door and yelped. 'Bloody hell, that's stiff.'

'Hey, language...' Beth threw back, laughed, then froze. 'Moll. What was that noise?'

'What noise?'

'Shhh.' Beth stood on her tiptoes, peered over the car in meerkat fashion. 'I heard something.' Stepping over the fallen fence, Beth walked along the path, towards where Molly stood, tiptoed around the house, disappeared out of sight. 'I'll be right back.'

'Beth. Please.' Feeling her anxiety rise, Molly stepped to one side, anxiously waited for Beth to come back, fought the urge to follow her. 'Beth... Beth... come and help me... I need you to help me open... this... door.' Molly gave intermittent shoves with her shoulder, tipped her head from side to side, constantly looking for Beth. 'There's something... stopping it.'

Reappearing, Beth walked back to the car, shook her head. 'Bloody hell, Moll. It's dark round there. I bet it gets real spooky at night, it'd be so easy to sleepwalk and fall off the cliff.' Using the car as a barrier, she slid down next to the wheel, crouched near the floor, let go of her hair, allowed her attention to return to her phone and frantically tapped at the screen, before glaring in Molly's direction. 'Moll, please tell me we have some bloody Wi-Fi.'

'Nope. No Wi-Fi. Sorry. Be a few days till it's sorted.' Standing back from the door, Molly crossed her arms and stared at her sister. 'Are you going to help me?' Molly almost sang the words, couldn't wait to get in, felt her whole body buzz with an excitement that was interspersed with trepidation. She didn't know whether to laugh or cry, whether it would be their best move ever, or their worst nightmare. All she really did know was that there was no time for indecision, and for now, they were both safe and together.

Giving the door another push, Molly looked over her shoulder at Beth. She'd walked away from the car and now stood staring up at the roof, at the old dormer windows.

'Is that... is that where he fell from?' Beth asked, pointing upwards, her face contorted with confusion. 'Can you imagine him lying there, screaming?'

Molly turned to where her sister pointed, swallowed hard and wished wholeheartedly that their mum had never revealed how Michael had died. 'It was raining. He slipped.' She spoke softly, but subconsciously she could hear his cries and wondered how long he'd lain on the patio at the back of the house before he was found.

Turning, she looked down the lane. She could easily see the house next door, but the other was a little further around the corner, just one edge of it remained in view. Carefully she tried to judge the distance, wondered if either were inhabited, if there would have been anyone home and even if they had been, whether they'd have heard his screams. She realised that with the cliff on one side and the sea on the other, it was more than doubtful. He'd been surrounded by the most perfect sound buffers, which could easily drown out any amount of noise and swallow it whole. 'It was just an accident, Beth, nothing more.'

'Well, the thought of him lying there for days, waiting to be found. It gives me the creeps.' Beth spoke with a hysterical squeal. 'And think of all the blood. There had to be some, didn't there?'

'Beth, you're freaking yourself out. In fact,' Molly waved a hand around in the air, 'enough of the dramatics. You're freaking me out.'

'Hey. You think I'm being dramatic? It's you that wants to live here. Not me. I wanted to stay at Dan's.' She kicked at the car wheel in a temper, pushed out her bottom lip, stared at her feet, then bent down and, with a tissue, polished the dirt from her shoe.

Turning her attention back to the door, Molly once again rammed it with her shoulder, until just a small gap appeared. Convinced it would move no further, she knelt down and nervously pushed her hand through the space between the door and the jamb. 'There has to be something trapped behind it.' She held her breath and closed her eyes, whilst almost lying on her side with one hand tentatively grasping at the space behind the door. 'I can feel...' She opened her eyes and looked up at the threatening sky. 'Oh, I think it's a carpet, I just need to...' Squeezing her arm further inside, she managed to wriggle her fingers until eventually she felt the door open to reveal what looked like a year's worth of post.

'Beth, we're in. Come look.' Scrambling to her feet, Molly stepped inside to see that one large piece of carpet had been purposely wedged behind the door. The rest of the carpet had been haphazardly hacked at and now just small, ragged remnants remained, still attached to the gripper.

Crouching down, she tentatively began to poke at the envelopes and pushed the paper mountain out of her way. 'Oh wow, so much post, so much crap and, oh boy, so many dead spiders.' She made a mental note to bring the vacuum in from the car and pulled at what was left of the carpet in an attempt to flatten it back down.

Pushing up the sleeves of her jumper, she stood up, walked along the hallway and, without a thought, began pulling at nails that were still randomly scattered across the wall. 'Looks like all these walls were full of pictures. Looks like Michael's niece emptied the place. Even went as far as to rip up the bloody carpet and take it with her.' Molly looked over her shoulder, caught sight of a small black and white picture that still hung on the wall. It was yellow with age, hung all by itself, forgotten, unwanted and half hidden by the door.

Lifting her hand, she ran a finger across the glass, where in the picture a young man was standing by the front door, smiling back at her. A child's bike lay at his feet. It was a picture full of sunshine, of family, and for a moment, Molly just stared at it, feeling as though she'd seen it before. 'Michael, was this you?' she whispered. Then she stepped back, regretting she hadn't seen him more often, got to know him better, liked him more. 'You were a good-looking guy. I'll give you that.' She paused, her fingertips hovering over the white picket fence, the same one she'd just destroyed.

Taking the picture down from its hook, Molly placed it on the windowsill. She tipped her head from side to side, suddenly felt sad and wondered if it might have been left behind on purpose. 'Your niece must have been really pissed that you didn't leave her the house, mustn't she?' Molly sighed, heard the sound of the rolling thunder, of incoming gales, then Beth's voice, anxious and annoyed.

'Yeah, yeah, we're here. It's okay. It's a million miles from civilisation and there isn't a shop anywhere in sight. And the wind up here, it bites. I might need to get a new coat 'cause I'm freezing my bloody bits off.'

Conscious that the light outside was fading fast, Molly turned, flicked on a light switch, and then another. 'Damn, there's no electric.' Moving up and down the hallway, she flicked at switches before turning back to the door. 'Beth, you need to come in here, the lights are out, we're gonna have to find the fuse box.'

Allowing her hand to graze the staircase, she studied the carved oak and what looked to be a narrow cupboard door that was almost hidden in its frame. Pressing her fingers firmly against the wooden panel, she felt the door click, opened it to reveal a small but empty space, a place where coat hooks lined the back wall and a full-length mirror was fixed to the back of the door. The sight of her reflection made her scowl.

'Urgh...!' Molly lifted a hand, pulled her sunglasses off her head, flicked her fingers through her shoulder-length hair, and studied the shape of her body. The weight loss didn't suit her, nor did the dark furrowed lines below her eyes. Startled by a cobweb brushing against her face, she jumped backwards. 'Urgh, and you need to bugger off, too. Go find somewhere else to live.'

'Oh, my God. What the hell did I do this time?' Beth wailed, and Molly turned to see her sister standing in the doorway, her eyes brimming with unshed tears.

'I wasn't talking to you, silly. I was talking to the damn spiders. They all need to go,' she said decisively.

'That was Gran on the phone.' Beth waved the phone round in the air. 'Says she hasn't seen us in forever, made me feel really guilty. I kind of promised we'd go over.' She raised both eyebrows, gave a half smile. 'Tomorrow, I said we'd go tomorrow.'

Molly caught the smug way Beth crossed her arms and chose to ignore the comment. 'I'm gonna bring the vacuum out of the car, get rid of those little suckers.' She looked at the place where all the spiders in North Yorkshire seemed to have taken up residence. 'Oh, and if we can't find the fuse box, we really need to hope we packed some candles. Otherwise, it could get really dark up here tonight.' She copied Beth's earlier mannerism, gave her a cheery thumbs up. 'We might even have to hide under the duvet with torches, pretend we're camping.'

Beth stepped back, placed a fist firmly on each hip. 'I don't wanna sleep here. Not while there's over a hundred spiders running round the house.' Inquisitively, she looked down the hallway, a slight smile of approval crossing her lips. 'So, I vote that we either go to the Travelodge or back to Dan's.'

'How about we do neither?' Molly chipped in.

'Okay, how about we order a pizza and camp in front of the fire, but only if there's electric and only if we get to suck the spiders up with the vacuum,' Beth tried to negotiate, looked hopefully towards the living room. 'There is a proper fire, right?'

Molly ran her fingers along the dado rail that circumnavigated the hall and cringed at the line in the dust she created. 'If there is, and provided we can find something to light it with, we'll make a fire.' She paused. 'As for the pizza, I doubt the delivery guy would find us. You said it yourself, we're "a million miles from civilisation".' She mimicked her sister's voice, gave her a sarcastic smile.

Sniffing at the air, Beth wrinkled her nose. 'What's that funny smell?'

'How should I know? House hasn't been lived in for ages.' Molly raised her eyebrows, flicked her hair to one side. 'I'm guessing the niece came and went, took what she wanted, including the damn carpet, maybe we got lucky and she cleaned a little on her way out.' Molly tapped her foot on the bare floorboards, while trying to mentally calculate how much money she had left in the bank, when her next payday would be and whether or not she'd have enough left to buy a carpet.

Pressing her hand against the kitchen door, Beth pushed it open. 'Jesus, Moll, have you been in here? Kitchen's sick, isn't it?'

Hearing the change in her sister's voice, Molly followed. The doorway had opened to reveal a kitchen that was almost empty, but perfectly clean. The smell of bleach hit the back of her throat, and oddly a bucket of steaming hot water stood to one side of the room, a mop leaning against the wall beside it.

To disperse the smell, Molly leaned over the sink, unlatched the window and pushed it open. The action caused a breeze to rush through the kitchen. A door slammed. The house shook, and Molly nervously spun around on full alert. 'What the...?' Instinctively she pushed Beth behind her. 'What was that?' With a pounding heart, she hurriedly grabbed at the mop, made her way to the utility door, stood perfectly still. Holding her breath, she allowed her hand to hover cautiously over the door handle. With her eyes fixed, she waited for the handle to move.

'Moll. Please don't.' Beth took a step backwards, the colour slowly draining from her face. 'Earlier, when I was by the car, I told you I heard something and you didn't believe me, did you?'

A shared glance was followed by a look of fear as flashing images of their mum flew through her mind... her unknown visitor... her subsequent murder... the pain they'd gone through. Trying to swallow, Molly's mouth went dry. Her breathing slowed. The taste of bile rose dramatically in her throat.

'Beth, it's probably nothing, probably just the niece, she'll have been cleaning, saying goodbye to the place. Now. You stay there and...' She tried to sound convincing, felt her fingers tightly wind around the mop, as she looked around for a better weapon. Finally, she took a deliberate breath, pressed the door handle down and jumped backwards as a utility room was revealed. The back door was wide open.

Swallowing hard, she watched it creak eerily back and forth in the breeze, a set of keys still hanging in the lock, their owners nowhere to be seen.

3

Recoiling, I quickly move into the shadows and hide in the undergrowth as I hear your voice yell out, your footsteps approach, and I hold my breath as a surge of euphoria builds in my chest. Holding my hand over my mouth, I try to hold back the laughter and fail miserably, as what started as a mere snigger bubbles up, until it erupts into an overwhelming, unrestrained laugh and I suddenly feel thankful for the storm, for the waves, the sound of which easily drowns out any noise I might make, makes it easier to move around, to get closer to where you both stand.

Half of me is fearful I'll be seen, the other half wants you to notice me, and I try to think up a plan, a reason for being here and a million stories flash through my mind. Fidgeting with anticipation, my feet step back and forth in the mud and I wonder which story you'll believe, and I quickly realise that the idea of stepping out of the shadows, revealing myself, excites my mind, especially when I know what I've just done.

Looking towards the shed, I see the rolled-up carpet. It's partially hidden down one side, a few logs and an old sheet of corrugated metal are balanced on top, along with an old spade I found in the shed. The irony of the find doesn't go unnoticed, and I quickly realise how useful a tool it will be.

Feeling a sense of power that I never want to lose, I continue to press my hand tightly over my mouth, and smirk as I see a pair of pale bare feet poking out from within the rolls of carpet. They're the same feet that tried to kick me, the same feet that went limp as I squeezed the last breath from her body and I'd smiled, felt as though I were holding onto a balloon that had suddenly begun to deflate itself – right before my eyes.

Then, without warning, my mood drops, anger takes the place of euphoria and I realise that it was an unnecessary death. She shouldn't have been here. Shouldn't have interfered. Today of all days I should have been here alone and allowed to search, to look for what I know he hid. But she wouldn't let it go, wouldn't give me the keys, didn't believe I'd been sent to collect them and for that, she paid the price. I couldn't risk her speaking to you, telling you I'd been here. And now, now I have the problem of hiding her body, of disposing of her, and I roll my eyes skyward to watch the rain and I wonder if I should have left her in there. In the house. Took my time to search and then, instead of cleaning the kitchen to cover my tracks, I should have burned the house down, with her in it.

Aching for the euphoria to return, I pull out my phone, wait for your back to be turned, begin taking photographs, one after the other and feel the power I have over you, over your life, your future. It's a power I can't live without, like a wild animal searching for food, for its next meal, to ensure its survival. Whereas you, you don't even realise that you need to survive. Not yet. You don't know how close you are to losing it all, to taking your final breath. It's something I never wanted to do, not to you. I was hoping you'd disappear, while you had the chance, you could have taken Beth with you, started a new life. But instead, you came to this house, to the one place I never wanted you to be and in doing so, you sealed your own fate, because now... I have no choice but to kill you both.

4

'Thanks for that, Beth.'

'Thanks for what?' Beth stood behind her, hands placed smugly on her hips. She made every attempt to look past her, around her and into the garden.

'For letting me practically break down the front door, when the back door was open.'

Huffing, Beth spun, stamped through the kitchen, towards the hall. 'What, do you think, I'm bloody psychic? How would I know the door was open?'

Trying to keep calm, Molly thought of the noise, how her sister had disappeared around the back, knew that if the door was open now, it must have been open then. She began counting to ten, her stomach twisted and she felt nervous that Michael's niece could still be around, that they might finally get to meet her. After all, they had spoken on the phone on numerous occasions. And strangely, Molly did feel inquisitive. Wanted to know what she was like. Especially after the frosty calls, where Carol had made it very clear that the house should have stayed in the family. That her father had helped Michael build it. The fact that she wasn't pleased had been quite an understatement, leaving Molly to wonder if she'd left the keys hanging on purpose. It was as though she'd had no intention of a face-to-face meeting and certainly hadn't made a point of welcoming them with open arms.

Pulling the keys from the lock, she turned them over and over in her hand, studied the ladybird keyring that was still attached. Puzzled, she decided that it looked expensive. It was something Carol might want back and nervously, Molly inched onto the doorstep, looked out, waited. The oncoming storm was getting closer, the sky full of clouds and the moon hidden from view, leaving the garden looking darker, more sinister, with darker, deeper and more foreboding shadows than she'd hoped. She found herself standing on her tiptoes and trying to look around corners, without actually leaving the safety of the house.

'Carol... are you out there?' She tossed the keys onto the worktop, cupped her hands around her mouth, shouted over thunderous waves that hit the rocks below and eventually, she took a step out. A step closer to the shed. 'Carol. It's Molly Winter, are you...' She was going to ask if she was in there, if she'd popped outside for a moment, but as the heavens opened and the rain began to fall in torrents, it was more than obvious that if Carol had been in the garden she'd have been seen running for cover.

Jumping inside the shed, Molly sheltered from the rain. She listened to the way the rain pelted against the roof and with eyes as wide as saucers, she scoured the roof, searched for holes. She kept an eye on the back door, on where Beth had previously stood. Wrapping her arms nervously around herself, she shuddered, noticed a few random logs. An old coal scuttle half full of black, oval rocks. It didn't look like the coal she'd known as a child. But she was sure it would burn and for that, she felt thankful.

'Yay... Beth, we will have a fire tonight,' she yelled, bent over to pick up the logs and then froze as she heard a loud, deafening bang, felt the shed door slam behind her. There was only a small polycarbonate window to give her some light. Pushing at the door, she felt its resistance, felt her heartbeat accelerate, her throat suddenly dry.

'Beth! Beth!' Her voice echoed back at her, the hammering of the rain on the roof enough to drown out any sound, and once again she thought of Michael, of how he'd have lain on the patio, all broken, in pain, with no one to help.

Her whole body began to tremble, her stomach faltered, threatened to rid itself of her lunch and she began taking deep yet rapid breaths. Nervously, she pushed at the door, then pushed again. Something was stopping it, something or someone had slammed it behind her, and in temper she began to kick at the door, could just about see through a small hole, where over the years the wood had disintegrated.

'Beth... seriously. I swear to God... this is no time for games.' Blinking, she held her breath, felt sure she could hear boots on gravel, tried to peer through the polycarbonate window. Gave her head a short, sharp shake. 'It's getting to you. You're finally imagining things,' she whispered to herself, thrust herself onto her feet and with a newfound energy she kicked at the door, began to hammer against it with tightly coiled fists.

'All right, all right! I'm coming,' Beth's voice shrieked, her footsteps splashed through the puddles and suddenly, the door was thrust open. 'What the hell are you doing in there?' Her eyes were wide, her face a mixture of shock and hysterics. 'What did our mum always tell you about going into strange buildings, on your own, at night?' She stood back in the rain, her hands on her hips. 'Well, come on...' She laughed. 'I've found the fuse box, lights are on and the living room, it does have a fire. So...' She looked down, spotted the scuttle. 'Great, you found some coal. I'll go make a start on the fire.' Pausing, Beth picked up the scuttle. 'Oh, and you might want to know. Removal van is here. He had to reverse the whole way down the lane, his clutch stinks like molten rubber. He's shouting about how he could have burned it out and, oh boy, he really isn't happy.'

Running for the house and locking the back door firmly behind her, Molly stood for a moment, stared at the shed. At her temporary prison. She couldn't help but wonder what had really happened out there. All she did know was that Beth was capable of anything, especially when she wanted her own way. And right now, she wanted to make sure that this house was the last place either of them wanted to be.

5

Determined to get Beth on side, Molly pulled the duvet up and under her chin, snuggled as close to her sister as she could get, gave her a loving squeeze.

'See, I told you we'd be okay, didn't I?' Since arriving, the job of moving them into the house had been exhausting, even with the help of the two grumpy removal men, who between them had moaned about every single item they'd carried in. The boxes had been too heavy, too wet, the path far too slippery, their vehicle parked much too far away and if anyone had told them how difficult the lane would be, they'd have probably had to charge even more than they already had.

And now, some six hours later, Molly and Beth were both lying in their makeshift bed. A double mattress positioned on top of a rug, in front of the fire, with their mum's two settees surrounding them like a fortress. One stood down the side of the mattress, with the other along the top, serving as an impromptu headboard, with a small space at the bottom of the temporary bed where they could crawl in or out, albeit only on their hands and knees.

'At least we got the room nice and clean.' Molly stretched, rubbed her back which still ached from the vacuuming, mopping and de-spidering. All of which had been done since the removal men had left. The mattress had been stowed in the hallway, carried in last, then carefully positioned between the two settees.

Leaning against the pillows, they both gazed longingly through the long curtainless window that during daylight would have given them the most perfect view of the entire bay. But right now, the view was distorted by the rain and hail that thrashed against the glass, along with the darkness beyond, where the faded lights of Filey intermittently poked through the thick murky sea fret, making Molly grateful for being inside. Even though the fuse box had been found, they'd turned the lights off and were lying in the firelight, with just a small number of carefully positioned candles, to give a warm and cosy ambience.

'Do you remember when we used to do this with Mum?' Beth pursed her lips, pulling at the duvet. 'It was the closest we ever got to camping, wasn't it?'

Molly slowly nodded. She remembered moving to the refuge, the times they'd all shared the same bed, because there had been no other option. It had been a quiet Sunday morning, with Molly reading a book and Beth sitting beside her at the table making a house for her dolls. It had stuck in her mind quite clearly because of the way their mum had been nervously pacing up and down, cigarette in hand, ash so long it arched toward the floor, before finally dropping off to land on the already grime covered carpet. Then, without warning, there had been an explosion of noise. Mum had screamed, ran towards them as though sheltering them from the sight of what appeared to be an army of police that had stormed through the house, all in search of Charlie.

'He'll be hiding in the loft,' their mother had yelled. 'You'll find him up there.' Her finger had pointed to the stairs, while she'd cowered beside the table, clinging to Beth.

Then, just a few minutes later, Molly remembered the emotions that had whizzed around in her mind as Charlie had been unceremoniously pushed down the stairs, out of the house and into a waiting police car where his screams and threats could be heard from a distance, even after the vehicle's doors had been slammed. She'd felt both relief and dread all at once. Relief that, for now, he was gone. But a sickening dread that, once he returned, he'd make them pay. After all, they were threats he'd spat at them so many times before. Times when moments of terror had turned into what had felt like hours of violence. The way he'd struck out, his face contorted with so much anger that his eyes had bulged, and saliva had dripped from his screaming, drunken mouth and then, just a few hours later, how he'd always begged for forgiveness, promising it would never, ever happen again. They were moments that Molly would never forget, moments that had haunted her since, times she'd thought him about to kill them all. She felt grateful that Beth had been so young, so naïve, completely oblivious.

Pulling Beth towards her, Molly dropped a kiss lightly on her sister's forehead. 'Our mum looked after us the only way she knew how.' A sob left her throat as she wondered how much Beth remembered. 'She had no choice. You do know that. Don't you?'

Beth nodded, her eyes brimming with tears too. 'The day it all happened, the day we left for the refuge.' She watched, waiting for Molly to nod before continuing. 'I didn't realise that that was it. That we'd never be going home. Not ever again.' Her voice quivered as she spoke. 'And I know you'd never really liked him, but he's my dad, and I didn't even get to say goodbye. And... then everything changed.' She paused and moved onto her side. 'I wanted to see him, but Mum said he was dangerous.'

'Beth, he was more than dangerous, and in my opinion, he was also a coward. Not many men would shoot a woman in the back. It was broad daylight, so he couldn't even try to pretend it was an accident, could he?' Molly chided, watched Beth's face, hoped she didn't ask too many questions that had no answers. Their mum had barely ever spoken of the case, of the woman, leaving Molly to assume, to try to find it on the internet. A search she'd made in vain; witness protection meant that the press had had their wings clipped and reporting had been kept to a minimum.

Turning away, Beth sniffed. 'I know what he did. I know it was horrid, that shooting someone isn't something most of us go around doing. But he was my dad and I really don't think he'd have been dangerous, not to me.'

Taking a deep breath, Molly pressed her lips tightly together, furrowed her brow. 'Do you know what, you're right. I didn't like him. My own dad died before I was born and for the first few years it was just me and Mum. Then Charlie appeared, he moved in, took over, made new rules. I saw what he did, how he was with Mum. How frightened both Mum and I were of him.' She turned, slowly breathed back out, tried to think how best to continue. 'Who knows how dangerous he really is or was and him being in prison all that time, well... whether you think he'd have hurt you or not, it didn't exactly make him father of the year, did it?'

Molly thought of the persistent phone calls. The harassment. The controlling attitude, along with his demands to see Beth and her mother's continual refusal to let him. 'He scares me, Beth. He scared our mum and I know you don't want to hear it, but she really was terrified of him. Not knowing what he'd do next. And, like it or not, I still think he had something to do with her being murdered.' Her eyes dropped to her phone. It lay on the mattress beside her, the screen lit up, the notification appeared. It was the same time and number as the night before and not one of her normal contacts. Closing her eyes, she growled internally. It was the second message she'd received. She tried to flick at the screen, felt sure Beth's dad, Charlie, was behind them and didn't want her to see.

Happy moving in day. Sleep well.

Staring at the screen. She felt her stomach plummet, her temper rise, her throat grow dryer by the second. She considered hitting the block button; her thumb hovered over the screen. In temper, she shook her head, knew she'd rather see what he was saying, what he was thinking. She had every intention of keeping him as far away from Beth as she could.

Beth sat upright and glared. 'You can't say that!' she snapped. 'You can't blame him for everything.' She emphasised the words. 'He was in prison when Mum was killed. He couldn't have been the one to hurt her. Could he?'

'Yeah, yeah, I know, the perfect alibi.' She could still see the policewoman's face, the way she'd described her mother's death as a tragedy. A burglary that had gone terribly wrong. But Molly had noticed the look of indecision on her face, her furrowed brow and the admission that things simply hadn't added up. The door hadn't been forced. All that had been missing was a watch. A Rolex. A gift that Michael had bought her. Then there had been the two untouched glasses of wine, both had been left on the worktop, the bottle of red open beside them, leaving Molly with the overwhelming wish that the visitor had taken just one sip of the wine and left their DNA behind. But they hadn't.

'I know you hate him, and I know he deserves to be in prison. But I really miss him.' Blinking repeatedly, Beth's hand brushed away the tears that were now rolling down her pale freckled face, her despair and teenage heartbreak more than obvious.

Pulling her sister towards her, Molly held her close. 'I promised Mum I'd always look after you, that I'd keep him away from you. And no matter how grown up you get, I will always do my best to keep that promise, because I don't trust him, and neither should you.' She dropped a kiss on her sister's forehead. 'Okay?'

Beth squirmed, nodded, and tried to smile. 'So, you took me to live on a cliff, miles away from anywhere?' She paused, looked thoughtful. 'Is that why you're hiding that letter, the one in your bag that says he's getting out. The one addressed to Mum. The one you didn't show me?'

Closing her eyes for a beat, Molly took in a cautious breath. Used both hands to push herself up. Tried to weigh up her emotions. Felt a surge of guilt, didn't know if it was because Beth had found the letter, or because she'd wanted to tell her herself. 'I would have told you. The removal men passed the letter to me. It had been at Mum's when they emptied the house. I'm sorry. But I didn't tell you for your own good, I don't want him near you and what's more, I didn't take you miles from anywhere. I took you to a house that our mum left to us in her will. And in the absence of having nowhere else to live, it seemed like as good a place as any.' She kept her eyes on her phone, wondered if she should admit to the text. Realised that whether she liked it or not, Charlie knew where they were.

'Moll, I want to see him.'

'Well, you can't.'

'But...'

'Beth. I'm not arguing. Mum begged me not to let you near him. Even made me promise.' She shook her head, held her sister's gaze. 'She must have said it for a reason and I can't break that promise, Beth. I just can't.' She sat calmly, waiting for an outburst. Hated the silence more. Eventually, she pointed through the window. 'Beth, we could have a good home here. We could be happy. Do you see over there? On a clear day you can see the whole of Filey.' Looking, they could see the harbour that rose up on a distant cliff before them. Small windows showed up like tiny dots of light, or stars that were trying to peek through the darkness, each one just a little more dulled than she'd have liked. 'Each of those little lights is at least one household, one person who could be looking right back at us, right now. Do you realise that?' She smiled and poked Beth in the ribs. 'So, if you think about it, there are hundreds of people, right there, right in front of you.'

Beth tutted and rolled her eyes. 'Seriously, Moll, those houses, they're at least two miles away.'

Molly squinted. 'It's not two miles away, is it?'

'If I stood on the cliff edge naked, I could guarantee that no one in Filey would see me.' Stretching forward, Beth grabbed at the cardboard box that lay abandoned on the hearth and pulled at the last piece of pizza. 'You want to share?'

Molly shook her head, smirking at the fact that Beth had won the 'takeaway' tea after all. The delivery man had found them within minutes, and even though they'd cleaned the whole house soon after the furniture had been delivered, Beth had still insisted on camping in front of the fire, just like they had at the refuge.

Pushing the last piece of cheese topping into her mouth, Beth picked up the can of soda and took a long slurp. 'I'm so full,' she announced as she flopped back against the pillows and massaged her stomach with a hand.

Molly relaxed too. Allowed her eyes to close. Heard the bleep of her phone, grabbed at it and read the message.

Hey Moll, how did the move go? You all unpacked? Dan xxx

Sighing, she thought of Dan. Of how he'd offered them both a home, somewhere to live. He'd been her friend, her former boyfriend, and she knew that a little part of her would always love him. Problem was, she could no longer trust him. They'd stayed friends, but things hadn't been right. Dan had changed. He'd become more secretive. Distant. None of it had made sense, until the week before. The day she'd driven to the solicitors. Into Scarborough. The day she'd spotted Dan standing by the sea front. The man who'd walked towards him. The handshake, the obvious transaction shared between them. It had been a moment of realisation. Of deep sadness. And if she hadn't already been planning on moving out just two days later, she'd have moved both her and Beth out immediately.

Every minute since, she'd been on her guard. Tried to decide whether or not to tell him what she'd seen, whether or not she should go to the police. Knew the consequences of what that meant.

It had been a heart-breaking decision. One she hadn't wanted to make. The relief she'd felt had been palpable when the furniture men had arrived. The van had already been filled with her mother's possessions and as the last of hers and Beth's things had been put inside, she'd noticed the look in his eyes as she'd climbed into her car and, for the very last time, she'd driven away without looking back. And by doing so she was breaking his heart, along with a little piece of hers.

Picking up her phone, she wondered how he was. Hated how much she cared, when she knew she shouldn't. Tapped out a message, told him about the move, the house, the oddity that had been the back door incident, the shed and, for a few moments, she stared at the screen, watched, waited, saw the three dancing dots appear, indicating that a response was imminent.

Ohhhh, are you missing me? Put the kettle on. I'll be right over. xxx

Panicking, she hastily replied.

Sorry. Probably not a good idea. Place is a mess. Me and Beth have resorted to sharing a mattress on the floor. But we have a fire. All is good. Don't worry. xxx

Holding her phone to her chest, she listened to the sounds of the house and took pleasure in hearing the rain thrash against the windows, the random creaks and bangs, along with the sound of the storm that blew violently down the chimney, making the flames lick and dance around half-charcoaled logs, before flying up the chimney in colours of golds and orange.

Supressing an involuntary shiver, Molly sat forward, stabbed at the fire with the poker, threw another log on top then lay back, and closed her eyes. 'Good job I found the logs.' She wanted to ask about the shed, wanted to ask why Beth would lock her inside, but bit down on her bottom lip, pondered the thoughts.

'Did you see that old hallway carpet? It was thrown down the side of the shed, under all the crap,' Beth whispered.

Molly's eyes shot open. 'Really? I wonder why she pulled it up, just to throw it away.' Pausing, she inched herself up against the pillow. 'Do you think we could salvage it?'

Beth shook her head, wrinkled her nose and pulled a face. 'Nah.' She pointed at the window where the storm still raged. 'It's been out there in the rain, it'll stink, and by now it'll be full of centipedes, slugs and God knows what else so, to be honest, I'm not sure I'd want it back.'

Molly moved onto her side, made a mental note to order more logs and then, out of habit, she began to stroke her sister's forehead and sighed. It suddenly occurred to her that Beth was no longer a child. Yet she wasn't an adult either and her daily frustration at being at the in between stage was becoming more and more apparent.

Settling down, Molly felt her breathing slow down and began to concentrate on the distant sound of the storm, on the rain that battered the rooftop and the annoying but hypnotic 'tap, tap, tap' of a tree branch that repeatedly caught against the window frame. Her exhausted mind began to drift into sleep, then a click, a new distinct noise, pulled her back to consciousness.

Grabbing hold of the settee, Molly used it to pull herself up. Listened nervously. Heard the distinct sound of footsteps while taking sharp intakes of breath. She picked up the poker and walked over to the door, where she moved the towel that had been their makeshift draught excluder. Then, with a hand on the door handle, she once again stopped and listened.

Holding onto the door, she looked down at where Beth peacefully slept, considered waking her, but shook her head. Wanted to let her sleep, to feel comfortable in her new home, and rather than give her something new to worry about, Molly made the decision to leave her be, swallowed hard and felt the taste of fear trickle down her throat, like a putrid acid that burned her all the way down. Her mind brought up a million flashing images, all at once, as she imagined her mother, how she must have felt, and what she'd have gone through, the moment she'd realised that someone was in the house, someone who wanted to hurt her.

Trying to shake the feelings off and with her back to the door, she listened to the house, to a distant thud that was masked by the storm. Felt her stomach lurch nervously, while all the time trying to remember what had happened when the pizza had arrived, and Beth had answered the door. 'Oh, thank you,' she'd shouted happily. 'There you go, keep the change.' Her voice had echoed in the hallway, the lack of carpet making it sound louder than it actually was.

Shaking her head, Molly bit down on her lip, tried to remember the door slamming, the loud bang it would have made, but couldn't, and with the poker still in her hand, she quietly opened the door, flicked on the hallway lights, held her breath, waited. Slowly and deliberately, she tiptoed along the hallway. The normal creaks and bangs of the house had suddenly dropped into silence, the only noise she could hear was the sound of her own heartbeat that boomed in her head at speed, like a bass drum.

Flicking on the kitchen light, she saw the boxes with their lids thrown to one side, the contents obviously disturbed. Searched through. Three different pictures of their mum had been placed around the kitchen, another on the windowsill. All oddly positioned, as though thrown into place. With her mind on high alert, her eyes immediately shot to the hallway, to the windowsill and to the empty space where Michael's picture had previously lain.

6

Laughing, I cower behind the shed, rub the grime from my hands down my jeans and close my eyes for just a minute. I'm listening to my heart, which is racing and beating so fast that the sound is scarily audible. I can barely breathe, the adrenaline is coursing through my veins and, for the first time in years, I feel alive. So alive that I want to laugh hysterically, knowing that I only just made it out of the house before you opened the door, knowing that I was so close, and if I'd have so wished, I could have murdered you both. Right there, while you slept.

Narrowing my eyes to see in the darkness, I look down at the picture. Wipe it clean. Stare at it. I don't know why I took it, but it feels like a trophy. A way of proving that I have the power, that I can take what I want. When I want it. Yet, for the second time today I wish I'd waited for the house to be empty. Realising now, I'll have to come back. Find a time when I can search the house properly. Without you being home.

The rain has stopped, the sky is dark, uncompromising, and it perfectly sums up my mood as, with frustration, I kick out at the cliff, feel the pain in my toes and jump backwards as I watch a few random stones topple downwards, to land heavily on top of the body. I realise I can't bury her here. I pick up the spade, then toss it to one side as the euphoria leaves, I feel the need to calm myself down and I sit down on wet rocks – watching the house – watching it through the darkness, where now I can see you walking up and down the hallway, poker in hand, as though you think it would help you. It's a sight that makes me laugh, especially when I know that I'm not going to hurt you – not today, maybe not even tomorrow – however, I do like the way I can control your mind – the way I can make you feel the fear!

7

After a long night of listening to Beth tossing and turning in her sleep, Molly reluctantly pushed the duvet down and crawled on her hands and knees to the bottom of the mattress. Every part of her ached. It was a pain she couldn't explain, didn't know if it had come from moving multiple boxes, or from sleeping on Beth's dodgy old mattress, on a wooden floor, surrounded by draughts. Taking a moment to roll her shoulders, she used the settee to pull herself up, stood and made an attempt at stretching each of her muscles in turn, before padding down the hallway in search of coffee.

Tentatively, she pushed the kitchen door open, peered around it. Gave a half smile and she shook her head as her gaze landed on the boxes, on the way the lids had been tossed to one side. Realised now that Beth would have been doing as she'd been asked, making herself at home, unpacking. Picking up the randomly placed photographs, Molly placed them on the windowsill, lined them up with equal spacing, smiled. 'If Beth wanted to see the pictures, then we'll put them out properly.' Casting an eye around the kitchen, she began opening cupboards searching for the picture of Michael. 'It has to be here.' She rolled her jaw, stared down the hallway to where Beth still slept, then back at the boxes that were piled up at the side of the room.

It occurred to her that the picture could now be hidden in any one of the boxes. She didn't have the energy or the inclination to look and instead she flicked on the kettle, stood and looked through the kitchen window. She could see that the worst of the storm had passed and sighed as she studied a small willowy tree that stood central to the front lawn. It still arced in the wind and overnight the last of its autumn leaves had been torn from its branches to lie haphazardly scattered around its trunk, waiting for the next breeze to come along and blow them over the cliff and into the sea.

After making a mug of coffee, Molly began pulling open drawer after drawer, still searching for the picture, wondering whether Beth really would have moved it. She lifted one of the box lids. Looked inside, then stood back, counted the many boxes that still circumnavigated the kitchen. Some had laptops, iPads and other electrical items lying on top, and now the idea that someone else could have been in the house seemed ridiculous and she laughed at herself, remembering the way she'd stalked around the house, poker in hand, ready to fight. 'They'd have taken a whole lot more than one scabby old photograph, wouldn't they?' she whispered as she moved along the boxes. Most were still sealed and she allowed her hand to move from one to the other, resting it on top of each as she went, palm down. It was as though by doing this she'd know the content, yet she still felt too afraid to open them and face the memory that would jump out from within.

Swallowing hard, she knew that every part of hers, Beth's and her mum's life was packed inside, and now she regretted not packing them herself, not labelling them properly. It wasn't as though she hadn't tried. She'd gone back to the rental and stood on the doorstep, daring herself to open the door, to place the key in the lock, but couldn't. Within minutes of arriving, her legs had turned to jelly. Her breathing had quickened. Her skin had turned hot and clammy. The rapid blinking had begun, and she'd found herself holding onto the door jamb, unable to breathe. The need to run had become overwhelming and, in desperation, she'd slowly slid down the wall, to sit on the wet doormat, in the rain, sobbing uncontrollably, too afraid to venture inside. The thought of walking into that kitchen, her mum's kitchen, seeing the exact spot where she'd died, had been simply unbearable.

Sitting there in the rain, she'd held onto her privacy for just a moment. Held a hand to the door, said her goodbyes. Then, as she'd looked up, she'd spotted the photographer. Frightened and alone, she'd scrambled around the house. Hiding in the garden, as unbelievably, she realised that the vultures were back, taking pictures, making money from her grief. Her only escape had been across a neighbouring garden. And feeling much too scared to go back, she'd arranged for the whole house to be cleaned and packed by a specialist team, only leaving her with the job of handing back the keys.

Moving from kitchen to hallway, Molly looked up the stairs, at the sloping roof, to where the small dormer window was perfectly positioned, and to the roofline that sloped haphazardly into the rooms. Furniture had been fitted sympathetically to make maximum use of the space and she smiled at the memory of the two small doors she'd found hidden inside each section of fitted wardrobes, two secret openings that led to the space within the eaves, two on each side of the house, one in each bedroom. The find had made her laugh and she'd imagined how lucky she was to have her very own entrance to Narnia, the perfect place to put all the boxes, all the parts of her life that she either had no wish to see or simply couldn't let go.

'Maybe I should step inside, look for Aslan,' she whispered between sips of coffee. Felt the liquid sear her throat. The events of the night before had played on her mind, left her tired. She'd tossed and turned, hardly slept and had waited patiently for the sun to rise. And now that it had, she wanted to get out there, to run, to burn some energy, and she wanted to do it on what felt like her very own private beach. Taking in a deep breath, she rolled her shoulders backwards, tentatively looked past the willowy tree and at the sky, tried to decide whether the rain, wind, thunder and lightning of the night before would return, or whether they might get a reprieve that would last long enough for her to go for that run.

Nodding, she placed her coffee cup on the counter, ran upstairs, dug around in one of her many suitcases, and quickly pulled her running clothes on, found her trainers from the depths of another bag, and added them to her outfit.

'Beth, I'm going for a run. I won't be long,' she shouted as she ran back down the stairs and along the bare floorboards that felt rough and cold beneath her feet. She heaved a sigh, wished for a new carpet, or even an old one. Knew she didn't have a hope, not until payday, and even then she'd have to budget, have to work out how much running a house would cost. It was something she'd never had to think about before, she'd always paid board, but her mum had dealt with the bills and the shopping. And carpets or other necessities needed for the house had always been provided by the many landlords they'd known over the years.

'You will be okay while I'm out, won't you?' She pushed her feet into her trainers. 'Beth, did you hear me?'

'Yes, the first time you growled.' The muffled sound of Beth's still half-asleep voice came from the makeshift bed, buried deep beneath a mountain of duvet. 'Moll, don't go. I—'

Molly took a deep breath. Thoughts of Charlie were fresh in her mind. She knew he was about to get out of prison and the thought was making her paranoid. Looking at her phone, she found the message. Furrowed her brow, shrugged it off. Knowing that it could have been sent from just about any one of her friends. Possibly one who'd changed their number and forgot to tell her. Worried she was reading into things that weren't really happening, she deleted the message with a satisfied swish of her finger, turned the key in the lock, held a hand over the handle. 'Hun. Don't be silly, you're perfectly safe and I won't be long, I need to run. When I get back, we'll start moving some of those boxes, find whatever it was you were looking for.'

'What are you talking about?' Beth shouted inquisitively.

'The pictures of Mum?'

'As normal, I have no idea what you're talking about.'

Molly shrugged. 'And the picture of Michael. Did you move it?'

'What?'

'His picture, Michael's picture, the one that was left behind, it's missing.' Molly rolled her eyes, once again stepped into the kitchen, began pulling cupboard doors open at speed, knowing that if Beth had hidden it, she wouldn't have put too much effort into doing so. 'Beth, come on. Help me look. This is serious.'

'Oh, it's serious, is it?' She flounced dramatically down the hallway. 'Actually, yeah, I remember moving it now. I put it on my bedside cabinet. Wanted a daily reminder of the man who fell off the bloody roof.'

'Beth,' she snapped, grabbed at the door.

Beth glared. 'If you want a serious answer, then ask a serious question. Why the hell would I want the picture? I didn't even want to move here. And now look at what's happening. You haven't stopped shouting at me since the minute we got here. Things are disappearing and we, we're creeping around, waiting for Mum's murderer to jump out of the understairs cupboard.' Her voice was loud and shrill. 'Before you know it, we'll be on the news, just like she was.'

Molly thought about what her sister had said and shook her head. 'Is that what all of this is about, Beth? Are you doing things to freak me out? Because if you are, you need to stop it right now. We are not going back to live at Dan's, and we're not moving house again. Do you hear me?' Angrily, she pressed her lips tightly together, felt her stomach twist with anxiety. 'And as for locking me in the shed, that was a new low, even for you.' Immediately she regretted her words, watched as Beth launched herself into the living room, slammed her phone down on the mattress, pulled at the duvet and held it protectively in front of her.

'You really think I did that, do you?' She paused, sobbing. 'Well. If you want to believe that, then that's fine. But, when we both get murdered in our sleep, you might want to remember – it was you that wanted to live here. Not me.'

8

Standing in the doorway, Molly tried to control her temper, tried to imagine what it must be like, to be just fifteen years old and to have lost so much, so quickly. Knuckle rubbing her eyes, she wished wholeheartedly that she could take back the words, turn back into being the sister, rather than the reluctant parent. Shaking her head, she poked the quilt with her toe, knelt down, laid a hand on Beth's back and hoped for a response that didn't come.

'Okay,' she said, standing back up, 'I'm going to go for a run. When I get back, we'll make some breakfast. I bought some bacon, some nice rolls. Oh, and some really nice tomatoes and lettuce, we could make BLTs with a big squirt of mayonnaise.' Hoping the thought of food would cheer Beth up, she opened the front door, stepped outside, stretched her arms up above her head and took in a long, deep breath of salty sea air. The cold wind hit her squarely in the face and she shuddered as the offshore breeze seemed to attack from all directions, cutting swiftly through her, with sharp, penetrating razor-like slices.

Thoughtfully, Molly glanced back at the house, considered

going back inside, talking to Beth. She was being so unpredictable, and she felt worried that the missing picture, the attitude, her reasons for hating the house so much were all her way of rebelling, of venting emotion. All of which left Molly at a loss; she didn't know what to do, wished she'd insisted that Beth join her for a run, but couldn't remember the last time Beth had run anywhere.

'She wouldn't thank you for dragging her out of bed, would she?' She tried to think logically, to clear her mind, felt the anticipation build up within her as she took deep breaths of sea air in the hope it would clear her lungs.

She looked to the sky. 'Please let her love it here.' She whispered the words in silent prayer, made excuses for the way Beth was acting, put the shed incident down to her having a little fun at her older, bossier sister's expense. 'She would love it if she'd known this place the way I had.' She recalled the memories, the way she and Mum had sat under an umbrella in the rain, refusing to move. How they'd planned a day on the beach and, rain or not, they were going to have a day at the beach. They'd often sat there eating fish and chips or a picnic that they'd spread out on a big blanket, laid on the sand. Sighing, Molly knew that she had to be the adult. That she had to rise above her sister's tantrums. After all, it was up to her to help Beth, to ensure she created new memories for them both and she had every intention of showing Beth how beautiful it really could and would be to live here – all she had to do was give it a chance.

9

Feeling her whole body begin to shudder, Beth might have thought she was cold, but the heat under the duvet had now become close to unbearable and not knowing what else to do, she peered over the edge of the covers and across the room, waited, listened.

'Moll... don't go,' she shouted to a hollow, empty house. 'Moll...' In disbelief, Beth furrowed her brow, inched her body upwards and carefully listened to the sounds of the house, where roof beams seemed to crack and move, along with the annoying tap, tap, tap of a branch that continually banged against the window.

Crawling to the bottom of the mattress on hands and knees, she leaned forward to scrutinise the hallway, fully expecting Molly to be standing there. Her face stern. Her arms crossed. Instead, she saw a long, empty, gloomy passage, with its tufts of carpet around the edges and a single shaft of light coming from the small panel that went down one side of the door.

'She... she really went...' Beth sighed, took in a deep breath and slowly made her way towards the door. 'Why did she do that?' She reached for the key, saw the unmistakable shaking of her own hand, and pulled it back just long enough to wipe her sweaty palm down her pyjama bottoms before locking the door.

'It has to be here,' she said as every cupboard was opened. Her eyes darted from one part of the kitchen to the other, settling on the storage boxes, all neatly stacked. Frantically, she grabbed at them, tore one open and stared at the cafetière and coffee mugs. Her mum's cafetière, the one she always got out when visitors came. Smiling, Beth remembered the way she'd been allowed to press down the plunger, how the smell of coffee would fill the room.

Spotting the pictures, she looked from one to the other, all stood on the windowsill, all perfectly lined up. Smiling slyly, she traced her mother's lips through the glass, blew her a kiss. Felt pleased with herself for having got them out the night before, knew that seeing them would have made Molly think. Mischievously, Beth spied the boxes, imagined what else was inside, what else she could sneak out, use to create doubt in her sister's mind.

'So...' Pursing her lips into a tight bud, she slammed the cupboard door shut. Opened the fridge. 'Molly wants to blame me for everything, does she? Well... we'll see what she thinks when she can't have her precious bacon sandwich.' Opening the back door and with a satisfied smirk, she dropped the meat into the dustbin. 'That'll show her,' she whispered, then jumped backwards as a plastic carrier bag blew past her feet like a ball of tumbleweed. Chasing after it, she picked it up, took in her surroundings and felt pleased that in daylight the garden looked so much more welcoming than it had the night before, during a storm.

Moving slowly along the path, she could see an old greenhouse, its door open. It looked full of used plant pots, still full of compost, their produce now perished from the months of trying to fend for themselves, not being watered, even though the hosepipe was on a reel by the back door and within easy reach. Red splodges stained the floor, where tomatoes most probably fell, only to be eaten by birds, or other passing animals.

She thought it was a waste that Carol hadn't tended the vegetables. Then thought back to the bacon, realised that that was a waste too and cursed herself for having thrown it away, now wishing she'd cooked it and either eaten it herself, or made a peace offering, in readiness for Molly's return.

Beside the greenhouse was the shed. It was the same shed that Molly had managed to lock herself inside, the one she'd walked past the day before in search of the noise. But now things looked different, the logs that had been previously scattered beside it had been moved, tossed to one side, and the carpet had gone. The sight made her stop. She began to retreat, slowly, one step at a time until, with eyes as wide as saucers, she stood on the doorstep scanning the garden, looking for anything else that could have been moved.

In one quick movement, she slammed the back door, locked it and stood with her back against it. Listening to the house, she tiptoed back into the kitchen and, fearful that someone could have got in without her seeing, she pulled open a drawer to grab at a wooden handled carving knife. Holding it close to her chest, she could hear nothing but the sound of her own breathing, the continuous hammering of her heart, the tap, tap, tap of the branch on the window. Someone had moved the old carpet and that someone hadn't been Molly, which meant that someone, a stranger, had been in the garden, while she... no, while they, had been sleeping. Panic took over; she couldn't concentrate and purposely she slipped to the floor, placed her hands over her ears and, hoping to mask the sound of her own heartbeat, she began to hum. 'It's just a carpet. Just an old piece of smelly, dirty old carpet. That's all. Nothing more. Nothing important.' Taking in huge gulps of air, she felt the bile rise in her throat, the acrid taste making her immediately jump up, spit in the sink and with the tap on full, she cupped her hands to scoop water into her mouth.

With her back to the units, she peered down the hallway, mentally measured its length. 'It's a long hallway. The carpet... it was hacked, probably cut into pieces.' She studied it, knelt down and pulled at the remnants still stuck to the carpet gripper. 'So, why some was some cut away, the rest left behind?'

10

With the breeze stronger than she'd thought, Molly began to tremble as the wind cut straight through her sports jacket. Once again, she thought about turning back. Tried to give herself an excuse not to run, but then laughed and strode forward. Determinedly, she made her way along the path and towards the beach where she hoped the overhang of the cliffs would shield her from the worst of the onslaught.

With a tingling sensation in her toes, she felt her pulse quicken with excitement. All of her senses, which had been so dormant for so long, were suddenly heightened, sprung into life and with enthusiasm. She took pleasure in every step, loved the way she could feel each cobble through her trainers, the roughness on her fingertips as they skimmed across the old wooden gate and the fresh sea air that hit the back of her throat with force. Laughing, she ducked to avoid the seagulls. They swooped and crooned and for a moment, she watched the mid-air dance that was playing out right before her eyes.

Spotting movement in one of the two distant gardens, Molly stood on tiptoes to study the neighbouring property. It was a house that the night before had been shrouded in darkness. She'd thought it deserted but now, in the morning sun, everything looked different. The house looked alive. Smoke came from the chimney, fresh, clean bedding hung on the line and a black sign written van was parked in the drive. It was just too far away to read what it said, but the sight made her smile and inquisitively, she hung around for a moment, hoped her neighbour would show themselves. Hoped she'd get the chance to say hello.

When they didn't, Molly disappointedly turned the corner and made her way towards the wooden steps that led down to the beach. They still looked a little old and rickety, just as she remembered, although now, some thirteen years since she'd last seen them, they looked as though they'd seen better days and so, doubting their rigidity and, with caution, her hand went out to give them a shake, felt surprised when they didn't move.

Carefully, she made her way down them, only to hesitate as she reached the bottom step, where she stood, motionless. With her eyes closed she cautiously, as though afraid to touch it, reached forward until just the toe of her trainer drew a line across the sand. It was a moment she wanted to cherish, to commit to memory and for the briefest time she couldn't help but feel her mother's arms wrap themselves tightly around her. She allowed her mind to envelop her in a warm, loving hug. One she took great pleasure in until her bottom lip began to quiver dramatically with emotion. Determined not to sob, she stepped forward, placed her whole foot squarely on the beach in the knowledge that she had miles of rugged coastline stretching out before her, with Filey in one direction and Flamborough in the other.

'I did it, Mum,' she announced to the sky. 'I came back to our beach, just like I promised.' The words were followed by another smile as a single tear rolled aimlessly down her cheek and with it, the feeling of her mother's arms deserted her, leaving her cold, vulnerable and alone.

'There you go, first sign of madness.' The man's Yorkshire accent came from nowhere. Molly's heart leapt in her chest and with a fear she didn't know possible, she felt a scream come from deep within her, as a huge black dog leapt down the steps towards her.

'What the?' She took a step backwards, held her hands in front of her face and watched as the dog dropped to the sand and began frantically bouncing up and down, his tongue lolloping to one side. 'Please—' Fear overtook the words and she pressed herself tightly to the cliff, unable to move.

'Dillon, *no*. The lady doesn't want to play.' The man's body was swiftly thrust between her and the dog, his back to her. 'Now – sit down, right now. Say hello nicely.' He pointed to the sand and the dog obediently sat, then the man looked over his shoulder to smile apologetically. 'That's right. Good dog. Good dog.' His hand fondly slapped the dog's side, ruffled his ears. 'Don't worry, he might look big and tough, but I promise he won't hurt you. Will you, boy?'

Even though the man's voice was reassuring, Molly cocked her head to one side and fearfully watched the German Shepherd's every move. 'Stay there. That's right, good boy, stay. Sorry about that...' He flashed her a smile. 'He's still a pup, thinks everyone wants to play and well, you did seem to be talking to yourself, looked like you needed the company.' He nervously glanced between her and Dillon who now lay with his head on his paws, whining.

Standing taller than her by a good six inches, the man had the build and looks of a sportsman. Broad shoulders, a square chiselled jawline and short dark hair that went well with his perfectly trimmed beard. The whole look was annoyingly handsome. Yet his hands, which he held up as though in prayer, looked like those of a workman, worn and hardened.

'Are you okay?' he whispered. "Cause I'm getting a little worried about the way you're eyeing me up and down.' He laughed nervously.

'Fine? Of course I'm not fine, your dog just frightened me half to death,' she snapped, turned away, felt the anger surge through her. The panic she'd felt had paralysed her with fear. It was a fear that was always there. A fear that had surrounded her for months, the not knowing who friend or foe was, the thought of an imminent attack high in her mind. The way daily events could quite easily turn into momentous and terrifying occasions. Staring at the sea, she felt aggrieved that he'd spoiled her moment, a moment she'd waited for, hoped for, dreamed about.

The man stepped away, ran a foot across the sand. 'Look, we're sorry we scared you. Aren't we, Dillon?'

She fixed her jaw and continued to glare as she looked him up and down. Couldn't shake the feeling she'd seen him somewhere before. Tried to remember where. 'He... he could have bitten me,' she finally grunted, with her back still connected firmly to the cliff.

He nodded, slowly. Took in a deep breath. 'He wouldn't have bitten you. Not unless I told him to. Which I might reconsider if you keep on shouting at me.' He gave her a half smile, arched an eyebrow.

Internally, she screamed for a second time. It was a long, shrill scream that came from deep within her, a scream that didn't actually leave her mouth, even though it desperately wanted to. Moving her gaze from him to the dog, she watched how he lay, like a petulant child who'd been placed on a naughty step, one eye on his owner just waiting for his command, telling him to play. Turning away, she did everything she could not to look at the man. She didn't trust herself to do that, because to do that would have meant looking at his face, his eyes, his annoyingly perfect smile.

'Well, if I'm allowed, I'm going to continue with my run... that's if you promise your dog won't chase me or bite me.' Her eyes went to the tide, to the curve of the beach, the town of Filey that stood prominently in her view, then back to the steps. Her initial thought was to retreat, to go back to the house, to lock the door, but with every ounce of energy she had, she fought the urge, knowing that if she went back now, she'd never come back out and instead, she'd end up cowering indoors and hiding forever.

Holding his hands out wide to his side, he laughed. 'Hey, no one's holding you prisoner, lady, are they?' He paused, rolled his jaw. 'I did however think it'd be kind of neighbourly to introduce myself before you went, but hey... seeing as you're in such a hurry.' Pausing, he studied her, stepped back. 'Look, can we start again? I'm sorry. I was out of order, I'd like to make it up to you.' He smiled, waited, when she didn't reply, he continued. 'The beach – it's normally empty, apart from the odd crazy surfer or two maybe, but they're far and few between.' He pointed to the water, to where a man sat straddling a board, staring out to sea, waiting for the perfect wave. 'God knows what they're doing out there today though, it's pretty Baltic.'

Molly looked up, surprised. 'Oh... I hadn't noticed him. I was miles away.'

'I bet you wish you were.' He laughed. Crouched down. Began to stroke Dillon, who, obviously pleased with the attention, sat up to rest a head against his owner's knee. 'Look, I'm Niall McCormick, we're neighbours.' He flashed her another perfect smile and without wanting to, she found herself smiling back. Since becoming a dentist, smiles meant everything. To her, good teeth meant good hygiene and it suddenly occurred to her that there was a distinct possibility that Niall might have been one of her patients. Even though she thought it improbable that the good people of Filey would travel all the way to York for a dental appointment. And on Monday, she'd have a whole new list of patients, a new surgery to work in, a new team around her.

'No, actually, I'm really pleased to be here. I came as a child with my mother. It was a long time ago and I was just taking a minute, trying to remember how it all used to look, and how much it has changed.' Grabbing at her shoulder-length hair, she dragged it upwards, tied it in a well-practised topknot. 'And how...' She suddenly realised what he'd said and eyed him suspiciously. 'How do you know we're neighbours?' Her mind did a somersault as she mentally rewound the conversation.

Niall pulled a ball from his pocket, threw it across the beach and smiled as Dillon happily took up the chase. 'I saw the removal van pull up last night. Saw you heading towards the beach this morning. Put two and two together. I was inquisitive and I followed you down here, thought it'd be nice to say hello.' He raised his eyebrows, smiled sheepishly. 'Obviously, once again, I got things wrong.' He paused. 'As I said, I'd really like to start over, 'cause this really isn't going the way I thought it would.'

Molly looked up at the house, recalled the black van, the smoke coming out of the chimney and the windows that looked as though they were all about to drop out, all by themselves. How she'd hoped for an introduction.

'I run the garden centre in town, we do everything from fresh flowers to landscape gardening.' Niall paused, crouched down beside her and pointed to the distant harbour. 'Centre's on the main road going out of town.'

'Well, I'm Molly, Molly Winter, a very cold amateur runner. And yes, we moved in yesterday.' She tried to smile, glanced at him sideways, then turned back to the sea. Purposely said as little about herself as she could.

'And your husband?' He arched his eyebrow in question, flashed her another perfect smile. 'Is he a runner too?'

'God, no, I live with my teenage sister, Beth.' She pointed to the cliff path. 'We arrived just as the storm did, so you could say that last night was a little more than interesting.' Holding back, she didn't mention the events, the noises, or the picture.

He looked thoughtful. 'Sorry. I thought I saw a man there yesterday, talking to Michael's relative.' His eyes rolled up at the sky thoughtfully. 'I think she's called Claire or Carol or something... I was down at the bottom of the lane with Dillon, so didn't get a close look.' Chewing his lip, he shook his head. 'Thought he was moving in.'

'Yes, Carol, she's Michael's niece. She emptied the place. Even took one of the damn carpets, only to throw it outside to get drenched in the storm,' Molly said, tried to make excuses. Thought about the text she'd received, about Charlie. Could he have already been there?

'Well, for what it's worth, I think you're brave. House does have a bit of a history. Not sure I'd have been plucky enough to buy it.'

Giving Niall a puzzled look, Molly watched as he once again rolled his eyes, defensively held his hands up, palms out in apology. 'Sorry... I shouldn't have said that. It's a great house.'

'Oh, I didn't buy it. I inherited it and as for Michael falling from the roof, that was hardly the house's fault, was it?'

Looking uncomfortable, he shrugged his shoulders, gave her a sidewards glance and began to walk towards the sea. 'Look, forget I said anything, you're right, can't be the house's fault, just a bit sad that the guy didn't have much luck in his life.'

The wind began to whip up as though on cue, clouds accumulated, turning dark and rolling together into one huge black mass. The atmosphere turned hot and humid, making every breath feel like an effort.

'What do you mean? What else happened?'

'Look, I've said too much...' He began to shake his head, ran across to Dillon, picked up the ball and threw it as far up the beach as he could.

'Oh no you don't...' Molly shouted, running after him. 'You can't say that much and not the rest.'

Looking up at the sky, Niall appeared to be nervously pondering his thoughts. 'Okay, there were two women, both died suspiciously. Although by the time his most recent wife was murdered, he'd died himself. So at least he didn't know about it and was spared the grief.'

Molly blew the air from her lungs and took a moment to respond. 'He wasn't married to the last one. She was my mum. And – you're right, she was murdered. But it didn't happen here. Not at this house.' She paused. 'Although by then, I guess she did own it. She just hadn't got around to moving in. So, I don't think it counts... does it?'

Niall stopped in his tracks, closed his eyes for a beat. 'Look, I shouldn't have said anything. I'm so sorry. I – well, I didn't know it was your mum, obviously.'

Molly pressed her lips together, gave a half smile and, thankful for the distraction, she tentatively reached out to Dillon who'd now positioned himself by her feet, looking up. Concentrating on the dog, she began to process the new information. She'd had no idea what Michael had been through previously, neither he or her mum had ever mentioned it, and knowing they'd kept the information from her left her feeling sick.

Allowing the breeze to blow in her face, Molly waited for the nausea to pass. Continually looked over her shoulder, at the house, at the roof from where Michael had fallen. Wished she knew what he'd been doing, why he'd been up there. 'Did you know him, Michael?' she eventually asked, desperate to glean even a tiny piece of information about the man whose house she now owned.

He paused, smiled. 'Sure. First time I came here was when Michael rang me. He wanted a quote. Needed his garden landscaping, spent a little time with him and while I was there, I looked at his garden. I spotted the property next door, fell in love with the place. Ended up moving here myself. So, in answer to your question, yes, I knew him. A little.' His hand swept outwards. 'The house is still a bit of a wreck, but... I guess I'll get it done, eventually, money permitting.' Pausing, he circled around. Looked up at the house. 'For the last year, I've been concentrating on the conversion. Turning the living space at the garden centre into self-contained flats, for the lads.'

'Oh,' Molly gasped. 'You have children?'

'Sure, twenty-two of them,' he quickly replied, laughed. 'Not mine, but they feel like they're mine some days. It's a community project. I employ former prisoners, give them a place to be. The flats will be somewhere for them to stay, you know, until they get sorted.' He pointed up to his house. 'I've got them starting work on my place later in the week, got a lot of jobs that need doing, both inside and out. There's nothing else in the diary and seeing as I'm paying them anyhow, I might as well do the place up a bit.' Niall glanced over his shoulder, looked her up and down with an appreciative glance, then turned his attention back to the dog, who ran excitedly between them, waiting for one of them to throw him the ball. 'And now that Dillon's your new best friend, you won't be worried about him any more. Will you?' He stood up, grabbed at the ball, gave it another long throw along the beach.

Molly smiled, appreciated the effort he'd just made to lighten the mood. 'Well, he certainly isn't the maneater I took him for.' Kneeling down, she waited for Dillon to run back towards her, rubbed his ears. Laughed as he rolled on the sand, exposed his stomach, waited for her to rub that too.

'Damn it.' Niall tapped his watch, turned to face the cliff, kicked at the sand, with annoyance. 'Sorry, late for work and if I don't get there soon and unlock the tool sheds, the men can't get on.' He laughed. 'They are ex-criminals, we lock the tools away at night,' he tried to explain, held her gaze, looked directly into her eyes, gave her a captivating smile. 'Maybe I'll catch you later,' he said softly. Then, as quickly as he arrived, he turned, jogged towards the steps and disappeared out of view.

11

With a hand on each knee, Molly stared at the sand, took deep steady breaths. She hadn't run for a long time; her stamina wasn't as good as she'd have liked, and annoyingly, her poor level of fitness was already beginning to show.

Her mind spun with a million questions. Niall's words had blown her mind; he'd told her things she hadn't known and now paranoia had begun to dominate her thoughts and she tried her best not to connect the coincidence of deaths, apart from the fact that they were all unusual. She wasn't sure she could link them all to the house. The thought that they were even remotely connected to the actual owning of a house was just stupid and illogical, wasn't it? Yet somehow a sense of anguish spun around her mind like a washing machine on its spin cycle. One that went faster and faster, each turn bringing a new thought, fear or memory.

Taking a breath, she watched the tide. It was becoming more and more volatile. Even the early morning surfer had climbed out of the water and retreated back to his car, where he'd pulled his wetsuit down to his waist and shrouded his upper body in a towel and a woolly hat.

In an attempt to change her mood, Molly continued her jog, found herself jumping over waves as they were systematically whipped up by the breeze and tossed themselves towards her where they crashed, one after the other, along the water's edge before receding back into the sea, where they belonged. They left the beach rippled and uneven, making every step feel like a dozen and, for a while, she enjoyed the simplicity of the game, dodging the waves, running a little closer to the water each time in the hope that the wet firmer sand would give her a more stable terrain. But the unpredictability of the rollers meant that her feet had quickly become sodden, her trainers uncomfortable and grainy with sand. All of which caused her to dramatically slow her pace, concentrate on her footing, and start to feel the burn that began in her lungs and moved to her legs.

Taking a deep, determined breath inward, she felt a sudden kick of adrenaline as it coursed through every part of her body giving her a strange pleasure with a fiery familiar sensation. The feeling made her think of Dan. Of the daily running routine they used to have. Their hope to run in a local marathon, a whole twenty-six miles. A hope that had ended the moment his Achilles had ruptured, followed by the disappointment they'd both felt at pulling out of the race.

'Go on, Molly, do it. Do it for both of us. I'll watch and cheer from the side lines,' he'd tried to insist, but running the marathon, along with scuba diving and climbing Mount Everest, were the things they were supposed to do together. All before they were thirty. All before everything changed.

Lost in thought, Molly spun around to see what had become an almost deserted beach, with the sky above turning from grey to black. The clouds had all mulled together and now appeared as one large dark mass, rather than the smaller individual clouds they'd been before.

'Time to go back,' she whispered, scanning the topography. She could just about make out the position of the house. The spot where it perched, high up on the cliff side. A place beyond the caravan site but not quite as far as Flamborough. A place she now got to call home. Smiling, she knew that right now, right at this moment, she got to live in what looked like the most perfect property on earth. She just wished it was perfect. That all the strange happenings could be forgotten, along with the new information she'd only just learned.

As she got close, the image of the house became clearer. It was no longer a dot on the horizon, and now she could make out both hers and Niall's homes, both surrounded by trees and bushes so overgrown that if you didn't know they were there, the houses would almost be hidden.

Squinting, she could just about make out a figure, someone standing by one of the trees, close to the cliff edge, looking out to sea, but from her position on the beach, she couldn't make out whether they were in her garden or Niall's.

'Is that...' She immediately thought of Beth. That something could be wrong, and without further thought she picked up her pace, felt the wind surround her like a mini tornado as the weather worsened and whipped itself up and into her face, making her blink repeatedly. Finally, when she glanced back up, the figure was gone.

12

Even though he was late for work, Niall found himself leaning against one of the trees, watching. The early morning surfer had now given up on the waves and had reluctantly taken refuge by the cliff, where he stood, debating the weather.

Catching sight of Molly, he watched her run, leap and laugh at the waves in a playful and almost childlike action. Meeting her had been fun, albeit a little planned and he thoughtfully sipped at the remnants of coffee. It had been made earlier, and was now only just drinkable, lukewarm at best, but the cup in his hands gave him something to hold onto, while silently chastising himself for saying too much. Shaking his head, he pushed himself away from the tree, threw the last remaining dregs of coffee on the grass and turned as a sudden blast of a car's horn disturbed his thoughts.

Looking towards the drive, he noticed the Audi, a distinctive sports car, one he'd seen before, but couldn't remember where. Debating the options, he realised that it could only really have been here or at the centre and he strode down his path towards it. Shrouded by trees, he took a closer look at the driver who, after catching the horn, now sat back in his seat with his chin angrily jutting forward, his frustration more than clear to see.

'I just knew she'd have a boyfriend, hidden away somewhere.' Niall took in the man's large, muscle-bound frame. The short, almost military haircut. The hands as big as shovels and, after a few minutes' indecision, he nodded, remembered the parole meetings, the prison officer with the sharp and uncompromising attitude and knew immediately that whether he was a neighbour or not, they wouldn't get along.

Turning his attention back to the beach and to Molly, he followed her path, saw her pull at her hair, watched how she tied it up on top of her head, before leaning over with her hands on her knees. Walking closer to the edge of the cliff, he pressed his lips tightly together, glanced between Molly and the Audi, which was still there, still parked, the boyfriend still sitting inside.

'Two is company, three is definitely a crowd,' he whispered to the boyfriend as he walked down the side of his house, towards his van. Climbing inside, he left the door open, started the engine. 'Dillon, here boy.' Watching Dillon jump into the seat beside him, he slammed the door and with one final look at the beach, he gave an appreciative smile. 'And you, I'll see you later,' he whispered to Molly.

13

Getting out of his car and walking through the garden, Dan stood and gazed at the sea, at the view, and then, through narrowed eyes, he looked up at the house that Molly now called home.

He knew she had fond memories of visiting this beach, had spoken of nothing else for months, and had told him repeatedly how much moving here had meant to her. It had been an excitement that had flown off the scale, especially during the past few days, and he'd become tired and restless as she'd explained continually that this house, this view, this beach would be her new beginning, a fresh start for both her and for Beth. She'd said it without a thought of what it would do to him. Of how lonely he would be and how every day he felt as though he were losing her just a little bit more.

Climbing back into the car, he held tightly to the Audi's steering wheel, stared down at the footwell, felt the frustration take over his mind and, in his temper, he slammed his hands hard against the wheel, inadvertently catching the horn. The sudden blast of noise made him jump and he sat forward, nervously looking at the sports car's bonnet as though willing it to be quiet, and for a moment he wished he hadn't come, didn't know what he'd achieve.

'You knew she was always going to leave.' He gritted his teeth, shook his head, picked up his phone, flicked back through the twenty plus texts they'd exchanged the previous night. 'But she still likes you, she wouldn't send the texts if she didn't. Would she?'

Sitting back in his seat, Dan studied the sky along with the looming dark clouds which were growing ever darker and moodier and from his position, he could just about see the tide rolling in. It was becoming more and more erratic by the minute and while watching it, he sat there, questioning his life, his happiness, Molly's happiness and what their future might or might not hold. How they'd been dramatically pulled together, and then drifted apart. It was something he had to put right. It was important that he kept her close.

Reaching across to the passenger seat, he picked up the new brass locks he'd just bought in town. She'd mentioned the doors the night before. How she'd been thinking of Charlie getting out, of her dread that he might turn up.

Turning the locks over and over in his hands, he punctured the packet. Pulled out the three keys. Took one for himself. 'There could be an emergency. She might need you to get in.' He tried to rationalise his thoughts, placed the key on his keyring.

Climbing out of the car, he saw the front door burst open. A nervous Beth peered around it, like a wild animal, cornered and afraid. Catching his eye, an immediate smile flashed across her face and enthusiastically, she beckoned to him, swinging the door open wide and jumping up and down on the old, tattered doormat, still wearing her pyjamas.

'Dan, what... what are you doing here?' Eagerly, she stepped off the mat and onto the path. 'Oh, it's so good to see you. I didn't know you were coming.'

She was smiling, but the tear-filled eyes told him a very different story and feeling concerned, he slammed the car door and practically ran towards her. 'Hey, kiddo.' Pulling her into a brotherly hug, Dan kissed her on the cheek and noted that her whole body was trembling. 'Thought I'd surprise you both,' he said. 'What's going on, are you okay?'

'I'm better now you're here and it's not much of a surprise when you go round blasting the damned horn, is it?' She poked him in the ribs, tried to look over his shoulder. 'Hey, what you got in your hands? Are they doughnuts? Let me see.'

Playfully, he ducked out of her way. 'Nope, not doughnuts, sorry. And you, young lady, you should stay indoors. You know, dressed like that.' Dan gave her a strict look, pointed to her pyjamas and quickly ushered her back over the doorstep and into the house. 'Go on. Inside. Any perv could be watching.'

Beth pulled a face, arched an eyebrow. 'For God's sake, Dan, who can see me, we're a million miles away from anyone. Not as though we have any real neighbours, is it?' She padded across the hallway, gestured for him to follow and watched as he closed the door behind them both.

'The beach is only down there; anyone could be walking along it.' He pointed through the window. 'They could look up and, well, you're growing up far too fast. Not everyone knows you like I do... so...' He waved a stern finger in her direction and looked over her shoulder, noticed the random carving knife that lay on the counter. 'Are you making breakfast?' He smiled. ''Cause I'm starving. Toast would be good, oh, and some bacon if there is any. In fact, I'll tell you what, a bacon butty would go down well. I'm sure it's your turn.' He thought of all the breakfasts he'd made her, how he'd practically had to force her to eat after her mother's death. How she'd loved his cooking.

Beth cockily rocked her head from side to side. 'Actually, I was just going to...' as though noticing the knife for the first time, she grabbed it, opened a drawer and pushed it inside, 'make toast. So, if you're nice, I might make you some too, but if you want bacon, you'll have to go to the shops.' Picking up the kettle she turned on the tap, allowed the water to run. 'Or we've got cereal. Cereal's easy.' She pointed to the cupboard above his head.

'Where's your sister?' Dan's eyes darted from kitchen to hall, even though he knew she was on the beach, running; it was as though he was half waiting for her to pop out, to greet him.

'Moll, she's down there. Went for a run, left me all by myself.' She pointed to the beach. 'And seeing as you're not dressed for running, I'll make you some coffee. I doubt she'll be long.'

Dan smiled, rested his hand on the worktop. 'Thanks.' Raising both eyebrows, he stared directly at her. 'So, you gonna tell me what's up?'

Beth froze, her hand lingered over the kettle and she stared at the floor. 'Can I come and live at yours?' she whispered, then looked up with red, tear-filled eyes that pleaded with his. 'Please Dan, I don't like it here. In fact, I hate it. I don't think it's safe. Someone was here, in the garden, they stole an old carpet and...' Her bottom lip began to tremble. 'Or... or... you should come live here, be with us?' she said with a hopeful smile.

Dan closed his eyes for a moment, tried to think rationally. He was caught between the devil and the deep blue sea. He wanted nothing more than to be here, with the two people he loved most in the world, two people he'd grown close to. But for so many reasons, he couldn't. Especially after Molly had made it clear that the move had just been for her and for Beth. A new start. A new start that didn't include him, no matter how much that terrified him.

Walking through the kitchen and into the utility, he studied the lock, shrugged and shook his head. 'Moll said she wanted the locks changing, I bought a couple of new ones,' he shouted loud enough for Beth to hear. 'Shall I make the coffee while you go get yourself dressed?' Without waiting for an answer, he went to the kettle, rearranged the mugs, looked through the cupboards, found the coffee and began spooning out the granules.

'Sure, make yourself at home. God knows we did at yours,' she shouted more cheerily as she went up the stairs. 'And the lock. I hope you're fitting it, cause the only drill our Molly knows how to use is the one in people's mouths and you know how that turns out...'

Dan smiled, made the coffee and a few minutes later, Beth trotted back down the stairs with her mouth wide open, pretending to be at the dentist, and Dan noticed that the tears had been dried and a light powdering of fresh make-up covered her face.

Making her way to the counter, Beth pulled herself up to sit on it. 'Oh, I missed your coffee this morning. It always tastes so much better than mine.' Taking one of the mugs, she blew the contents and took a long, satisfying slurp.

Dan smiled. 'Ah, you're just gonna miss me making all your dinners, your lunch box, oh and don't forget your breakfast, supper, snacks. Actually,' he teased, 'don't you think it's time you learned to cook for yourself?' He turned to the lock, pulled it from the packet. 'And yes, I had every intention of fitting the lock. Wanna make sure my two favourite girls are safe now, don't I?' He winked and pulled a face at the obstinate packaging.

Sighing, Beth pursed her lips. 'Seriously, Dan. You and our Moll, you should get back together, then you could come and live here. That'd be good, wouldn't it?' She gave him a hopeful look. 'I'd feel so much safer.'

Dan walked to stand by her side, leaned against the unit and bumped shoulders. 'It isn't that easy, is it? Me and Molly, well, it's complicated. Since your mum, too much happened and...' He gave her an easy smile, cast his eyes around the kitchen, along the hallway and into the living room where he could see the mattress and duvet still on the floor. Padding along the hallway, he glanced up the stairs. 'Besides, I'll be around – all the time, you'll see.'

14

Leaning against her grandparents' porch, Molly held her breath, supressed a nervous giggle and felt for Beth's hand in the dark. Giving it a reassuring squeeze, she felt the familiar three consecutive squeezes back, the secret code they'd had as children, a way of saying 'I love you' or 'sorry', a simple gesture that brought tears to her eyes.

'Hold on, hold on, I'm coming.' Their gran's cheery voice came from within. The bright red farmhouse door flew open and Molly and Beth found themselves pulled into a series of bear hugs and kisses. 'Oh, my girls, there you are. Now let me look at you.' Holding each in turn and at arm's length, Rose looked them up and down. 'Gorgeous, my gorgeous, sweet girls.'

For what seemed like the hundredth time, Molly fell back into her gran's arms, closed her eyes and took in the familiar scent of the floral perfume, a scent that immediately brought back a tidal wave of memories, of similar all-consuming hugs. Standing back, Molly held onto her grandmother's hands, stared into her eyes. An unspoken apology passed between them, but not before she saw the pain, the worry lines that had appeared on her face, her age that now showed.

'Your grandad,' she began, 'he shouldn't be long. He's out back checking the sheep.' She looked nervous, smiled, kept her eyes on the door. 'You know what he's like, will keep looking after those darn animals till he's a hundred and one.' She gave a short but anxious laugh and held Molly's gaze, until suddenly Beth threw off her coat, ran across the stone floor and slid onto her knees.

'Oh, my God, you have a new puppy.' Her voice went up an octave as she held out her arms to the tiny liver and white spaniel that emerged from beneath the long, oak table. Jumping up, he scampered towards her. He was all ears and paws. Each paw trying take a different direction, giving him the look of being all floppy and out of control.

'Well,' their gran said, 'he was the runt of the litter, you know what I'm like... the minute I saw him, I just fell in love.' She laughed, kicked at a pair of muddy wellingtons, then beckoned them into the living kitchen, a room where the whole family mingled. For as long as Molly could remember, life on the farm had always revolved around this huge, warm and homely room with its long farmhouse table. A table that over the years had been used for everything, from the whole family sitting at it to eat Christmas dinner, to the traditional Sunday morning baking fest where they would make cakes and buns to last all week.

'Wow, you still have my favourite settees,' Molly whispered as she spotted the two identical velour sofas that stood opposite each other, both still piled high with cushions, and a huge inglenook fireplace that dwarfed just about everything else in the room, apart from the Aga, which had to be one of the biggest ovens Molly had ever seen in her life. The only thing that had changed in all the years were the randomly bought rugs, her gran's charity shop finds, that were scattered all over the quarry tiled floor, and seemed to come in all colours, shapes and sizes.

'Now then, come on, stand up, let me look at you.' The warmth in her gran's words came out as a shriek as she spoke to Beth, pulled both her and the puppy into a second all-embracing hold. 'I've missed you so much, my girl, so much.' She rocked her gently back and forth, kissed her repeatedly on the cheek, looked her up and down and hugged her again. 'It's just forever since I last saw you.' Taking a single step back, she lifted a hand to touch Beth's cheek, wiped away her tears, then lovingly held her hand there and looked tenderly into her eyes. 'You look so grown up. How did that happen? One day you're my little girl and now, now you're a young woman.' She paused as the back door sprang open and the cold night air rushed in. 'Ah, Henry, right on time. Look who's here.'

Feeling pensive, Molly watched as her grandfather spun in the doorway, took in the sight, grunted, pulled off the old, waxed jacket and hung it by the door that he purposely held ajar. 'Come on, Meg. In you come,' he said as an old black and white sheepdog sauntered in, realised they had visitors and an excited round of welcomes began. 'So, you finally decided to show your face, did you?' Her grandfather's words were slow and deliberate. Then, with thoughtful nods of his head, he stared directly at Molly, then looked down at where Beth had once again taken her position on the floor, her hand hovering cautiously over the puppy, unsure of what to say or how to react.

Turning away, Molly felt her eyes fill with tears. She wasn't used to her grandfather's wrath, saw the renewed pain in her gran's face and took note that her smile didn't quite reach her eyes, not any more. The sparkle that had always been there had gone. She'd grown thin, gaunt and her normal lust for life had disappeared, replaced by the look of hope and gratitude that they'd spared her the time to visit. The difference in her was palpable and Molly felt every part of her ache, knowing she'd contributed in some way to that pain. 'We're in touch all the time. We phone, don't we, Gran?' she said apologetically, knowing that the mediocre explanation just wouldn't be enough. That her grandfather expected more.

'Oh, you phone, do you?' Henry arched his eyebrows, pushed off his wellingtons. 'You're breaking her damned heart. Don't you see that? Don't you think she lost enough, all those years of keeping everyone's business, your mother's damn secrets, pretending everything's okay, when it isn't?' He threw the boots at the boot box and pulled off his cap to reveal a fringe of grey hair around his balding, mottled scalp. 'That house, urgh, it's been nothing but trouble for years and now, now you've gone to live in it, for God's sake... give... me... strength.'

'Oh, Henry. Please don't. They're here now... and, well, I'm ashamed of you, launching straight in.' She paused, gave him a stern, controlling look. 'Now, isn't it time you hugged your girls and showed them some love, rather than that sharp, bitter and twisted old tongue of yours?'

Again, he stood and stared. Then smiled awkwardly and held out his arms. 'Of course, you're right, you always are. Come here, give this silly old man a hug. God knows he could do with one.'

Dutifully, Molly stepped into his arms, felt them surround her. Felt comfort in his hold and took in the familiar earthy aroma that always came with farm work. 'I'm so sorry we haven't been. I really didn't mean to hurt you, honestly I didn't.' She felt the tears that had threatened earlier, suddenly begin to cascade. She was embarrassed, knew her grandfather was right, that there was no excuse. They'd stayed away, hurting everyone. Including themselves. 'It's just,' she rolled her eyes towards the ceiling, 'since Mum, I...'

'I know, I know... as your gran says, you're here now.' For a big man, the words were gentle, loving and heart-breaking, all at once. He'd always been there, the one whose knee she'd sat on so very often as a child, the one who'd read to her, hugged her to sleep and in her teenage years had become her very own taxi service, collecting her from nightclubs, when in reality she'd been far too young to go into them.

'I told you we should have been, Moll. Didn't I?' Beth growled accusingly, catching Molly's eye with a glare, the blame within them clear to see. 'If I could drive, I'd be here every single day. In fact, that new school Molly's making me go to has a bus that goes right past, so maybe I'll come on my own, after school, to see the puppy.' She lay back on the carpet, giggling as the puppy jumped all over her. 'That'd be okay, wouldn't it, Gran?'

Molly's hand went up to wipe the tears from her grandfather's eyes, before kissing his cheek. Sighing, she let go and watched as Beth jumped up from the floor and rushed in, childlike, to take her place. Taking a moment, she slid to the floor, sat on the rug, leaned her back against the sofa and began tickling the hyperactive pup that playfully jumped all around her. 'It's just...' She stared at the floor, took in a deep breath, bit down on her lip. She didn't know where to begin, didn't know how to explain. She loved her grandparents with all her heart and didn't want to hurt them but since her mum died, she'd done just that, she'd pushed them away, she'd pushed everyone away.

She hadn't been able to get over the idea that her mother had known her murderer. All the evidence had pointed to it. The door had been willingly opened. Two glasses of wine had been poured, ready to drink. A million thoughts and nightmares had whizzed around her mind like a fast-spinning drill and she'd constantly looked at all their friends, their neighbours, and work colleagues. She'd seen them all as suspects. *Was it you? Did you do it? Did you take her away from me? Was it an accident? Were you sorry? Did you watch her die, steal her Rolex and if you did, why?* She hadn't known who to trust. Who not to trust. And now, deep down, she knew that to have even considered her own grandparents with those same accusing eyes had been a deep and unnecessary injustice.

'She should be here, shouldn't she?' Pushing herself up to perch on the edge of the settee, Molly paused. Her hand went outward to sweep the room until finally it pointed at the fire. 'She should be in this room, right now, and she's not and every part of this house reminds me of her,' Molly finally whispered, feeling her gran sit down beside her and pull her into all-encompassing and loving hug.

'Hey, you remind me of her too. You're her absolute double. But that doesn't mean I don't want to see you,' Gran whispered with compassionate eyes. 'And, Moll, she's...' The words caught in her throat, and she closed her eyes, puffed her cheeks up and blew out while waiting for the moment to pass, then continued. 'She's gone, Moll. And it breaks my heart that she's gone. But – do you know what feels worse?' Holding Molly at arm's length, she raised her eyebrows, gave her a half smile, searched her eyes. 'What's worse is that I feel like you've gone too, that I didn't just lose her, I lost you two, too.' Forcing a smile, she tapped her hand to her heart. 'Right now, we all need each other, we all need to stay close, look out for each other, right?'

Molly closed her eyes as she lay in her gran's arms, which surrounded her like an old, familiar blanket. One that gave love, comfort and warmth and, for once, she didn't mind being held, rocked and loved like a baby. After what seemed like an age, she opened her eyes, stared into the flames of the log burner, watched them dance and imagined her mother sat there. She was perched beside the hearth, laughing and sipping hot chocolate, with the glow of the fire lighting up her face. It was an image she'd seen at least a thousand times and she smiled wistfully at the memory. 'Why didn't we come here, instead of going to the refuge. You know, when Beth's dad was arrested?'

Gran sat back, lifted a hand to cup Molly's face and, with tears in her eyes, shook her head, glanced at Beth and stood up. 'Now, tell me, have you been eating properly? 'Cause looking at you both, you look much too thin.' Brushing down her skirt, Gran pressed her lips together as though weighing up the situation, and without waiting for either of them to speak, she continued. 'I've got a big meat and potato pie in the oven. Much too much for the two of us, isn't there, Henry, and it'll go to waste if you don't have some.' She smiled and walked towards the Aga, as though a piece of her pie would be the best solution for them all.

'There sure would be; you know your gran's pies, they're big enough to feed the whole darn village.' Rubbing his stomach, their grandfather walked to the door. 'I'll go and shower, get rid of the smell of sheep before we eat and give you ladies some time to chat.' He gave them an easy smile, nodded as though satisfied with the situation and left the room, taking Meg with him.

'But... we did stay here, didn't we?' Beth suddenly chipped in. 'I remember you teaching me to ride my bike, and the next day you decided that if I could ride the bike, I could ride a horse and up I went.' She laughed, her eyes never leaving the puppy, who ran around her in ever decreasing circles.

Molly felt the breath catch in her throat as she looked up at Gran, knowing that Beth was right. They had stayed here for a while. She just couldn't remember when. Was it after Beth's dad had gone into prison, or before, during a time when their mother had been taken to hospital, fighting for her life? A time that both she and Beth had been protected from and a time her gran obviously still didn't want to talk about.

'Sure. We'd love to stay for dinner, wouldn't we, Beth?' She swallowed hard, trying to change the subject as Beth moved to sit beside her on the settee, her whole body as far back into the cushions as she could get, until she looked as though the settee were about to swallow her whole. With her legs curled up beside her, the conversation about staying at the farm forgotten, she giggled as the boisterous puppy stood with its front legs by her knee, its back legs frantically bicycle kicking, in an attempt to climb up and sit beside her.

'Come here, boy,' Gran shouted. 'Let's have you behaving yourself for just a few minutes.' She patted her leg, tried not to laugh as the puppy hurtled towards her, went far too fast, skidded onto its chin, then jumped up quickly to weave itself around her ankles, its paws reaching upwards with its head comically disappearing beneath Gran's long voluminous cotton skirt. 'And yes, I know, you want feeding too. I didn't forget.'

Molly leaned into the settee with a sense of contentment. She'd spent most of her life in this very kitchen, surrounded by dogs, cats, the occasional house rabbit and God only knows how many budgies. It had always been the most welcoming, animal-filled kingdom she'd ever known, and she smiled, knowing that right now this house was exactly what both she and Beth needed, that their visit had been the perfect way to build bridges and to spend time with their down-to-earth grandfather, who said everything just as it was, which was a refreshing change to most people she knew. Then in comparison, there was her more than wonderful, eccentric grandmother, who still dressed and acted like the world's last remaining hippy and said everything she could to keep the peace.

'And you were cooking that just for the two of you, were you?' Molly questioned suspiciously as her gran pulled the biggest pie she'd ever seen out of the oven and placed it on a big cast iron trivet in the middle of the table, looking overly proud, just as she had so many times before.

Staring at the pie and at the depth of the crust, Molly found herself trying to work out how many extra miles she'd have to run the following day to negate all the piled on calories, because where there was pie, there was always a pudding to follow. She sat down at the long oak table, leaned on her elbows and listened to the contagious sound of her sister's giggling. It was a sound that made Molly realise that one small puppy was bringing her more happiness than Beth had had in months and the guilt tore through her like a sharp but jagged knife.

Standing up, Molly moved to the dresser, pulled knives and forks from within, picked up a tea towel and started to polish each one before placing it on the table. Staring thoughtfully at her reflection in the last of the knives, her mind flicked back to how she'd met Niall on the beach, to his face that had intrigued and annoyed her in equal quantities. Sighing, she could see his perfect looks, that flawless smile and his man-mountain of a physique that was just about as good as they came. Then, without thinking, she compared him to Dan, who was also a good-looking guy, had kept himself physically fit, had a great body, big muscles and a smile to match. In fact, Dan was what most women would class as the perfect catch, so why didn't she see it, what was it that had changed so dramatically between them?

Sighing, she looked up, stared at the fire, tried to dismiss all thoughts of men and relationships. She had Beth to consider. Had to be the one constant in her sister's life, without distractions. Shaking her head, she took in a deep breath, watched the flames that licked the back of the chimney and suddenly became aware of the smell of rich caramelised beef, garlic, mushrooms and onion that filled the kitchen. Molly's mouth began to salivate.

'Oh, my God, how do you do that?' she said to her gran. 'I

wasn't even hungry and now – now I'm absolutely starving.' Making her way to the table, she watched her gran turn the pie around on the trivet, as though by turning it she'd get a different perspective. Then, as she'd done so many times before, she plunged her knife into its crusty middle, placed a large piece into her deep, earthenware bowl and poured the thick, dark beef gravy from the jug.

Less than a half hour later, Molly sat by the fire, gave an involuntary shudder, crossed her arms around herself and used a hand from each arm to rub the other. Closing her eyes for a beat, she listened as the logs crackled and an easy silence filled the room, the only noise coming from the puppy whose whole back end was almost bending double with excitement as he wagged his tail. Once again, Molly noticed the joy in Beth's eyes as he jumped up and over her legs into her arms and finally landed on the floor in a heap, nestled his head into the folds of her gran's skirt and fell into a deep, restful and immediate sleep. It was as though someone had pulled the plug out and through half closed eyes, Molly raised her eyebrows, glanced across to Beth, who, like the puppy, had lain down, closed her eyes and with her head on her grandad's lap had fallen into a deep, peaceful sleep.

15

'So, you've gone out, have you?' I stand in the shadow of a large oak. Its branches reach out, far and wide above me, like long, spindly fingers trying to grab at the houses. It's a tree I've seen so many times before. A tree that I've leaned against to admire the view, to watch what you're doing, just like I watched Michael, his niece, your mother.

Quietly, I step over the fence, across the grass and onto the path, where my feet land heavily on the cobbles, the sound of my footsteps echoing eerily. I notice that the tide is still out, the waves are not rolling or crashing against the rocks and tonight, there are no seagulls, no dogs barking, and certainly no children hollering or whooping on the beach below.

Pulling the roll of tissue from inside my coat, I unwrap the long stemmed white longiflorum lily from within. Curl my lip in a sly smile, then lay it on the doorstep, carefully positioned to look natural, as though it could have blown in on the wind rather than been placed purposely.

With the garden suddenly illuminated by distant headlights, I take my leave, edge around the garden to step over the fence and position *myself to one side of the tree, take pleasure in watching you and the way you sit, staring at the house, and by the look on your face, you're wishing you were just about anywhere in the world but here.*

16

Sitting alone in the car in the darkness, Molly stared at the house, could hear Beth's words still ringing in her ears. 'Place really is knackered, isn't it?'

Knuckle rubbing her eyes, she slumped back in her seat, realised how true Beth's words had been, felt the happiness and excitement of living here dissipate. Taking a deep breath, she began to wonder whether she really had been excited or whether the thought of getting away, of living independently and away from Dan had clouded her judgement. Because the reality of living here wasn't anywhere near the 'dream' or the 'return to happier days' she'd hoped for.

Running her hands around the steering wheel, she squinted, followed the line of her headlights to the edge of the garden, tried to work out how hard it would be to make the garden safe, to stop anyone falling over the edge and, if it were possible, how they'd manage to erect a fence or barrier so close to a cliff. She cursed, remembered how beautiful the garden had been, knew how much it would take to restore it and all the hidden costs that would come with such a project.

Feeling overwhelmed, she puffed out her cheeks, switched off the engine and gave a gasp as the brightness faded and disappeared, leaving her sitting in near pitch darkness with just the moon and stars to light her way. It made the idea of leaving the car to walk to the house in the dark, alone, less than ideal.

Grabbing at her handbag, she pulled out the letter she thought she'd hid, the letter Beth had inadvertently found. Reading it again, she scowled. 'Well, you're out, Charlie...' She gave a thoughtful nod, closed her eyes to see his evil, scowling face. Once again, she'd received a text. A single line, non-incriminating, that could have been from anyone. Deep down, she felt sure it was him. Felt sure it was something he'd do. Ensuring that when he did turn up, looking for Beth, she'd already be on her guard, watching every car, fearing every knock on the door. With her blood boiling inside, she could feel her pulse quicken. No matter what, she had to keep him away. Felt proud that she'd managed so far, but that was before he'd been released and now, everything had changed, he was free to walk the streets, to approach Beth whenever he wanted. Molly felt a sense of relief that she'd secretly gone through Beth's phone, her social media settings, increased her privacy. It had been a job she'd hated doing. A necessary evil. 'It had to be done,' she said with a nod, convincing herself that what she'd done was right, it's what their mum would have wanted, what she'd have done herself, if only she'd been here.

Glancing over her shoulder she nervously peered back along the lane, her eyes constantly searching the shadows, looking for movement. Looking for Charlie. From where she sat, she could just about see the side of Niall's property, the small but welcoming floodlight that lit up a small part of his drive. A small glimmer of light that peeked its way through heavily drawn upstairs curtains. In comparison, her own house was shrouded in darkness, making her wish that she'd thought to leave a lamp on in the hallway, or the bedroom, anything that might have made it look just a little more homely and welcoming.

Climbing out of the car, she watched the gate blow back and forth in the breeze but stood and squinted at the rickety old shed, its broken window that reflected the moonlight back at her and the huge pile of logs that had been delivered and were now strewn all over the area that used to be a lawn.

'Damn it.' She bit down on her lip. The hopes of a hot bubble bath, a book and an early night disappeared. 'I could ignore it. I could get up early, move them tomorrow,' she whispered into the darkness, pulled open the gate, felt the first drops of rain land on her face and roll down her cheek. 'Oh, for God's sake,' she growled, marching up to the front door as she felt her pocket begin to vibrate, the sound of Snow Patrol immediately filling the air. Delving into her pocket, she pulled out the mobile and smiled at the screen.

'Hi, Dan, how are you doing?'

'I'm good. Where are you?' He sounded edgy. The unusual tone of his voice spoke volumes and she balanced the phone on her shoulder, unlocked the front door. Then froze as she spotted a flower. It was wilted, bruised, lying on the doorstep with nothing around it but fallen autumn leaves that had blown in on the breeze. Turning, she looked over her shoulder. Felt sure she heard someone whisper her name, shrugged it off, determined not to be put off by the eeriness of being so remote. 'It's just a flower.' She checked the flowerbed to the side of the door, where all the previous year's flowers had withered and died, and her fingers went out to touch the climbing plant which had lost its leaves and all that remained was the twisted, woody stems that reached up for the eaves.

'What?' Dan's voice cut through the darkness, jolting her back to the conversation.

'Nothing,' she began. 'There was a flower on the doorstep, some kind of lily that had obviously blown in on the breeze.' Again, she heard a whisper, distant, remote. Felt her heartbeat accelerate. Her mouth grew dry, her eyes searching the darkness. 'And now I'm imagining things. Thought I heard someone calling me. Argh.'

'Molly, I think you should go inside, lock the door,' he insisted, 'till I get there.'

'Dan, it's a bloody flower. Now, are you going to tell me what's wrong?'

With her mind filled with unanswered questions she ignored his pleas, knew he'd do anything he could to be here, to be a part of their lives. With a determination not to be fazed, she threw her handbag over the bottom of the balustrade, stood for a moment and waited nervously, listening to the house. Heard the normal creaks, bangs and knocking of the branch on the window. Realised how strange the house felt at night, how different it was to be alone.

'Where's Beth?' he asked, his voice soft, gentle, inquisitive. 'She with you?'

Pulling the understairs cupboard open, she quickly grabbed at her wellingtons and a pair of gloves. 'Dan, I know you so much better than that, what are you not saying?'

Standing still, Molly switched on the kitchen light and checked the room. Again, it was as she'd left it and if it wasn't for Dan sounding quite so edgy, she'd feel a sense of relief, but right now, she could almost imagine him pacing the floor as he pondered over his words. 'Beth stayed at Gran's. Is there a problem?'

'So, you're at the house, alone?'

Dropping her boots onto the floor, Molly pushed her feet inside. 'Dan, now you're freaking me out. Are you going to tell me what's going on, or not? 'Cause I know there's something.'

'Look.' He paused, took a breath. 'You know he's been released, don't you?'

'Sure, they sent Mum a letter. It was in a box full of post that had been at Mum's.' She still had no idea how she'd managed to open the post, to read each letter in turn. There had been so many claims, so much money, all owed in her mum's name. Money she still had to find a way of paying back, just as soon as the estate was settled.

'Well, that's the thing. He got out a few days ago.' She heard him sigh. 'I swear, Moll. I only just heard, or I'd have said something sooner.' When she didn't speak, he continued. 'I had to transport one of the prisoners to the hospital this afternoon and you know what it's like, the hours of boredom. Charlie got mentioned. I checked when I got back, and his cell was empty. New guy already in his place. Word has it, he got out Wednesday.'

Taking the phone away from her ear, Molly stared at the flower, the bruised, wilted flower, felt the air leave her lungs, darkness surround her mind, and she spun around on the spot, fully expecting to see Charlie O'Connor's broad frame standing in the doorway, a wide, nasty sneer crossing his face. She knew he was getting out, knew it had been planned for some time, but had tried to push the thought to the back of her mind, secretly hoping it wouldn't happen, that his release would be delayed or that somehow, he'd disappear, without trace. And vehemently she hoped she'd never again have to hear his name or worry about him contacting Beth.

'Moll, you there?' Dan's deep voice echoed from the handset and, for a moment, she simply held it at arm's length, her fingers numb with fear.

She pulled the phone back to her ear, felt a sob leave her throat. 'Dan... could he have been here? I mean, where is he now? Where is he living?' Searching the darkness, she followed the line of the trees, the space where her car was parked, saw nothing but shadows.

'Moll, your guess is as good as mine. His parole officer would have an address, but even criminals have data protection. I could ask around, see if anyone knows.'

Slamming the door behind her, she angrily stamped down the path. 'No, Dan. There's no point is there. Wherever he is, bloody psychopath is bound to turn up here, looking for Beth. And what if he does come here, to this house? What if he convinces her he's changed, reformed, whatever you call it? She's close to becoming an adult, Dan, and I won't be able to stop her seeing him, will I?' She knew she was rambling, talking at speed, but couldn't stop. Slowing her pace, she eyed the trees, the bushes, the shadows, thought about the picture, of how it had gone missing. 'I think he's already been here. Too many things have happened and now, now I have a lily, dumped on my doorstep.'

Pacing back and forth, she tried to work out what Charlie was planning, what his end goal would be, whether he really would have left a flower on her doorstep. He'd always been resourceful, a little more than elusive. Which meant that he would definitely be up to something, and Molly knew that he had all the time in the world, not to mention all the wrong friends in all the right places. Some were still on the inside and others on the streets. Most willing to do just about anything to earn a quick buck.

As far as she knew he hadn't known where she and Beth lived. She hadn't told anyone she was moving, apart from her grandparents and Dan. And of course, with him living next door, Niall knew they were there too. Which meant the chances of Charlie having found them already were slim, but not impossible, and the thought that he could have already been here was now digging away in the back of her mind.

'Where did you say she was?'

'Who, Beth? She's at Gran's, conveniently fell asleep on the settee. Accidentally on purpose I'd say. So I left her there for the night, she hasn't seen them for a long time, and I thought Gran would talk some sense into her about trying to settle.' Picking up a log, she threw it across the shed floor and watched it as it came to rest at the back, where long bamboo poles stood in a corner, most probably waiting patiently to hold up next year's crop of beans or tomatoes.

'Jesus, Moll, what's the banging?'

'Oh, it's nothing, you know, just throwing logs into a shed in near pitch darkness, like you do. Delivery guy left them all over the bloody grass. Right by the shed door, trapping it open and, on cue, it's raining.'

'What logs?'

'A whole tonne of them, for the fire, I even paid extra for the kiln dried type and right now they're getting absolutely drenched, so...' Another log was tossed. 'Dan, I'd better go, I need to get this done, I don't want to be out here any longer than necessary, not if that psycho is out and about.'

17

Pushing the phone into her pocket, she nervously wedged the door open. Piled a few logs in front of it. Made sure it couldn't slam to a close. Being locked back in wasn't an experience she wanted to repeat, especially as tonight she was alone, Beth couldn't turn up and unlock it for her, unless of course it had been Beth who had locked it in the first place.

Picking up another log, she began throwing them with force into the depths of the shed, one at a time, and felt thankful for the window which, although broken, let in just enough moonlight for her to see where the logs were landing. Even though there was no order or assemblance, she knew that they'd at least be dry and out of the rain.

With her senses, already on high alert, Molly listened for every noise, immediately picked up on a cough followed by footsteps. Her whole body froze with terror and automatically she reached out, lifted a log, felt ready to use it as a weapon. Nervously watched through the corner of her eye as a pair of jet-black boots strode towards her.

'Don't come any closer!' she screamed, turned, lifted the log up ready to throw.

'Hey... woah... I come in peace and, if you don't mind, I'd rather you didn't throw anything at me.'

Laughing nervously, Molly dropped the wood, held a hand to her chest. 'Bloody hell, Niall. You just frightened me half to death.' She paused, took in a breath. 'I just lost ten years off my damn life. Again.' Leaning against the shed door, she saw Dillon running towards her, tongue lolloping to one side. Instead of being fearful, this time she bent down, fussed him while his whole body rocked from side to side. 'How come you're out so late?'

'Me and Dillon, well, we went to the shops. Seems like I can't go anywhere without him.' Niall placed a shopping bag on the ground beside where Dillon patiently sat. 'I was going to take him for a last-minute stroll on the beach, but then, well... we saw you.' He paused. 'Actually, if truth be known, I saw the guy delivering the logs this afternoon and when we heard you trying to launch the logs from a great distance, we realised what you were doing and... I knew I'd never settle with that racket going on, so rather than get pissed off by the noise, I thought I'd best stroll over and give you a hand.' He smiled and rolled his eyes upwards as the drops of rain increased in size. 'And, yep, they did say it'd rain.' His hands went out, palms up, then looked from Molly to the logs and back again. 'Give me a minute – Dillon, come on.' He tapped his leg twice. Disappeared into the darkness.

Continuing with her mission, Molly picked the logs up, threw them into the shed. Then heard Niall's boots return to the path. 'Bit of a wimp is our Dillon, hates the thunder, so I took him home,' he said with a smile, flexed his fingers. 'Right, let's get this done.'

'Seriously. You don't have to,' she said. 'I can do it, and it really won't take me that long.' The words fell unconvincingly from her mouth and even as she said them, she stood to one side, allowed Niall to step forward to look into the shed. Then, after summing up the situation, he began grabbing at the logs, two at a time, and with one foot in and one foot out of the doorway, he began launching them inward, as the deluge of rain continued.

'You're getting soaked,' she shouted, but the weather masked her voice and she stood back, then looked down to see her own jumper clinging intimately to her.

As though noticing her discomfort, Niall wiped the rain from his face, gave her an easy smile. 'Here,' he shouted, 'stand inside.' He took her hand, pulled her towards the shed. He looked her up and down, and quickly averting his eyes, pulled off his jacket. 'Here. You might wanna wear this...'

Gratefully, Molly took the jacket, pulled it on and zipped it up. 'Thanks.' Blushing, she anxiously stepped inside, stared into the moonlit shadows and to take her mind off of once again being trapped, she paid far too much attention to a twisted old spade that hung by the shed's broken polycarbonate window, felt sure she hadn't seen it before but knew that it was just another item that had been discarded, forgotten and left behind. Another part of the people that had lived there. Gingerly, her hand went out to touch the tool. The plastic coating had long since dropped away from the metal handle, the blade all damaged, obviously well used, and she struggled to hold back an overwhelming sob that left her throat. Had her mother done the same? Had she stood in this tiny little shed, picked up this spade, planted flowers and vegetables? Closing her eyes, she pictured her mother's face, her smile, the way her eyes would sparkle when she spoke. It was a sight that gave her immeasurable happiness and sadness, in a tidal wave of emotions that threw themselves around in her memories, all at once.

Then, as a jet-propelled log flew past her wellington clad ankles, she found herself back in the present. Fearful that the door was about to slam, that once again she'd be locked inside, she jumped forward and with her balance unsettled felt herself fall.

'Steady there.' With lightning reactions, Niall's hand shot forward. 'You all right?' His fingers twisted with hers, his touch firm, but gentle.

'Oh my God, thanks, yes, I'm fine, I...' She blew out, slow and steady. 'Thank you.' Nervously she released her hand from his, ran it through her hair to push the wet tendrils back from her face, wished for an elastic to tie it back, then nervously knuckle rubbed her eyes. She realised her mistake and that a combination of being out in the rain and rubbing her eyes probably meant that she now had make-up smeared all over her face like a tsunami of colour in all the wrong places.

Embarrassed, she turned away, pulled a sodden tissue from her pocket, quickly swiped at her eyes, then for something to do, she began moving the randomly scattered logs into a much neater pile at the back of the shed, as she continued to dodge the others that flew in through the door behind her.

As the last log was thrown, Niall stepped in, purposely leaned against the top of the door and silently gazed at the garden.

'What are the chances you'd let me design it?' he suddenly blurted out, tipping his head to one side and pointing. 'After all, Michael already paid for the plans, they're already drawn. Ready to go.'

'What, you drew plans for a garden?'

'Yep. We measure, plan, produce 3D drawings, everything.' He began to laugh. 'The vegetable plot, it's in the wrong place. We were going to push it further that way, into the far corner, where it'd get the right amount of sun and shade, it'd also be closer to the outside tap. Making it easier to set up a sprinkling device, save you having to water it by hand.' His finger waved at the area of the garden he spoke about. 'Raised beds would be better, save you bending too much, we could fill them with topsoil, plant small bushes around the sides, make it look visually pretty, create an edible garden. It's always good to grow your own.' He turned, smiled. 'And over there you need trees, they'd create a natural barrier, protect you from the elements and the greenhouse, well, if I'm honest, I'm kind of surprised it's still standing, 'cause the wind up here is brutal and right there, where it's been standing, it takes a battering every time it blows a hooley.'

Taking a step back, Molly looked over his shoulder, admired his silhouette, the translucency of his shirt, and with just enough moonlight she took in the shape of each and every one of his muscles and felt herself blush as he turned to fill the doorway. His body was hovering far too close to hers and now in the shadows, she could only imagine the look on his face, the smile, the way his lips formed a perfect pout.

Rubbing a hand across his neatly trimmed beard he turned back to the garden, seemed to study the terrain. 'If it were mine, I'd move the greenhouse right out of view. Put it next to the cliff. Lay a new base.' He nodded decisively, turned, caught her eye. 'Come here, look.' His arm went to her, rested easily on her shoulder. 'It needs to go over there and instead of a fence next to the cliff, I'd build a wall, but not with bricks, they'd crack with the movement, so instead, I'd keep it natural, create a raised bed out of sleepers, with plants that are not too high, obviously, you want the view, but you also need the safety. It'd create a natural barrier, stop anyone from accidentally dropping over the edge,' he joked, pointed to the area behind the house. 'And over there, that's where the patio should be, the hot tub, the garden furniture, a lawn, borders, one or two small trees, bushes, bamboo that would make a lovely rustling noise in the wind and hopefully, on a good day, it'd create a bit of a sun trap.'

Molly could see his excitement, the buzz of ideas that flowed from him and nodded appreciatively. 'You have no idea how much I'd love for you to do all of that, especially the idea of the hot tub, I can't think of anything nicer, but...' She looked down at the shed's floorboards, thought of the debts her mother had left behind. Had no idea how she'd ever pay them back. 'There's no way I could ever afford it. Our mum's estate, it hasn't been settled yet. I'm still trying to work out what does and doesn't need paying.' She rolled her eyes upward, caught his gaze, held it for a moment too long. 'Sorry,' she whispered. 'Don't know why I told you that, but the truth is... the garden will have to wait.'

Feeling self-conscious, she ducked under his arm, stood just outside the door. The rain had stopped as quickly as it had started and with relief, she held her arms outward, palms up. 'Well, look at that, it stopped right on cue.'

Trudging across the grass, Niall walked with her. His eyes were cast down, and as they came to stop close to her front door, he went quiet, nervously stepped from foot to foot, making Molly wonder if he were waiting for an invitation, for a 'Will you come in for a coffee? A cosy night in? A night of mad passionate sex?' Shocked by her thoughts and with eyes as big as saucers, she stared across the bay, thought of how her life had been and how just a few years before, at a time when she'd been young, free and single, she'd have happily invited him in, made him coffee, thought about the rest.

Since Dan, she'd kept herself to herself. Hadn't wanted to get involved, not with anyone. Her mum's death had made her wary and living in Dan's house had made it impossible. After all, they'd once been a couple. Bringing another man home would have been like rubbing salt into the wound, especially when he hadn't wanted the split. Taking slow, deliberate breaths, Molly stood, watched the way the waves rolled up and over themselves, their silver tops, with only the moonlight to highlight their path. The only sound louder than the crashing of waves was that of the branch which annoyingly still tapped against the front window of the house, disturbing her thoughts, bringing her back to the moment.

Rolling her eyes, she pressed her lips together, smiled nervously. 'I know, I know, it's annoying, isn't it? Another job I've added to the ever-growing list. I'll get round to it...'

Stepping forward, he studied the tree. Its proximity to both the house and the edge. 'You'd be a bit crazy if you tackled that. It isn't hanging on by much, looks as though it could fall at any minute and if you grabbed it, well... I reckon you could topple right over the edge.' He walked across to the tree, pressed a hand against it. 'Why don't you let me sort it out for you, wouldn't take me a minute?'

Breathing in, she gave Niall what she hoped was a casual smile, didn't want to take advantage. 'Look, no. It's fine. You've done enough.' With the shed in her sights, she pointed across the garden. 'It would have taken me ages to clear the logs and the branch...' She stretched, her heart pounded, her stomach twisted with nerves. 'It's only annoying when its windy.' She laughed. 'Which of course is just about all the time up here, but then... serves me right for going to live on the edge of a cliff, doesn't it?'

Pausing, Niall took the time to think about his words. 'You know, I really didn't mind helping you...' He threw her a smile, kept his eyes fixed on hers. 'And leave the branch. I'll bring the safety gear over. Chainsaw will sort it in seconds.' He laughed. 'Besides...'

Molly felt her heart race, saw the way his eyes drew her in, held onto hers for a moment too long. Catching her breath, she nervously took a step backward, realised she was still wearing his jacket and went to unzip it.

'Seriously.' He paused, held out a hand, caught her fingers with his. 'Please – don't take it off... I mean, I'm not complaining, but for the sake of your modesty...' he winked, 'I'd keep it on.'

Seeing the amusement in his words, Molly couldn't help but smile back, caught the way the moonlight lit up his face, the unmistakable, sensual way he pursed his lips and even though he'd been drenched by the rain, what was left of his aftershave still played with her senses. 'But...' She looked down at their conjoined hands, forced herself to breathe, felt his lips precipitously touch hers. Just a graze at first, then with his hand cupping her chin. Then, with clear, defined movement, he began gently surrounding her mouth with soft, tender kisses. The headiness of his aftershave stimulated her senses, she felt alive for the first time in months, felt his lips leave hers momentarily, only to begin searing a path down her neck. Closing her eyes, she moaned with desire, allowed him to take control. Then, without warning, his lips returned to hers. Moving sensually, he captured them in a passionate, more demanding way. His tongue gently teased to send shivers racing through her body, like mini electric shocks. With each kiss the intensity deepened, the warmth spread through his fingers, moved over her shoulder, down her back, traced the curvature of her spine. Then he stopped. Held his face close to hers, the onyx sparkle of his eyes reflecting in the moonlight.

Self-consciously, Molly began to twist her fingers around themselves. Closed her eyes for a beat, inhaled the sea air, blew out through puffed up cheeks, then looked everywhere she could to evade his gaze. 'Oh, you forgot your shopping.' She watched as he walked towards it, lifted the shopping bag, reached inside, pulled out the bottle of red wine. Waved it in the air.

'You fancy a drink?' He pouted, his mouth still red, almost bruised from kissing.

Quickly, Molly's eyes went from his mouth to the bottle, her gaze landing on the silver label, the deep red swirly letters. The exact brand that had been left on the side at her mum's on the night she was killed. With the air squeezing itself out of her lungs, she did everything she could to force it back in. Tried desperately to calm herself. Didn't want him to see her panic, tried to think logically. It was just wine. A single bottle of wine. Nothing more. It was a popular brand. All the shops sold it. What's more, she should have known that one day she'd come across it again. So why did she feel as though it were poignant. Why was she suddenly terrified of inviting him in and why was she standing here, looking for Charlie, waiting for him to walk up the path, shake Niall's hand. After all, he knew criminals, he employed them. Which meant there was a chance they could have met.

Shaking her head, she kept her eyes on the bag, swallowed hard, felt incapable of shifting her gaze, of catching his eye. 'It's late, I need to go in… I need to call my sister,' she heard herself making excuses. 'I need to make sure she's okay. You know, before she goes to sleep.' She paused, grabbed at air. 'I left her at our gran's and…' She felt her breathing accelerate and with eyes fixed on the bottle, she inched slowly backwards, gained space between her and the door.

Sensing her indecision, Niall looked down, to one side, held his hands out, palm forward. 'Hey. No worries. It's fine. All is good and I'm gonna… you know.' He pointed to the gate, looked around, gave her a pensive smile. 'I'm gonna go.'

Nodding, Molly practically threw herself at the door, closed it behind her and slid down the wall to sit on the bare floorboards, held a hand to her chest.

With air that was already difficult to breathe, the sudden and loud knocking at the door behind her brought her a new, deeper sense of trepidation. For a moment, she simply sat, closed her eyes. Unable to move. Wished she'd turned off the light. Then slowly, she began shuffling, inch by inch across the floor, towards the kitchen.

'Moll...' Another short, sharp, knock vibrated behind her. 'Moll, you in there, come on, open the door. It's me, it's Dan...'

18

Smugly, Charlie O'Connor walked slowly along the lane, towards the coastal path and meandered between the cars that were already parked, most empty of their occupants who'd already gone to the beach and were riding the waves or walking along the cliff tops. He glanced cautiously from one vehicle to the other, all the time checking that they were empty, that he hadn't been seen.

Taking his time, he made his way to a small wooden bench that stood by the cliff. Dropping onto it heavily, and with slumped shoulders, he concentrated on the sunrise, took deep inward breaths. Suddenly, he realised how long it had been since he'd smelled the sea air, how different it was to how he remembered. That in the ten years he'd been inside, everything had changed, and he curled his lip angrily, knowing what he'd lost. What he needed to get back.

For a moment, he stared through tired, narrowed eyes at the dormer bungalow that stood in the distance. Its position on the cliff top precarious, yet perfectly surrounded by a natural landscape that he'd love to admire, and would have, if only that house hadn't brought him so much misery, caused him so much loss. A loss that still wasn't over.

Holding a hip flask up in the air, he swirled the whisky around inside, held it up in salute. 'To my daughter,' he whispered, laughed and finally, after much deliberation he lifted it to his lips and held it there thoughtfully. Then tipped the flask in a fast, upward motion, before swallowing with a satisfied, 'Arghhhh.'

Wiping his mouth on his sleeve, he screwed the cap back on. He dropped the flask onto the grass beside him, and with his hands hooked behind his head he leaned back, closed his eyes, took pleasure in the early morning sunshine warming his face. In his mind, he could hear every sound. Found himself homing in on every voice, every person that walked along the beach. Listened carefully, wondered if Beth would be one of them.

Turning on his seat, Charlie caught sight of the old black BMW as it pulled into the car park. Watched the way it steered into position between two other cars. The driver, a bald, stocky man sat within, glaring in Charlie's direction with a furrowed brow and dark, piercing eyes. Climbing out, he limped uncomfortably across the grass, a long wooden walking stick held aloft in his hand. It barely touched the floor, giving Charlie the impression that it had been brought as a weapon.

Standing up, Charlie cautiously held out a hand, saw the man's indecision, thrust it back into his pocket where his own weapon hid. Rolling the pen knife over in his fingers, he stood his ground, waited until the man reached him.

'Took your damn time, didn't you?' Sitting back down on the bench, Charlie moved to one edge, rested an arm across the backrest, indicated the seat beside him.

'I haven't got long,' Matt Kelly snapped, waved his stick in the air. 'So whatever it is you want, you need to make it fast.'

Nervously, he paced back and forth. Took a step towards the cliff edge, anxiously looked over and, with the colour draining from his face, he stepped away and stood behind the bench as though using it as a protective barrier. Holding on tightly, Charlie noticed the way his fingers turned white, his nails unconsciously digging into the wood. 'Don't even know why I'm here. I owe you nothing, O'Connor, do you hear that? Nothing.'

'Matt, come on. Chill out, you're gonna give yourself a heart attack. Now, sit down, take in the sunrise,' Charlie whispered, almost dreamily. He sighed. 'See that.' He pointed at the sea. 'That boat. I'd like to go on a boat one day, wouldn't you? A cruise maybe, or just on a cruiser, round the bay.' He laughed. 'Can't see me ever getting on a damn cruise, can you? Now, please, enjoy the moment.'

'Sit down, enjoy the moment?' he spat. 'I'd rather jump off the bloody cliff than sit with you. Now. You either tell me what you want, or I leave.' Anxiously, he turned, looked over his shoulder, rubbed the palms of his sweaty hands down his jeans, tugged at the collar of his shirt. 'Well?'

Launching himself over the bench, Charlie took Matt by surprise. Knocked the walking stick out of his hand, grabbed him by the throat and slowly squeezed. All the time, adding more and more pressure. 'You need to sit down when I ask, or I might just throw you off the fucking cliff. Blink twice if you understand me?' They stood nose to nose and Charlie smiled as Matt blinked, then forcibly walked him around the bench and eased him onto the seat. 'There you go, that wasn't hard, was it?' Slapping him on the side of his face, Charlie winked, gave him a sarcastic smile. 'Next time, you do as I say, first time. Got it?'

'What the fuck do you want, O'Connor? I won't ask again.' He shuffled along the seat, until he balanced stiffly on the edge.

'I want to see my daughter,' Charlie growled. 'I want to see

Beth. She has something I want. And you, you're going to make it happen.' Charlie knew he was treading a fine line. His parole had restrictions and he knew that by taking one step within a half mile of Beth he could easily end up back inside. But he'd waited years to see her, to set things straight. To get what he wanted and now... now he had every intention of doing just that. Just as soon as he knew where she'd be. All he had to do was get her on her own. Without her sister. He pointed across the cliff, to the house perched on the edge. 'See that house, that's where she lives.'

Puzzled, Matt sat forward, wiped beads of sweat from his brow in relief. Pulled at his collar, undid the top button. 'So, if you know where she is, what the hell do you need me for?' he said with his eyes firmly fixed on the walking stick.

'Well, I can't just walk up and knock on the door, can I?' Rolling his jaw, Charlie looked down, saw two women walking along the beach, their arms hooked together, their feet touching the edge of the water. 'Against my parole.' He stood up, took a step towards the cliff and inquisitively, he picked up a stone, threw it at the beach and watched as the girls turned, looked up. With disappointment crossing his face, he shook his head, sighed. 'Your sister,' he said decisively, 'she lives around here, doesn't she?'

Matt nodded, slowly. Then jumped up from his seat. 'Oh, no. Not a chance. You're not bringing our Shirley into this. I won't have it, she's a good kid, never been in any trouble with the police. I won't have her working for you.'

Looking directly into Matt's eyes, Charlie saw the beads of sweat that continued to roll annoyingly down his forehead, the twitch of his eye, the trembling of his lower lip. 'No, Matt, not your Shirley, I wouldn't do that.' Charlie spoke calmly, paused, lifted a hand, tapped the side of his nose. 'But that nephew of yours,' Charlie dropped in. 'He owes me. I got him out the crap a couple of years ago. Saved him from going down. Didn't I?'

Throwing his head back, he let out a loud, humourless laugh. 'What is he now? Sixteen?' Looking back at the sea, Charlie waved a hand in the air, then leaned forward to pick the hip flask up from the grass, took another long, satisfying slurp. 'I think it's time you give him a call. Tell him I need a word.'

19

Waving to her grandad, Beth held onto the gate until her knuckles went white. Tutting, she watched miserably as his car turned the corner and his taillights slowly ambled down the lane, disappeared out of sight.

Standing there for a moment, she considered the day, the amount of unpacking they still had to do and wished she were back at her gran's, playing with the puppy, lying on the rug in front of the fire, or eating another bowl full of her grandad's homemade 'whisky butter porridge'. It was a smell and taste of home. A flash of happiness that had been broken the moment Molly had phoned and insisted she came back to the house.

'I'll take you,' her grandad had quickly said. 'Let me get my boots on.' He'd made a play of finding his boots, allowing the puppy to chase his laces. 'I could do with a bit of fish for tomorrow's tea, so if we go now, I'll take a drive by the harbour, see if any of the local fishermen have anything good to offer.'

At first, the idea of her grandad coming to the house had made her smile. She loved the thought that he'd see the place. See how much there was to do. And in his own generous way, she thought he might stay for an hour or two, help them unpack. But he'd refused.

'I don't want to come in,' he'd said. 'Bloody house, it's caused me enough trouble to last me a lifetime. Last thing I ever want to do is step foot inside it.'

'Hey kiddo?' The front door sprang open and Dan's voice suddenly burst through her thoughts, making her jump with surprise, then squeal with delight.

'Hey, you, what you are doing here?' She gave him an over exaggerated wink, a cheeky half smile. 'You two have a good night?' she questioned in a whisper, quickly realising that her plan had worked and felt pleased with herself for pretending to fall asleep and texting Dan the moment Molly left. Smugly, she reached up, kissed him on the cheek. 'So good to see you, but...' she pointed to the sand, 'if you want another half hour or so, I could always bog off down the beach.' She began to smirk, poked him in the ribs. 'Unless of course, you know, you're a bit exhausted...' Her teenage giggles infiltrated the hallway.

'Beth, enough of that. Now, have you seen the bacon?' Molly's voice bellowed from the kitchen, making Beth freeze on the spot. 'I know there definitely was some. It was right there, in the drawer. Put it there myself, Friday night, as soon as the men brought the fridge in.'

'Welcome home, Beth,' she mimicked, took a deep breath, gave Dan a look that would have melted butter and whispered with a giggle, 'What makes her think that I know where it is?' She stood on the step, peered in through the door, spoke to Molly. 'How should I know, maybe you just thought you put it there. I mean, did you check the cupboards, or... or oh, oh, I know, maybe it's at the side of my bed right next to that picture of dear old Michael.' Rolling her eyes at her sister, Beth flounced up the stairs. She went into the room that she'd chosen for herself and began rummaging through the bags of clothes that still stood piled up in the corner.

After dragging on a pair of clean jeans, a hoodie and a pair of old denim trainers, Beth stamped back down the stairs. 'See what I've had to do. Double denim.' She pulled a face. Held a foot out for Molly to see. 'I'm going out,' she yelled, heard the door slam behind her, smirked.

Zipping up her jacket, Beth skipped along the cobbled path, headed for the lane. Dodged the puddles and tutted as her feet slipped from side to side. Her hand went out to hold onto one of the tall, willowy trees. Its branches reached so far over the path that she almost had to duck to walk beneath them. Holding her position, she stooped to wipe the mud from her trainer, peered through the fence and into the neighbouring property. 'So, that's where the man-mountain lives, is it?' Pursing her lips, she looked from one irregular sized window to the next. Not one looked to be the same shape, there was a mishmash of styles, all screaming out to be changed, replaced. Tipping her head to one side, she tried to imagine what kind of a man he was, what he actually looked like. She cursed the way Molly had gushed about him for a whole hour after she'd met him.

Angrily, she stood up and kicked out at his six-foot gate, heard it swing open with a loud, distinctive groan. The unexpected sound made her duck behind an overgrown privet, where she clasped a hand over her mouth, hoping he wasn't at home.

Whilst cowering, she held onto the edge of the gate, took in a deep breath in and with one eye on her own house, and one eye on his, she began forming a plan. If she were to get Dan and Molly back together, the man-mountain had to stay away, and with a smirk on her face and a final glance at the house, Beth turned the corner, saw the wooden steps and stood at the top, looking down.

'So, this is the famous beach, is it?' Warily, she made her way down to the sand, immediately pushed her hands in her pockets, felt a shiver travel up from her toes. 'Jesus...' she yelped, wished she'd worn her ski jacket. 'And Molly reckons it'd be fun to walk on the beach, does she?' She huffed. 'Well, I've got news for her. It isn't.'

Keeping her back to the sea and the oncoming breeze, she faced the cliff, looked vertically upward, tried to work out where their garden began and ended and eventually, after much deliberation, she spotted the overhanging tree, the one whose branch tapped on the window.

'Hey...'

Holding her breath, Beth slowly turned. She smiled with relief as a young, half dressed man ran towards her. Pushing a hand through his curly blond hair, he balanced a surfboard precariously under the other, gave her a cheeky smile and propped his surfboard up against the cliff. Throwing his towel at the sand and pulling at the neoprene wet suit, he carefully stretched it up and onto his arms. 'So, you're either new around here, or you're trying to work out how to scale that cliff and burgle that house?' He pointed, wrinkled his nose and shook his head. 'I wouldn't bother, cliff doesn't look too safe.'

Laughing, Beth shook her head. 'Not at all. I was just trying to work out how easily I could blow the cliff up and watch the whole thing disappear into the sea.'

He took a step back, reached behind his back, zipped his wetsuit. 'Okay...' He paused, laughed. 'I'm taking it you're not too keen on the new owners?'

'Sure, I am,' she chortled. 'I guess I am the new owner, along with my sister. We only got here Friday. Right in the middle of the storm and...' She swept an arm outward as though beckoning the sea. 'There's nothing to do around here.'

He began to walk across the beach, picked up a small pebble and tossed it towards the water. 'You could always come surfing? Water's great.' He gave her what looked like a pensive yet inviting smile. 'Or...' Arching his eyebrow, he winked, cheekily. 'There's always other stuff we could do. Places we could go.'

Beth quickly took a step back, felt the colour rise to her cheeks. 'Hey, stop it. I'm fifteen. I hate it here, and my sister, I think she'd like to ground me for at least a year.' She looked up, caught his eye.

Moving cautiously, he sat down, inched closer. 'We're almost the same age, it was my sixteenth birthday a couple of weeks ago.' He leaned against her, bumped shoulders. 'I'm Jackson, live in the village.' His hand went up, pointed to the steps. 'I'm down here most days. 'Cause, as you say, nothing much else to do...'

Feeling the heat rise within, Beth casually put a hand to each side of her face, squeezed her elbows inwards, and gave herself a silent but much needed hug to hide her embarrassment. She couldn't believe he'd spoken to her. Didn't know why he had. Searching the beach, she looked at the other people who walked and played on the sand, realised how many others he could have spoken to. But he hadn't. He'd spoken to her. The thought made her quiver with excitement, making Beth openly preen herself and flick her hair backwards.

With waves that were increasing by the minute, Jackson moved a little closer, rested an arm casually across her shoulder. 'Seriously, you'd love it out there. Getting your balance is the tricky thing. Once you've learned how to do that, it's easy.' He dusted the sand from his feet, pulled a pair of tight-fitting neoprene pumps on.

Quickly wrapping her arms back around her knees, Beth leaned against the rock face, used it to shelter her from the breeze, watched the waves as they rolled towards her and felt uncharacteristically tempted by his offer. 'Jackson, how would I learn, you know, to surf?' She eyed the board. 'Would I have to get in the water?'

Jumping up, Jackson lowered the board to the sand. Stood on it, his hands held outwards. 'Nah, you could do it here.' He held out a hand, pulled her up to stand on the board in front of him. 'That's right, keep your head up.' His arm went around her waist. 'Put your arms out, chin up, don't look down... and don't move too quickly and if you lean forward, close your mouth and expect the board to shoot backwards... if you don't keep your mouth shut, expect to swallow the sea and everything that floats around in it.'

She felt herself topple. 'Oh my God... see, I told you I wouldn't be able to do it!' She stepped onto the sand, felt happy that the landing was solid, remembered the plastic straws – they were still out there, floating around in the sea – and felt nervous of taking the board on the water.

'Come on, back on the board.' He held out an encouraging hand. 'Try it again.'

Feeling his arm slip around her waist for a second time, Beth's stomach turned with excitement, she could barely breathe, enjoyed the sensation of his touch. 'Ohhhhh,' Beth squealed, gripped tightly to his hand, began to laugh. 'Thought I was about to fall again.' She took a deep breath, felt his chin on her shoulder, his face next to hers.

'That's right, perfect. Imagine the wave, see it coming, steer the board.' His arm tightened around her waist. His body rocked sensually behind hers, making her gasp.

Laughing, Beth quickly stepped off the board, out of his grasp. 'Well...' She looked him up and down, admired the shape of his arms, the way the wetsuit hugged his legs. 'I think that's today's lesson over.'

'Well, that's a shame, 'cause I think you were just about

picking it up.' Suddenly, his arms were around her. 'Watch out,' he yelled, and Beth heard a prolonged crunch, followed by a thunderous bang. Her whole body was propelled across the sand. She landed against the cliff. Pain shot up her spine. The air left her lungs and her eyes became fixed on the tree that had fallen from the cliff top and landed on the beach beside them.

'What the hell just happened?' Taking short, sharp, exasperated breaths, she looked up to see exactly where it had fallen from. Quickly realised that she wouldn't be bothered by the branch ever again, nor would it tap on their living room window the next time they had a storm.

Jackson sat forward. 'I'd say that if I hadn't just saved your life... you'd be under that tree,' he said smugly. 'Which means... now...' He cupped her chin with a hand, pulled her towards him, stared into her eyes. 'Now, you owe me. Big style.'

20

My fingers press heavily against the ground. I'm sneaking through the undergrowth, keeping one eye firmly on the house, and feel a spark of nervous adrenaline as the back door opens and Molly slowly steps out. She's just a few feet from me. If I reached out, I could almost touch her barely dressed body. Her dressing gown is splayed open. The short pale green satin nightwear rides up on her thigh and I catch my breath, hold it in, notice the way she looks wistfully at the shed, the trees and then, right at the area where I'm crouching behind conifers, a deep red autumn viburnum, and I take in a sharp intake of breath, allowing the aroma to captivate my senses.

After just a few seconds, I hear the door close. I'm unsure as to whether she's gone back in, or stepped further out and I take a risk, lift my head above the proverbial parapet, crawl forward and while taking careful considered steps along the border, I make sure that I don't stand on the ground covering honeysuckle, the small crocus or the lavender that blows haphazardly in the breeze.

Tiptoeing nervously around the back of the greenhouse with my feet perilously close to the edge of the cliff, I look over, feel the fear and unease rise within me, crouch down to balance on a small ledge and wait patiently until I hear the youthful voices on the beach below.

Smiling slyly, I close my eyes as I eavesdrop, take a pleasure in the pure, innocent giggles as they turn into loud spouts of raucous laughter. The sound battles with that of the sea, the waves crashing on the beach below, seagulls crooning as they swoop and, without realising the danger, I hang my legs over the edge of the cliff, allow myself to peep at the beach.

Wondering how and why my life has come to this – to watching others. I'm saddened by the fact that my path has already been determined. Soon, both my life and theirs will be very different. And I sigh, wish for a day when there will be no more looking over my shoulder, or thoughts of murder. It occurs to me that I've fought with my conscience for far too long, and angrily I lift my hands, rub viciously at my head, bang my fists into my skull. Hear an undignified, but muffled growl that leaves my throat and I battle with the rights and wrongs of what I've done, wonder if I can really go through with it and kill them both? It's a task I don't want, there's been one too many deaths already and I find myself staring at the horizon, focusing my mind, knowing that it won't be over – not until I put the deed behind me, just as I have before.

Peering at the two youngsters, I enjoy the battle of wits between them. It's more than obvious that Beth likes him, her smile is lighting up her face. She's young, playful, her mannerisms are coy and innocent. What's more, he doesn't seem to mind. And neither do I, until the moment when she gives him the look of a she-devil, steps off the surfboard, pouts her lips and allows him to wrap his arms around her, moves her body sensually against his.

Through narrowed eyes, I press my lips tightly together. Stop myself from shouting, from screaming at him, from telling him she's only fifteen, a mere child, and in my temper I stand up. My hands automatically gravitate towards the tree, which is already balancing precariously, its life literally hanging on the edge, and with every ounce of energy I have, I push at the trunk. Then laugh as a thunderous noise is heard and the tree topples over the edge and directly towards Beth and her boyfriend.

For a single moment in time, I really don't care which one of them it hits.

21

The keen gardeners of Filey had all come out in force, meaning that Daniel's Audi TT, albeit noticeable, had been easily hidden between all the other cars. Sitting in the driver's seat, he slouched, pulled his collar up and his baseball cap down.

Watching, he found amusement in the mix of people who flooded through the double doors, pushing trolleys full of late flowering perennials, huge bags of decorative bark, pea gravel and an abundance of plants that would no doubt all die before the winter was over. The oversized trolleys added to the hilarity, as it appeared that most of the customers had completely underestimated the size of their cars, and stood scratching their heads before struggling to safely fill their car boots, with quite a few purchases ending up on back seats, in footwells, on passenger knees or were left on the trolley while the car was packed, unpacked and repacked.

Dan nodded thoughtfully. He knew he was losing Molly, she didn't look at him the same, or speak to him the same, not any more. That playful attitude he'd always loved about her had gone and he tried to come up with a plan of how to ensure he was at the house as often as he possibly could be. What's more, he had to make sure Niall saw him, every time he was there. Hoped he'd take the hint and keep a distance. The last thing he wanted was for Molly to get used to her new neighbour dropping in and out. Helping out around the house, the garden, becoming useful, or getting friendly. He gave a sharp shake of his head; Niall McCormick wasn't part of his plan and he certainly didn't want him to become part of Molly's plan either.

Giving himself a wry smile, he congratulated himself on turning up the night before. The way he'd sat next to her, held her close. Once again comforted her at a time she'd needed it the most.

'Not every man's a murderer, are they? I mean, if he wanted to kill me, he could have done it in the shed, couldn't he?' It had been more of a statement than a question, but the words had given Dan every opportunity to play on her emotions.

'Hey, I totally agree. But you barely know the guy. You only just met him and maybe he is a neighbour... but seriously, the people he mixes with...' He'd paused, wiped a hand across her cheeks in a feeble attempt to dry her tears, thought carefully about his words. 'They're criminals, Moll. They may have been released, let out into the world, but I know how their minds work and you have to trust me on this one. Just because they've been let out, it doesn't suddenly make them law-abiding citizens now, does it?' He'd sat with her until the tears had subsided, all the time fearful of leaving her alone. Fearful of Niall coming back to her door, of him taking his place. 'Moll, maybe I should stay tonight, stay with you,' he'd finally suggested, felt pleased with the indecision in her eyes. The way she'd nodded in approval.

'With Beth being at Gran's, I guess you could take her room,'

Molly had said, before jumping up and running down the hallway. 'I'll just go check her room, she'd be mortified if she left any personal stuff lying around, if you know what I mean.'

Reluctantly, he'd taken up the offer of the spare room, would have preferred the offer of her bed, of sleeping with her, knew not to push, to give her the space, and made every effort he could to be the person she needed. Determined that he'd be the one to comfort her in all the right ways. At all the right moments.

And now, now he had to alter the chain of events that had already begun, he had to find a way to build back the trust, to be a part of her life.

'So,' he thought desperately. 'Do I make a play of sorting the garden? Give myself a reason to be there, a reason for her to like me again?' He thought of his own tiny garden, his lack of enthusiasm for cutting grass. The impulsive purchase of forty slabs, all of which still stood against a wall, waiting to be laid. 'So, do the garden over the winter. Get Molly to trust you again, take her out, be the man she fell in love with the first time. Get her to fall in love with you again. That way, you can look out for her, protect her.' He knew that it had been his own stupidity that had pushed her away, his own actions had caused the rift, and mentally he kicked himself for not using the time better. He should have been delighted when she ran to him, when she moved back in, bringing Beth with her. Instead, he'd recoiled and thought of himself.

Sighing, he felt his whole body go tense as he saw the double sliding doors of the garden centre slide open, and Niall McCormick walked out. He stood in the doorway, hands on hips, sunglasses on his head. He looked smug. Full of his own importance. And while checking his domain, he wore nothing but a polo shirt and jeans, on a day when the temperature was more suited to an overcoat and gloves.

'What the hell does any woman see in you?' Dan whispered as he remembered the way Molly had returned from her run, her voice high-pitched with excitement.

'You'll never guess what just happened. I just met my new neighbour, Niall.' She'd practically danced on the spot. 'And what's more, he has the most beautiful dog, Dillon.' She'd spoken without taking a breath, beamed with happiness and had spent the next hour talking about him, about everything he'd told her.

'Perfect smile, perfect teeth, great frame, urgh...' Dan growled, picked up his phone, realised how bitter he sounded and for the second time that week, he began to google Niall McCormick, studied the results. 'No Twitter. No Facebook. No Instagram.' He furrowed his brow. 'Who the hell are you?' Flicking down the screen, he looked through various posts, the newspaper articles all singing his praises.

'On paper, you look like a real knight in shining fucking armour, don't you?' Dan scowled. Moved further down the screen, clicked in and out of posts. Nothing was out of the ordinary. Yet, in his eyes, nothing seemed quite right. Niall McCormick was literally too good to be true, which probably meant that he was. Even the way he strode across the car park was a little too perfect. Three men, all former criminals, climbed out of their vans and Dan took pleasure in the battle of the body language that began between them. Hovering head and shoulders above the others, McCormick smiled, pointed to a large pile of railway sleepers, spoke and then watched as the men, like over-enthusiastic puppy dogs, jumped to attention. Each one nodded, smiled, began the task of carrying sleepers from one side of the yard to the other.

Recognising one of the men, Dan lifted his phone, began to take photographs. 'Not the man I used to know, Grant, are you? Can't seem to remember you ever taking orders from anyone before.' He flicked through the pictures, waited for the conversation to be over, for Niall to disappear inside. Then, with purpose and a fixed gaze, he climbed out of the car and marched across the car park.

'Grant... over here, I need a word.'

22

Sliding her seat closer to her patient, Molly glanced up at the window. The dense, dark clouds that had been accumulating earlier had now parted. The rain had finally stopped, and she smiled as the low afternoon sun shone between vertical blinds to cast a bright orange hue around the brilliant white surgical environment.

For what seemed like the hundredth time that day, Molly felt herself squinting at the clock, swallowing impatiently and consciously counting the minutes. Her new assistant, Tasha, who had been very friendly at first, had suddenly begun throwing questions across the room in rapid succession. She seemed to have an insatiable appetite to find out all she could, in as much detail as you were willing to give.

While pretending to study an X-ray, Molly carefully slid open her personal drawer, made an attempt to covertly check her phone, looked for messages.

'Oh, didn't he message you yet?' Tasha quickly dropped in, with both shoulders hunched and a smirk crossed her face, then, when no answer came, she raised both eyebrows in question, tapped her pen against her teeth.

Throwing a hard stare across the room, Molly took a deep breath and looked for something to do, other than turn back to both Tasha and the patient. She switched on the light box, studied the orthopantomogram. Then, restlessly, she glanced across at her computer, wondered how many more patients she had booked in that day, how many more questions she'd have to answer before escaping for the evening. Tapping her screen forward to study her list, she gave a half smile as she realised there was just one more patient left to see. But then, in direct comparison, she felt the blood drain from her face as she saw Carol Cooper's name filling that appointment.

Holding onto the thin leather seat with trembling fingers, she leaned forward, felt her frustration levels rise as she tore off her glove, her face shield, then anxiously tapped at the keyboard, only to furrow her brow as she quickly read through the notes at speed. Saw the numerous appointments that Carol Cooper had booked.

'Oh, that one – she might not be turning up.' Tasha leaned across, placed a hand next to the keyboard, uncomfortably close. 'She didn't turn up for the appointment she had last Friday, which isn't like her at all. She's normally really early, and she chats for England, so she does. Drives Ginny in reception a little bit mad with all her tales and stories. But after her not coming in on Friday, I'm thinking she'll not come in today either.'

'Friday... the Friday just gone?' Molly could barely breathe. Carol should have been here on Friday. Somewhere else she should have been other than at the house. Haunted, she thought of the keys, the way they'd been hanging in the door, the bucket of hot steaming water. If she'd been there cleaning, knowing they were about to arrive, why wouldn't she wait, why would she leave before they got there, especially as they'd only ever spoken on the telephone. As Tasha had said, she had been very chatty, even though they'd had their disagreements, where she'd made it very clear that as executor of the property she'd felt very badly done by, that she should have come away with something for her time and effort. Yet she certainly hadn't been rude, which made it strange that she'd acted in such a way.

'We were parked on the lane, looking at the sea. But she got past us, without us seeing her?' Molly whispered out loud. Stared at the stainless-steel sink, turned on the tap, watched the water swirl around it, the steam rise up. 'The water in the bucket was still hot.' Shaking her head, Molly tried to make sense of the madness that was spiralling around her mind, the thoughts that stacked up, dropped into place, then scattered again.

'Molly, are you all right?' Tasha asked with an edge of concern. Her hand went out, pressed down lightly on Molly's shoulder. 'I could ask one of the other surgeons to take over...'

Snapping back to reality, Molly felt her skin flush. 'No, sorry. I'm... I'm fine,' she whispered, took a deep breath, inched her chair close to her patient, made a pretence of adjusting the light. 'Okay, Mr Elvin, if you'd open wide.' Holding a mirror in one hand, a probe in the other, she stared into the older man's mouth, at the limited range of decalcified, yellowing, misshapen teeth.

'Err... Molly...' Tasha whispered, wriggled her fingers surreptitiously behind the patient's back. Lifted the box of gloves towards her.

Staring at her hands. Molly immediately realised what Tasha was telling her, silently chastised herself for not replacing the glove and dropped the mirror and probe back into the stainless-steel tray, pulled at the box.

'...Upper left one, two and three are all missing, four we have an occlusal composite, five distal composite, six missing, seven...'

She blew a jet of compressed air onto the tooth, poked at it with a probe, tipped her head to one side and pressed her lips tightly together. 'The seven has a large mesial occlusal amalgam in it. I'd like to put a watch on it distally until next time. Upper left eight is missing.' She sat back, studied the X-ray and watched as Tasha quietly keyed the information into the computer.

Jumping up from her seat, Molly leaned across the man, carefully replaced his denture. 'There you go,' she said softly as she pressed her fingers under his jaw, closed his teeth together and checked his alignment. Once satisfied, she moved the chair into an upright position. 'If you'd like to give your mouth a rinse.'

'Am I done?' He picked up the thymol flavoured water, sipped, spat out, swiped at his mouth with the back of a shaking, aged hand.

'Yes, Mr Elvin, you are.' Molly removed her gloves and watched Tasha as she leaned forward to unclip the paper bib that covered the front of his shirt, gave him a genuine smile and watched him shuffle across the surgery and out of the room, with Tasha closely behind him.

Breathing out as the door closed behind him, Molly felt the pressure of the day rest heavily on her shoulders. She had to get a grip, had to calm herself down. Methodically, she turned to the sink, held her hands under the hot running water for as long as she could endure, dispensed three generous squirts of soap and began scrubbing at her hands with more vigour than normal.

Coming back into the room, Tasha perched on the edge of the patient's chair. 'Come on then, are you going to spill the beans? I'd love to know who he is, so I would.' Searching Molly's face for answers that didn't come, she sighed with disappointment, stood up and with a professionalism that Molly admired, she began to clean and organise the surgery. Sides were wiped, the spittoon sprayed with generous amounts of antibacterial spray and instruments, aspirator tubes, used drill heads and burrs were all placed on a metal tray in readiness for taking to the scrub room.

Closing her eyes for a beat, Molly took a breath. Knew she was unconsciously listening for the front door, for Carol Cooper to arrive and walk in, full of life. But deep down, she knew it wouldn't happen. Like Friday, she felt a little disappointed. She'd wanted to meet her, and even though she had an empty bank balance, she'd wanted to put things right. The strange happenings had made the whole event of moving into the house one to be remembered and momentarily she was back on the beach, with Niall, looking into his eyes, being captivated by his smile, his lips, the way his eyes had been deep, dark and unyielding, and he was telling her about the house and how everyone associated with it had ended up dying in a violent or mysterious way.

Sighing, Tasha broke through her thoughts. 'I don't think Carol Cooper is coming. She's never this late, normally sat in the waiting room for so long before her appointment we often feel as though we should offer her coffee, so we do.' She clicked at the keyboard with a long, pointed finger, watched the screen turn from bright opal to black, then tipped her head to one side to catch Molly's eye. 'Now then, are you okay? I'm a bit worried about you. You went awfully pale back then. I thought I was going to be picking you up off the floor, using me mammy's old smelling salts to get you back up.'

Raising both eyebrows, Molly rolled her eyes, knew an explanation of sorts was necessary. 'Sorry, it's no excuse, not in this job. But I have a lot on my mind.' She paused, thought. 'I'm hoping my fifteen-year-old sister will send me a message.' She once again checked her phone, waved it around in the air. 'Since our mum died, she's lived with me and today is her first day at a new school and she went off this morning in a mood. Apparently, I'm ruining her life.' She emphasised the word 'ruining', and sighed.

Uncannily, Molly thought, Beth had always messaged. After their mum's death, she'd messaged constantly, panicking if a response hadn't been immediately returned. Which confirmed her thoughts. Beth was still in a mood and it was going to take more than a phone call, text or the promise of pizza or new shoes to make things right. Which would be a great way of making it up, if only her bank balance hadn't been dwindling by the minute.

Standing up, Tasha continued to clean, her slender frame moving around the surgery with ease. 'I mean, come on, for the love of God, she can't really think that you're ruining her life, can she?'

'Who knows? She's a teenager.' Molly picked up her drill, detached it from the high-pressure hose, squirted ample amounts of oil through the hand piece and shook it. After carefully reattaching it, she pressed her foot on the pedal and watched as pressurised water sped back through it and into the sink where, once again, she watched the water flow, swirl around the bowl.

'I'll just pop these to the scrub room.' Tasha picked up the metal tray, opened the door. 'You want a coffee?'

'Sure, that'd be great, thank you.' Molly smiled. She didn't want coffee. What she did want was a moment alone, a moment to decide what to do. Standing up, she walked across the room, stared aimlessly out of the window, waited until she could hear Tasha in the room next door, the sound of instruments hitting the sink, water running and the sound of an autoclave door slamming to a close. These were followed by Tasha's heels clicking along the tiled corridor to disappear into the kitchen, where she'd probably spend the next ten minutes chatting to the other girls, making coffee.

Sitting back down, Molly quickly pulled her phone from the drawer. Then, with her lips pressed tightly together, she turned back to the computer, felt the anxiety begin as she flicked through the unfamiliar screens of the new system, tried to navigate her way back to where she'd been earlier, to Carol Cooper's notes. Once located, she held her phone up to the monitor, took a series of photographs. Hoped that one of them would show her a clear, concise picture of Carol's address. New data protection meant that her wings had been clipped. Taking the address wouldn't have previously been a problem, but now, the guidelines were blurred, and she couldn't risk being caught.

'Here you go, a lovely mug of coffee. Just the thing before you finish for the day and drive all the way home,' Tasha said as she passed her the mug. 'Did your sister get hold of you yet?' She perched on the chair, raised both eyebrows at the mobile phone Molly still held in her hand.

Shaking her head, Molly pressed the messenger icon. Hoped somehow a message would be there, that in her flicking and clicking at screens it had been opened and closed without reading it. Then, as covertly as she could, she tapped on the photographs, scanned the ones she'd just taken, flew quickly past them to one of the house, of the view, of Niall's property in the distance. Guilt seared through her. He hadn't deserved the way she'd treated him. The events of that night had played over and over in her mind and she began to wonder what would have happened if she hadn't seen the bottle. If it hadn't been the same make that had been on her mum's worktop the night she'd been killed. Would she have reacted differently? Would she have invited him in for a drink? Would he have kissed her again? How far would things have gone before Dan had turned up, knocked on the door like a knight in shining armour, fully expecting to stay the night? And now, she regretted that too.

'Wow, it takes a certain kind of memory to make a woman blush like that,' Tasha said, still perched on the chair. 'So, what do you say. Are you gonna share the gossip with me, or do I have to go and pretend to check the autoclave again?' She pointed to the door, laughed, picked up her mug and took a slurp.

Feeling her skin continue to radiate, Molly bit down on her bottom lip, considered the pros and cons of sharing gossip and paused before speaking. 'My new neighbour. I met him the other day and – well, you could say he's kind of cute.' She hesitated, laughed. 'To be honest, he's more than cute and I think I owe him an apology.'

Tasha nodded, excitedly. 'Really? So, what did you go and do, 'cause by the look of your cheeks, it had to be something?' She stood up, continued to wipe the surfaces, shuffle instruments and tidied paperwork.

Molly continued to weigh up her new assistant, began to relax in her company. Liked the way she'd stood up, almost danced on the spot, swayed with excitement. 'We were getting along quite well, I guess, but I completely blew it. And now, along with my little sister, he probably hates me.'

'Really... so why would he be hating you? Come on, tell Tasha all about it.' She went to the door, opened it, checked the corridor, clicked it to a close. 'Looks like the others have all gone home, so it's just you and me and a pair of coffee mugs.' Pulling the elastic from her hair, she shook her head to let her strawberry blonde locks drop loosely onto her shoulders.

Molly shook her head. 'Oh, it's nothing.' Sighing, she blew the coffee. Realised she'd wanted it after all and took a long swallow before placing it down on the side.

'Hmm. Doesn't look like nothing. I've seen that kind of look before... I bet you'd like to take him for a roll in the hay, so you would?' She picked up the empty mugs, went to stand by the door.

'Who, Niall? Huh, maybe a couple of years ago I would have. But now, now it's just the wrong time, the wrong place, the wrong everything.' She thought of his smile, his lips, how they'd taken control of hers. How she could have easily kissed him repeatedly. Until she'd spotted the bag, made a fool of herself and watched as he'd respectfully backed away, given her some space. 'Besides, he's just too good-looking for his own good. He'd break my heart and then where would I be?' She waved a hand rapidly in front of her face, dismissing the words.

Pondering, Tasha walked around the chair, her eyes travelling over it, ensuring it was spotless. 'Wait a minute, did you say his name was Niall?' She raised her eyebrows. 'Describe him. What does this Niall look like?'

'Oh, I don't know,' she lied. 'Tall. Dark hair. Trimmed beard, real neat and a square jawline.' She closed her eyes, thought. 'And the deepest, most beautiful eyes I ever saw,' she said, sighing audibly. 'A complete mountain of a man, landscape gardener... why, do you know him?'

'Oh, for the love of God, Molly. For someone you apparently barely know, you sure as hell give him a great description now, don't you? I thought the name was an unusual one for round here, and yes, I know him. He did my mammy's landscaping last year.' She nodded appreciatively. 'I can't believe you turned him down, most of the women in Filey would do him in an instant, so they would.'

Molly closed her eyes, remembered the kiss.

'They did a good job of my mammy's garden and all that, but she was on the edge of her nerves the whole time they were around. Felt as though she was always having to watch what they were up to. Checked all her tools and jewellery were there at the end of each day, so she did.' Walking across the room, Tasha ripped at the paper towelling, cursed as more than she'd wanted fell from the dispenser. 'So, when I think about it, you probably should take a wide berth. Good-looking or not, it does make you wonder what his allegiance is to all the ex-cons, him giving them all jobs and all that?'

'Allegiance?'

'Sure. No one really knows him, do they? Keeps himself to himself, don't think I've ever heard any gossip about him – most think he could have been a former prisoner himself, although he'd have had to be a wealthy one with all his money.' She laughed, threw the paper towels in the bin. 'Hey, maybe he could have robbed a bank or two?'

'Seriously, do you think that's true?' Molly's fingers automatically went to her lips, traced the exact spot where his lips had first met hers.

'What, that he robbed a bank, or that he used to be a prisoner?' She paused, smiled. 'Don't look so afraid. It's not like you had a full-blown affair with him now, is it?'

'Good God, no, what do you take me for?' Molly felt her stomach roll, saw the look of disbelief on Tasha's face. 'Okay, okay, he might have accidentally brushed his lips across mine... it was nothing.' She blushed, thoughts of the kiss rolled over and over in her mind. She could still see the onyx sparkle in his eyes, the touch of his fingers as his hand had gently cupped her chin, wholeheartedly wished the evening had ended differently. That he'd come inside, even if that had only been for a coffee. The idea of doing just that left her feeling exhausted. She couldn't imagine having a man around the house. One who was capable of making decisions, something she could have really done with the day before, when it had taken her over two hours to choose a colour to paint the hallway. Confused, she'd eventually mixed three half tins of paint together in a bucket, created her own shade of cream and had then spent the whole afternoon trying to eke the paint out, making sure she covered all the walls, while leaving the facing wall until last, just in case she needed to paint it a different colour and pretend it had been a feature.

After Molly had found the bacon in the bin, Beth had felt that decorating for the afternoon had been a punishment. Resulting in them spending a whole afternoon skirting around one another. Painting the walls in silence, while Beth had practically stared out of the window, her eyes fixed on the lane. 'Why do you keep going on about the new damned neighbour?' she'd asked repeatedly. 'For God's sake, Moll, I have no idea what's wrong with you, you should like Dan. He's perfect for you. In fact, I'd say he probably still loves you. Although I have no idea why.' The paintbrush had been slammed down in the tray, paint had jumped up and spattered itself across the floorboards. 'You had the perfect opportunity with me at Gran's. You had the house all to yourself, yet still...' She'd tutted and rolled her eyes, leaving Molly to spend the whole afternoon thinking about Niall, about the kiss, the way the warmth had quickly spread through her and the feeling of happiness she'd initially felt and sadness that had quickly taken its place.

Moving forward, she knew she should speak to Beth, discuss living at the house, the décor, the security. She had to speak to her about Dan. Convince her that they'd never become a couple and that no amount of Beth wishing for it was going to make it happen. Which would lead to another conversation, one about other men and how she'd feel if Molly met someone and brought them home. It was bound to happen one day and giving Beth choices and decisions had to be a good thing. And talking about it now would give her the time she needed time to process the idea for herself, before it happened.

'Why don't you get off, see how that sister of yours is doing? I can lock up here.' Tasha interrupted her thoughts, opened a cupboard, threw Molly her coat. 'I'll be seeing you in the morning, and don't forget, there's not only your sister to sort things out with, go sort things out with that man of yours too.' Waving a young, but knowledgeable, finger in the air, she shooed her out of the door, leaving Molly to wonder which man she needed to sort things out with. Dan or Niall?

23

Frustrated with herself, Beth knuckle rubbed her eyes and screamed internally. It had been much too early to leave school and already she'd thought up a million different explanations, reasons why she'd simply walked out of the gate. Each explanation more ludicrous than the one before. She could imagine Molly's face when she tried to explain, could already see the look of annoyance and disappointment, felt her skin prickle with anticipation.

'I couldn't do it, I couldn't stay,' Beth whispered as she climbed from the service bus, thought about every new town their mother had moved them to, every new school she'd attended. From an early age, she'd quickly found out that being the new girl hadn't been much fun. She'd often become the target, the one person everyone had wanted to know and on more than one occasion she'd found herself standing in a corner, her back against a wall, with questions thrown at her from all directions, fired like bullets from a hundred different guns. Until a time when they'd learned enough, and she suddenly turned into the person they all took a great delight in hating.

For some reason, today's new school had been worse than any of the others. Year Ten had been a whole new kind of hell where all the girls were pubescent teenagers, all had hormones bouncing off the walls and had strutted around school like prize hens. Ones whose pecking order would have been decided at preschool and they'd made it more than obvious that a new girl infiltrating their group wasn't welcomed.

Feeling very alone, she'd spent the whole morning looking out of the classroom window. She'd found herself so bored, she'd even counted the leaves as they'd fallen from trees, watched the changing mood of the sky beyond and with her stomach full of knots, she'd headed out of the school gates with eyes full of tears.

Formulating a plan on the bus ride home, she'd thought about Dan. Of his house. Of how she was sure he'd let her move back in, sleep in her old room. The one she'd shared for the past six months with Molly. It still had the grey tartan curtains she'd loved so much, the bank of ivory wardrobes. All the drawers. The cupboard space. Which meant that all her shoes would once again have somewhere to go. What's more, she'd be close to the city, to her friends. Friends she wanted back.

'If I lived with Dan, I wouldn't have to walk down that damn lane,' she scoffed, but knew deep down that Molly would be hurt if she left, couldn't decide how to tell her, how to make her understand. 'I can't stay,' she whispered. 'I know it'll hurt you, but I just can't.' She shook her head. 'I don't want to.'

Hitching her school bag higher up on her shoulder, she came to the junction, stood on the kerb and looked down the road where Jackson lived, felt sure he'd mentioned something pertinent that would help her find him and for a moment she stood, waited, hoping he'd miraculously appear. Give her just a few minutes to say goodbye. Before she went back to the house, packed and left.

Disappointed, she turned to the coastline, to the wooden steps where the breeze had increased. While using a hand to stop her hair from blowing around wildly in the wind, she took huge gasps of air. The beach, as far as she could see, was practically empty. There was one man walking his dog. Another sat bobbing up and down on a surfboard. He was patiently waiting for the sea to change, for the waves to grow and she stared hopefully, wanting it to be Jackson. Quickly, as she realised it wasn't, she slumped her shoulders, turned and stared back at the dreaded, puddle-filled lane that led to her house.

Tentatively, and placing her feet on the small patches of solid ground, she took one step at a time, carefully planned her route. Felt herself wobble, held her breath, cursed the mud as it splashed up and onto her shoes.

Finally, within sight of home, she spotted the piles of aggregate. It blocked a part of the lane, along with a van that was precariously parked on an angle in front of the neighbour's house.

Feeling her stomach lurch, she heard a loud, angry bark. Saw the dog Molly had spoken of, its nose poking through the rusty metal bars of the gate. Taking a quick step back, her feet moved from beneath her, she tipped to one side, wobbled and with a loud, piercing scream, she slipped. Fell onto her side and felt pain surge through her hip. Cold water seeped through her school clothes and angrily she shouted at the dog, which now sat and whined with its tail beating heavily against the drive. 'Urgh, it's all right you wagging at me now, you bloody thing.' She eyed him suspiciously, cautiously pulled herself to her feet. Heard footsteps approaching the gate.

'Dillon, what you up to? Come on, let's go find Niall.' A man's voice summoned the dog, who jumped up excitedly and disappeared behind the hedge, leaving Beth to stare nervously at the gate. She waited for him to return, or for the man to show himself and at least apologise.

'Don't worry, I'm fine. Covered in bloody mud, thanks to your damn dog,' she yelled, 'but hey... don't mind me. I only live here.' Stumbling towards the gate that stood with no fence to either side, she saw the irony in opening and closing it, limped up the path, where she hesitated and listened. Since the tree had fallen over the edge of the cliff, the house had sounded different. The continuous tap, tap, tap had gone and in its place was the sound of the waves that could be heard crashing onto the beach, making her wonder if the surfer had got his wish, that his perfect wave had miraculously appeared, and, more importantly, whether Jackson was down there with him.

Distantly, she could hear men working next door. The sound of spades banging against the dirt and aggregate, jokes being shared, the uninhibited laughter that followed. The fact they were having fun while they worked added to Beth's annoyance and she pushed her key into the door, kicked her muddy shoes off on the doormat and made her way up the stairs and straight into the gleaming white bathroom. It was a clear reminder that Molly had been in there. Its spotless nature resembled one of her surgeries, where both cleanliness and sterility were part of her lifestyle. It was a trait that Beth had always liked about her sister. The fact that Molly constantly cleaned meant that she didn't have to. And intentionally, she washed her hands, laughing as the mud splattered all over the sink, then as she smeared the brown droplets of water that had remained on her hands across the pure white towel. Something else that Molly would be annoyed about. Like a petulant child, she stripped off her mud-soaked clothes, dropped them on the floor, right next to the basket. 'We'll see what you think to your neighbour's wonderful bloody dog now, shall we?' She scowled, rubbed what was left of the mud from her face with the towel, draped it across the bath for Molly to see.

Sitting on the edge of her bed, Beth dug through her clothes. She pulled on a clean pair of ripped designer jeans, a pair of sturdy fur lined boots and her favourite thick winter jumper. If she was going to get to Dan's, to York, she'd need to be prepared to catch another bus, another bus that cost money she didn't have. Wishing she'd called at the cash point on her way through town, she stamped from her room to Molly's, began rummaging through bags. Coat pockets. Her jewellery box. They were all the places Molly dropped her small change. An odd pound here, a fiver there. Laughing, she counted her find, pushed it into her jeans pocket. Pausing, she felt guilty for taking the money, then she furrowed her brow. Hadn't Molly often said that the money Mum had left them was hers too? She arched her eyebrows, looked out of the window, 'So, it's not stealing, is it? It's just a loan, till Mum's money comes through.' Satisfied with the explanation, she went back to her own room, began to carefully and decisively fill both her school bag and a small wheelie case with all the things she'd need, along with all the things she couldn't possibly live without and then eyed her shoes, knew she couldn't carry them too.

With the case in one hand and her schoolbag on her shoulder, she carefully tiptoed along the lane. The last thing she needed was to alert the dog, or to fall back in the mud, and she gave herself a congratulatory smile as she successfully inched herself past the gate.

Taking a moment, she stood under the biggest, most twisted tree, turned and looked back at the house. Sniffing, she pulled a tissue from her pocket and blew her nose as it occurred to her that she'd never left home before. Not alone. No matter how horrible or hard things had got, she'd never packed a bag, and now even though she'd tried to justify her reasons, she felt more than ashamed that she'd stolen the money, and with eyes full of tears she tried to imagine what Molly would think, how disappointed she'd be and what she'd do when she learned where she'd gone.

'Beth, you all right?'

Looking up, she saw Jackson stride towards her, his eyes searching hers. With his hands reaching for her shoulders, he pressed down, squeezed hard, kept eye contact.

'Beth, speak to me.' His voice sounded distant, almost an echo that came from somewhere above, somewhere so far away, yet so close that she heard. 'Beth… come on, I've got you. Tell me what happened.'

Trembling inside, Beth blinked purposely, fell against him, closed her eyes for a beat and felt a sob leave her throat. 'Nothing… everything, I don't know,' she admitted, felt relief as the case was taken from her hand.

'Let's take you home.' Jackson began to usher her back towards the house, towards the gate where the dog had barked, to the spot where she'd fallen, and with the anxiety rising, she stopped abruptly.

'No… please, I can't go back in there.' She frantically looked back up the lane. 'Please, I don't want to.'

Hesitating, Jackson pulled her into a hug. He stepped from foot to foot, bit down on his lip. 'Are you going to tell me what happened?'

Shaking her head, Beth grabbed the case from him. 'I can't say it, 'cause if I do, it'll be real.' She pulled herself out of his hold, began marching up the lane.

'Beth, stop, you can't…' He ran behind her, his hand gently

covering hers on the handle of the case. 'Here, it looks heavy. Give it to me.'

Silently, they walked, stepped carefully between the puddles, along the grass verge until they reached the last of the properties. Standing thoughtfully by the gate, he looked at the house, then back at Beth. 'Okay,' he said, 'come on, I have an idea.'

Trudging through fallen leaves, she held onto Jackson's hand, felt the bottom of her jeans getting wetter by the minute, cursed the fact that she'd worn the good ones as she tripped over random items that lay scattered around the garden. Old tyres were half hidden in the undergrowth, a car had been parked and stood for so long that the ivy had begun to grow over the top of it and within just a few metres of the back door, there was a sheer drop over the cliff edge, to the beach below. 'Jackson, where are we going?' she whispered, eyeing the property with its dirty windows, frames so rotten they'd crumbled away to show a corner of the glass poking out from beneath.

'Don't worry, I'm not breaking in.' He laughed as they neared the door, where he turned to look her in the eye. 'Beth, wait here. Let me just...' He gave an apologetic look, rushed on ahead, leaving Beth to hover nervously on the doorstep.

The room beyond looked as though it used to be a kitchen, two taps hung from a wall over a paint-splattered plastic bowl which stood on top of an old mahogany dropleaf table. Next to the table was a wooden chair, a flat two-ring camping stove balanced on the seat. A white plastic carrier bag lay beneath it. The windowsill was littered with objects. A chipped ceramic mug, half filled with congealed coffee. An ashtray that overflowed with cigarette butts, the ash scattered all around as though it had fallen out as more and more butts were added. A half bottle of whisky stood on the linoleum floor. A pair of mud-covered boots and a silver hip flask were carelessly discarded beside it.

Appearing in the doorway, Jackson beckoned her in, walked to her, picked up the case. 'Hey, don't look so terrified, come on in.' He led her through the stark kitchen, and into a hallway beyond, where anaglypta wallpaper looked welded to the walls, shelves and doors had been thickly covered with paint that had turned yellow with age and the brown, threadbare carpet stuck to her feet as she walked.

'In here, we've got some bean bags in here.' His hand went to her arm. He hooked his fingers around her elbow, carefully manoeuvred her across the room, pushing the door to a close behind her. 'There you go, now... do you wanna tell me what's going on?' He pointed to the case. 'Or...' His eyes rolled towards the door.

'Who's we? Who lives here?' Beth asked, and afraid to touch anything she kept her hands close to her sides. She moved from one foot to the other, carefully stepped between piles of boxes and watched Jackson as he ignored her question, picked up one bean bag, then the other, Jackson cringed as the plume of dust billowed outwards which made Beth wince, seeing as everything in the house was covered in dust, including a high-back green velour chair that was pulled up in front of the hearth. The hearth, which had once been covered in tiles, was now covered in cigarette ash, mug rings with dark, ingrained dirt. A bucket sat on the corner of the fireplace, screwed and twisted lengths of newspaper lay in the grate and a log balanced precariously against a black metal poker.

Inching towards the window, Beth saw a camp bed. It leaned against the wall. A sleeping bag neatly folded up on top. Both looked out of place, much too tidy for a room full of chaos. Sniffing at the air, she wrinkled her nose, reeled at the smell. 'Jesus Christ, Jackson, did something die in here?' She tipped her head to one side, felt herself being ushered towards a dark brown corduroy bean bag.

Sitting down, she gingerly wrapped her arms around her knees and nervously picked at the frayed tears of her jeans with a finger. 'I... I was about to leave, you know. When you saw me. I was going to catch the bus, to York, to live at Dan's house.' She took in a deep breath, watched Jackson kneel down in front of the fire where he lit a match, set fire to the curled-up twists of newspaper, threw a handful of sticks on top, along with pieces of coal that he carefully placed around the edges. Then, thoughtfully, he waited, watched for the sticks to catch light, pulled a sheet of newspaper from a pile and held it in front of the fire until it turned from white to beige, beige to scorched and then burst into flames. Quickly, he tossed it into the fire, laughed as small pieces flew upwards and into the chimney.

'Beth, you can't leave...' he finally said, before standing up and facing her. Arching an eyebrow, he gave her a puzzled smile, began to pace around the room, around the boxes, occasionally moving one from place to place. 'You need to stay. You live here now.' He went to the closed door, leaned against it.

'I was...' Keeping one eye on the door, she tried to decide what to do, felt her bottom lip begin to tremble. 'I lived at Dan's before, with Molly.' She paused as tears welled in her eyes. 'He's like a brother and... and I'm sure he'd let me stay. He just has to. 'Cause if he doesn't, I'm not sure where else I'd go... but...'

'But what?' Turning, Jackson stepped back towards her, looked from Beth to the door, knelt down, took her hands in his.

'I never thought to ask him, I just presumed it'd be okay but now I'm scared.' Her bottom lip protruded like a petulant child. 'What if he won't let me stay? What if I go all the way to York and he puts me straight in the car, brings me back? Or worse, he could phone Molly. She might come and get me, and I'd have to listen to her lecture me all the way back home.' Pausing, she brushed the hair away from her face, pressed the heels of her hands against her temples. 'I'd better go. Our Molly, she's already gonna ground me for a year when she finds out I cut school.' Sitting forward, her hand went to the bottom of her jeans, the material still wet, and involuntarily she began to shiver.

'Don't go.' Jackson turned, began to move things around, placed the second bean bag next to hers, sat down and took her hand in his. 'Beth... please don't go to Dan's.' His eyes searched hers. 'I want you to stay here, with me. I'm gonna teach you how to surf, there's your end of year prom. That would be this year, wouldn't it? I could take you if you like?' He nodded enthusiastically. 'You'd like that, wouldn't you?'

Feeling the warmth of his hand, Beth felt herself blush, and although she'd been shivering, a heat had now begun to travel through her. Smiling, she used her other hand to pull at the collar of her jumper, to pull it up around her face where she buried her nose in the fabric, all in the hope he wouldn't see the colour seeping into her cheeks. Nodding, she flicked her eyes up to his, then back at the fire that had begun to crackle and spit.

'I hate school. Not even sure I want to go to prom. It's not like I'll know anyone.' She paused, kept her eyes down. 'Apart from you and, if I'm honest, I don't want to go back to that school, not ever. But our Molly, she'll make me go,' she said and, ever thoughtful of the time, she pulled her phone from her pocket and looked at the screen. Took a moment to imagine herself in a pretty dress and the most beautiful shoes. Holding onto Jackson's arm she'd feel like a princess, but knew how little money Molly had and that buying a dress would be a luxury they could live without. Automatically, her hand went to her pocket. To the money she'd taken from Molly's room, felt another bout of guilt flood through her. Now, she wished wholeheartedly that she hadn't taken it, that she hadn't thrown bacon away that they could barely afford and vowed to put it back, to use her own money to replace the bacon.

'Aww, every girl has to go to the prom. It's a tradition, a bit like your dad walking you down the aisle and all that.' Letting go of her hand, Jackson sheepishly turned, picked up the log, tossed it on top of the coal. Then, with the poker in his hand he waved it around in the air. 'And talking of your dad, you've never really said. Do you get on with him, visit? You could go and live with him, couldn't you?' He tipped his head to one side, nervously looked over his shoulder and into the hall.

'I don't think that'd be a good idea,' Beth said, puzzled. She thought back to the continual messages she and Jackson had shared since their meeting on the beach, felt sure that at some point she must have mentioned her dad, but couldn't for the life of her remember when. 'My dad. My relationship with him, its complicated.' She tried to explain, rolled her eyes. 'And to be honest, he just got out of prison. My mum was scared of him, told me that I should be scared too.'

Coughing, Jackson began to rattle the poker noisily in the grate. Grabbed the bucket. 'I'll just go and get some more coal. Get the place warmed up for us.'

Ignoring his outburst, she slid forward, held her hands out in front of the fire. 'Who lives here?' she asked. ''Cause I know someone does.' Her eyes shot to the door. 'Is someone else here?'

'No. Don't be daft.' He jumped up, and with the bucket in his hands he walked back to the door. 'Place used to be my grandad's. He died a few years ago and my dad couldn't bear to sell it. So...' He paused. 'He stays here sometimes. Just to keep an eye on things and on a weekend, he lets me come down here, sleep over. It's close to the beach and I throw the surfboard in the hallway, come and go as I please.'

Watching as he walked out of the room, Beth stood up and moved to the door, saw his surfboard like he'd said, standing in the hallway with his wetsuit hung on a peg beside it. His neoprene pumps had been dropped by the door along with an odd pair of older, tatty looking shoes, an overcoat. They were much too big for Jackson and creepily, she wondered if they'd belonged to his grandad. Whether they too were something his dad had held onto.

Catching his eye as he walked back towards her, she smiled nervously. 'What's down there?' She ducked past him, her fingers grazed the door across the passage, the door began to swing backwards.

'Beth, don't...' He jumped backwards, stood in her way, held his arm across the door, his fingers gripping the jamb, to block her route.

Feeling uneasy, she held her breath, furrowed her brow, spotted the edge of a rolled-up carpet. It was distinct, noticeable and matched perfectly in colour to the tufts that were still attached to lengths of gripper in their hallway. 'What's that doing here?' She pointed to the carpet, felt a breeze gush down the hallway towards her, took a step back apprehensively and eyed the closed windows and door that stood beyond him. 'It was down the back of our shed the other day. Came from the hallway in our house.'

'What, that?' Chewing his lip, he pointed to the carpet, shook his head. 'As I said, it was my grandad's house, all the stuff here belonged to him and if I remember rightly, he bought that from a door-to-door salesman, he was going round with rolls of it on the back of his van. Maybe the bloke who owned the house down there bought some too.' He nodded convincingly. Hooked his arm around her shoulder, walked her back to the room at the front of the house.

Deep in thought, Beth plonked herself back down. Thought about the carpet, about what Jackson had said, seemed to remember her mum once buying a carpet in the same way. A traveller had pulled up on the street, his van full of everything from carpet to microwaves. Smiling the thought of the way her mum had haggled, getting the small bedroom carpet down from a hundred and fifty pounds to just sixty. 'Bargain,' she'd announced, as she'd dragged the carpet up the path, into the refuge. 'We can put this in the bedroom, make it all snug and warm.'

'Penny for them?'

Shaking herself back to the present, she once again pulled her phone from her pocket, stared at the time. 'Damn, Jackson, I have to go...' She realised how late it had got, fixed her eyes on the door, could hear each breath she took, knew she didn't have time to get back to the house and change back into school clothes. 'Molly, she'll be waiting.' She paused, felt her bottom lip begin to tremble. 'She's gonna kill me for skipping school.'

Pondering her words, Jackson pulled her into a hug, his hand gently pushed the hair away from her face and for a few seconds, she thought he was about to kiss her. Instead, he rocked her back and forth. 'Please don't leave.'

'I have to. Molly, she'll be parked outside and already she's gonna see me come out of this house; she'll freak out at me for leaving school early and I probably won't see you for the next six weeks, while I'm banished to my bedroom.'

Laughing, Jackson leaned back. 'No, silly. I meant don't leave, don't go to Dan's.' He pointed to the case. 'We – we're just getting to know each other and if you left, you'd miss out on learning to surf.' He nodded, placed his hands on both of her shoulders, looked directly into her eyes. 'Let's make a plan. You could sneak your things out, few bits at a time. Then, when you're sixteen, when they won't arrest me for it, you could move in.' He let go of her, spun on the spot. 'We could make the place real nice, spend our days on the beach.'

As he gave her a smile that melted her heart, Beth couldn't work out if her stomach had flipped with excitement or relief. What she did know was that she had a plan. They had a plan. A reason to stay.

24

With a cautious glance at Carol Cooper's house, Molly was immediately aware that something was wrong.

There was a Qashqai parked on the drive and three pints of milk all scattered on the doorstep. One glass bottle that still looked fresh. Another leaned against the step, half lying down, its silver top pecked at by birds, the milk inside vastly diminished, and the third had completely toppled. The milk had spilled, and a ginger cat was crouched beside it, licking hungrily at the spillage. As Molly pushed at the gate, the cat sped across the drive, found a safe place to hide below the car, and eyed her suspiciously.

'Who you lookin' for?' An abrupt Yorkshire voice came from a man in the next-door garden who limped toward the fence with his woollen hat pulled down over his ears and his scarf wrapped tightly around his face, leaving only the inquisitive look in his eyes for her to see.

With colour rising to her cheeks, and for something to do with her hands, she waved her phone around in the air, pointed to the screen, read from it. 'Carol Cooper? I was sent her address,' she lied, 'I believe she lives here.'

'Urgh,' he huffed, 'she certainly does. But you'll have a job. No one's seen her for days. I've been feeding her damn cat since last Friday, I have.' He shook his head with annoyance. 'If she'd said she was going away, I wouldn't have minded. But to just up and go, well...' He kicked out at the fence, stamped down his path, pulled open the wheelie bin lid and dropped a handful of rubbish inside. 'It isn't right, is it? If she was going away, she should have told me, left me some cat food, but this time, I've had to run up and down to the shop, and buy it myself and I haven't got a car like she has, although,' he looked thoughtful, 'don't know where the hell she'd have gone without the car.'

With a sense of unease, Molly waved a thank you, felt her legs begin to weaken. The man's words, 'No one's seen her for days,' played over and over in her mind. She remembered what Tasha had said, that Carol Cooper was always on time, that she'd never missed an appointment. Not until now. Grabbing hold of the car door handle, Molly dragged it open, felt her legs finally buckle as she dropped inside, locked the doors behind her.

Staring at the house, her head began to swim with a tidal wave of emotions as the ginger cat came from under the car, strolled towards her. It gave off a shrill and high-pitched squeal, arched its back. It was obviously loved and cared for, which made it even more improbable that Carol would have abandoned it.

Molly considered going to the shop, buying some food, even if that was just to save the old man from doing it. With her indecision, she began to twist her fingers together, wishing for pain. At least with pain, she'd feel alive, she'd feel something other than this monotonous spiral of emotion that poked at her heart and penetrated her thoughts.

Then suddenly, an involuntary sob released itself from her throat, in a loud, audible moan. 'History's gonna repeat itself, whether I like it or not...' she wailed, 'and there's nothing, nothing I can do to stop it.'

25

Pressing on the brakes and with her foot tapping anxiously against the pedal, Molly looked down at the clock. Even with her diversion and subsequent meltdown, she'd managed to arrive at the top of the lane in good time. Taking a moment, she noticed the twenty plus cars that were all parked near her. Parents sat in them, patiently waiting, tapping at steering wheels, snoozing or staring aimlessly at the coastline, which told her that the school bus was running ever so slightly late.

Trying to calm her thoughts, she wiped at her eyes, picked up her mobile. Went to the keypad and considered phoning the police. She had no idea what she'd say. How she'd even try to explain that Carol Cooper was missing. What she suspected, or how much of a lunatic she'd sound if she accused her stepfather of being involved, the same stepfather she hadn't seen for the past ten years. Nervously, she began to press the numbers, then, with thoughts of Beth and of how she'd feel if she climbed into the car halfway through the conversation, she stopped. Couldn't allow that to happen, not today. She'd already been in a mood that morning and the silent treatment she'd thrown around the house hadn't been appreciated. Milk had splashed up and out of the plastic container as it had hit the worktop with force, her cereal had been eaten at speed, the bowl tossed into the sink and the front door slammed so hard behind her that the old rickety windows had once again shaken in their frames, which had been another unwelcome reminder of how much work needed doing to the house and of the bottomless money pit it would take to make it right.

Ready and waiting for another moody onslaught, Molly began flicking through her phone. The Wi-Fi still hadn't been connected at home and she took any opportunity she could to grab a connection without draining her allowance. Tapping on her bank app, she began to mentally calculate what she still had to pay out that month but looked at her balance and blinked repeatedly at the screen. Screwing up her eyes, she squeezed them together, then opened them again, took another look at the screen and felt an unexpected wave of relief as she took in the new, higher balance. A numbness spread through her, like a wave rolling in. She didn't know whether to feel happy or sad and, eventually, she came to the conclusion that she felt neither. The poison chalice that denoted all of her mother's savings, insurance policies and the tiny amount of private pension were now all in her account, minus the solicitor's fee. A sum of four and a half thousand pounds was all that was left of her mother's life.

'Oh, Mum,' Molly whispered to the phone. Swallowing, she began adding up the cost of repairs. Tried to work out how much a carpet for the hallway would be, curtains for that huge picture window, anything to make the house warmer and more homely, in the hope that Beth might eventually feel happier about living there.

Taking in a deep breath, she thought about selling. 'It'd be easy. We could sell and we could run,' she whispered to the car, knew how easy running would be. It was something she'd done for the whole of her life, something her mother had done for years and, with a determined flick of her hair, she stared ahead. Knew that if she ran, if she let Charlie win, she'd always be running. 'You're not chasing me away, Charlie. Not this time.' As she spoke, she nervously eyed the crowd. Wondered if he was there, if he was watching, wondered what she'd say to him if he came near her.

Checking that the car doors were locked, she leaned back, closed her eyes, concentrated on her breathing, tried to compose herself before she saw Beth. With long intakes of breath, she felt the pressure of the day begin to diminish. Over the past few months and on top of everything else, she'd had no choice but to keep working. To take all the stress that came with being a dentist, which always included the one or more treatments a day that would turn into the unexpected. A toothache that would turn into a filling. A filling that would turn into a root canal. And then, lo and behold, a root canal that she hadn't had time to do in the first place would turn into a simple extraction, a surgical extraction, suturing, packing, X-rays. Depending on which tooth and how badly decayed it was, the extra treatment could put her back by anything up to an hour. Every time this happened, every patient that followed would tut, look at their watch and comment about how long they'd been kept waiting. Meaning that on most days, she'd simply pray for 'damage limitation' and that the 'unexpected treatment' would occur at the end of the day, rather than at the beginning.

Hearing the school bus pull up, Molly opened one eye, watched it through the rear-view mirror. She could see it standing there, its engine revving, the twenty or so teenagers all disembarking. Most were laughing, walking in pairs, making their way towards their parents' cars. But the odd one or two walked alone and stared at phones or made a pretence of listening to music. Feeling the air leave her lungs, she noticed that Beth wasn't amongst them. Jumping up in her seat, she spun around. Unlocked the door, threw it open, then recoiled quickly with relief as she spotted Beth, running towards the bus from the direction of the lane. Her school bag was thrown over her shoulder. The pale blue torn jeans and jumper she wore were definitely not school issue.

'Okay, keep calm. What has she been up to?' Molly queried as she saw Beth disappear behind the bus, only to emerge two minutes later looking tired and disgruntled, pretending she'd just got off. Trudging across the road, Beth looked up, stopped, caught Molly's eye and then purposefully marched past her at speed.

Molly dropped the window. 'Beth... come on, get in. I have news.' Biting down on her lip, she tried to weigh up what she'd seen. The lane was long, at least two thirds of it could be seen from the road, only the last part as it turned around corner was hidden and even though she'd been resting her eyes, Molly felt sure she would have seen her if she'd come from home.

'If I have to go to the house, I'd rather walk. It'll postpone my getting there,' she snapped over her shoulder, jutted out her chin and then forged ahead, with what looked like the heaviest school bag ever. 'Oh, and for your information, the only place worse than the house is that shitty, horrid school that you made me go to. I hate it. I'm not going back. You can't make me.'

Molly took in a deep breath, started the car, wound down the window and began to manoeuvre it alongside her sister. 'Beth, it's not my fault you have to go to school, and you can't stay pissed at me forever, can you? Now, come on, do us both a favour, get in the damn car...' She paused, waited for a response, spoke again. 'I mean, it'd be nice if you at least told me what you're pissed at me for. Because most days I'm really not that sure.'

'You're ruining my life,' Beth snapped. 'I didn't want to move here. I didn't want to move schools. But you made me. You took control. You went along with it regardless, whether I liked it or not.' She kicked out at the sandstone. 'And Dan. Why did things have to change? I'm sure he still loves you. Yet still, it was you that made us move out and from the way you keep looking across at the new neighbour's house, you seem more interested in a man you barely know than a man who gave us both a home. It's disgusting.' She spun and glared at the car.

'Beth, please.'

'Don't "please" me. Dan has always been there for us, and Moll, I really like him. He's kind. The other day, he came over to fit the locks and all you talked about was the bloody man you'd just met on the beach, how interesting he was, how beautiful his dog was. It was cruel. I thought you'd have known better.' She paused, dropped the bag from her shoulder, where it landed heavily on the ground. 'And Saturday, you had every opportunity, to, you know... but didn't take it.' She rolled her eyes, turned and stared at the sea. 'He loves you, Moll, so why on God's Earth can't you just love him back?'

Molly considered her sister's words; they were the words of a teenager. A teenager who thought that life was simple, and she was right, Dan had always been kind to them, even after they'd broken up as a couple. He'd stayed around, offered them a home, and he and Beth got along just fine, probably better than she and Beth did. But Beth didn't know the whole truth, telling her would have broken her heart, it would have been another person who'd let her down and Molly empathised with her feelings. They were feelings of being the youngest of three siblings. The little one of the three who was unable to stop the older two from quarrelling or falling out.

'Okay. I'm sorry. Maybe I'll invite him over at the weekend?'

she shouted over the sound of the sea. Still choosing not to mention the lack of school clothes. 'We could spend some time with him, do a BBQ, make a fuss.'

Even though she was a few steps ahead, Beth stopped in her tracks, visibly sighed. 'Moll, he isn't a bloody puppy.' She paused and tutted. 'And why you like the neighbour and not Dan, is beyond me.'

'Right. That's enough,' Molly snapped, took in a deep breath. 'Who the hell I like or don't is my own goddamn business. Do you get that?' Molly stared out to sea, thought about Niall, the way he'd made her feel, the way she'd thought of the kiss ever since, the way she'd hoped it might happen again.

Slowly, Beth turned to look at the car, her gaze landing somewhere around the wheel arch. 'Okay, fine. I won't say another word. You like who you want. But Moll.' A soft choked cry left her lips. 'The picture. It wasn't me. I didn't move it.' She kicked out at the floor. 'And I'm scared because someone did.' A sob left her throat. 'What if someone had been in the house while we slept? What if they come back? What if... what if they kill us... take a knife from the kitchen and stab us, just like they did our mum?'

Beth looked distraught, her pain palpable, a pain that Molly fully understood. She felt it too. The thought that someone could have been walking through their house, just a few feet away from where both she and Beth had lain snoozing, had gone through her mind over and over, like a nightmare on fast forward.

Pulling the handbrake on, Molly turned off the engine, climbed out of the car and walked over to where her sister stood. 'Come here.' She pulled Beth into a hug and held her close. 'I'm so, so sorry. I really didn't mean to blame you about the picture, honestly I didn't.' She paused, leaned back and swept a loose strand of hair from in front of Beth's cute, freckled face. 'It was...

oh, I don't know, the heat of the moment, I guess. I was scared. I didn't know what else to think.'

Holding her breath and with Beth's words firmly in her mind, Molly stared up the lane, towards the house. Thoughts of Charlie ever present. 'You... you haven't heard anything... from your dad, have you?' she asked, cautiously. Couldn't help but think he'd been around, watching, planning, carefully scheming, knew that if he had, Beth would be the first person he'd contact.

Shaking her head, Beth shrugged. Gave a half smile and turned in Molly's arms. For a short while, they both stared at the continually rolling breakers, the numerous surf boards that bobbed up and down.

'Okay. How about we call a truce,' Molly suggested. 'How about you tell me why you didn't go to school today, or at least how you ended up in your jeans and I won't shout?'

She paused, felt Beth physically sigh with relief.

'And...?' Beth whispered.

'How do you know there will be an and...' Molly said, poked her in the ribs and made her shriek with laughter.

'Stop it... I know what you're like, there's always an and... so, you may as well tell me what it is.' She turned, arched an eyebrow, gave Molly an inquisitive smile.

'Okay, maybe there is an and... What I was thinking was that we agree to give the house a year, make it nice and homely. Mum's money came through today. If we're careful with it, we could probably get a security system, put one of those really strong front doors on it. Make it real cosy and... if you still don't like it once it's done, we'll sell it. Where we live is your choice, too. Half the house and the money belongs to you... so...' She looked across the bay, at the town, desperately hoping that Beth would come to love this view as much as she did. 'So, the minute you're old enough you get to decide.' She paused. 'Is it a deal?'

'I have a caveat.' She paused, looked through her long, dark eyelashes. 'I want you to make things right with Dan,' Beth urged hopefully.

Hesitating, Molly rolled her eyes, she didn't want to lie, didn't want to give Beth a false hope. 'I'll phone him. He'll always be a friend, Beth. But I can't promise more than that. Please understand?' She paused, kissed Beth on the cheek. 'Do we now have a deal?'

'Deal.' Beth turned, snuggled in. "Cause I just know you'll love him eventually, Moll. You just have to.'

Molly bit down on her lip. The last thing she wanted was for Beth to be angry or unsettled, and instead she decided to change the subject. 'Hey. How about we go into town, grab a takeaway, do something fun, like... let's go look for a new bed for your room, a double one that you can spread out in, new curtains, bedding, and... and if we get the time, we could try to find the perfect dressing table. Every young woman should have the perfect place to get herself ready for dates, shouldn't she?'

Molly thought of her new bank balance, of how useful that money would be. And as she'd said, it was Beth's money too. She deserved to be happy. 'You can choose some wallpaper and paint. We'll make your room all lovely, buy you some new shoes and fill that wardrobe of yours. We could even get some fairy lights, hang them around the headboard. Once it's decorated, you might like it more.' She smiled. 'Hey, we might even pop into that little shop near the supermarket and see if we can get a new carpet for the hallway. What do you think?'

Beth laughed and, for the first time in days, Molly felt at peace with her sister. Hugged her tightly as they both stood on the edge of the cliff, looking outwards at the rugged, craggy coastline. What she wanted more than anything was for the constant arguments of the past six months to be over. For Beth to go back to being the sweet, anxiety free teenager she'd been before their mother's death. For them to go back to acting like siblings, the way it had been before she'd had no choice but to become Beth's impromptu and reluctant parent. But Molly knew it was a wish too many, that Charlie was still out there, that he'd more than likely been in their home, while they slept, digging through their things. The question was: why had he been there?

Hearing the ping of her phone, Molly reluctantly pulled it from her pocket, read the message.

Isn't it sweet... you two, stood together like that? Real sweet.

Taking a fast intake of breath, Molly spun on the spot, searched the topography, the beach, the car park. Moving Beth towards the car she opened the door, pushed her inside. Then, taking a moment, she swallowed hard, stood on her tiptoes and stared along the cliff top. 'Okay, Charlie... you want to play games, do you?' She gave a determined nod. 'You just made your first mistake.'

26

'Beth, come get your breakfast.' Molly stood by the kitchen door, looking at the newly laid carpet. 'Beth!'

'You don't have to keep shouting.' Beth sauntered down the stairs, flicked back her unbrushed hair and pulled lightly at the bottom of her pyjama top. 'I heard you.'

'I know you did.' Molly laughed. 'I just like how nice it sounds in here now with the carpet and the door curtain.' She turned back to the toast, attacked it with butter, placed it on a plate and tipped the beans on top. 'I'm still gobsmacked they fit it last night, I mean, we only went in the day before, didn't we?'

Beth smiled, picked up the plate and slid onto the leather-look stool that stood at the counter. 'Yeah, he either really needed the sale or felt sorry for you when you almost sobbed in the shop, told him how horrid it was without a carpet and how you couldn't possibly live in such a heinous way for a minute longer.'

'I did not,' Molly said, but knew she had. In two days, she'd organised a carpet, Beth's bedroom furniture, and an alarm system for the house. In just one week, it would all be fitted. The house would be secure and both she and Beth would sleep peacefully knowing that if anyone so much as tapped on the window, the alarms would go off.

'You did so.' Beth pushed a piece of toast into her mouth and chewed. 'As well as batting your eyes at him, you practically begged.' She looked up at the clock. Paused.

Carefully watching, Molly waited for the excuse. It was more than obvious Beth was struggling with the new school. Since receiving the message, Molly had taken her back and forth to the school bus, noticed the pair of jeans and the jumper that had been hidden inside her rucksack. Her books lying on top. Her sly disappearance the night before that had left Molly in fear, wondering where she'd gone and why.

'I just went to the wooden steps and back,' she'd said defiantly on her return. 'I am allowed out, Moll, aren't I, or would you rather I was a prisoner, kept in my room?' Molly bit down on her tongue, hadn't wanted to come over as overbearing or strict, but also knew that Charlie was out there, that she was sure the message had come from him but hadn't wanted to alarm Beth by telling her anything about it.

'Just till we get the alarm system, I'd just rather you stay local. Stay near the house, where I can see you.' She'd watched as her sister had huffed and puffed. Thrown her schoolbooks onto the settee, sat down in a temper to do her homework.

'Moll?' The word was a question in itself. 'I have sport today, hockey and...'

'And what?'

'I don't feel well.' She glanced up with a look of despair, both hands went to her stomach and her bottom lip protruded in an attempt to show her misery. 'You know how I get. I feel like I'm going to pass out, throw up or do both, all at once. I really don't know my way round the school yet, no idea where the toilets are.

And today, it'd be the first time I'd have had to do sport at this school, and...'

Molly began to eat her own breakfast. Took note of how Beth had stopped speaking mid-sentence, how she looked close to tears. Knew that if she didn't allow her the day off, she'd take it anyhow and that the last thing she needed was Beth going AWOL, doing her own thing. At least by being here, with the doors locked, she'd know where she was, what she was doing and who she was with.

'Beth, you've only been at that school for two days, it's a little soon to be taking a sicky, isn't it?' She threw in the question, already knew she'd let her stay home, but didn't want her to think that getting a day off school had come too easily.

'People don't choose when to be sick, Moll. It could be genuine, couldn't it?' Again, her face was solemn, her eyes pleaded, and Molly could imagine her holding her breath, waiting for the response.

'Okay, you can stay home. On the understanding that you go tomorrow. No excuses.' She paused, gave her a half smile. 'I'll phone your gran, see if she'll come over.' She knew she was being overly cautious, but after what had happened with her mum, and the thought that Charlie could have been so close, she didn't want Beth alone, not in this house, not for too long. 'Plus, you can unpack a few boxes.' As she said the words, she saw the instant look of relief cross Beth's face. It was a look that stayed there for a whole minute before a second wave of despair took its place. 'What now?'

Nervously, Beth looked at the front door. 'Couldn't you stay home too?' Again, she gave her a pitiful look. 'Or... or I could phone Jackson. He could come over and sit with me, you know, till Gran gets here, couldn't he?' She smiled. Her fingers went up together, steepled, as though in prayer.

'Not a chance. You know I can't stay home with you. It's my third day in my new job and I have patients who can't look after themselves and before we go any further, who the hell is Jackson?' Registering the look on Beth's face, the shrug of her shoulders, Molly pushed her plate to one side, walked to the pile of boxes, lifted the lid of one. Then another. 'Is he the reason you're skipping school?'

'I didn't...'

'No more lies,' Molly snapped. 'From now on, I want the truth, even if it isn't a truth I want to hear, do you understand?' She glanced up, saw her mother's pictures lining the windowsill. Wondered how her mother would handle Beth's truanting. 'And what about the day before? The day you pretended to get off the school bus. Were you with Jackson that day too?'

'He's my friend. He's sixteen... lives up on Gap Road, I promise, you'll like him.'

Beth's words hit her like a stone. Gap Road, the road she'd driven down to get to Carol's. Images flashed through her mind, the milk on the doorstep, the feeling of unease, the subsequent meltdown. She'd been sure Charlie had been involved, had been going to phone the police. Couldn't believe she still hadn't.

27

Needing to find Beth a distraction, Molly quickly moved around the kitchen, began to search through the packing boxes. 'Ah, here we go. While I'm at work, why don't you and Gran take charge of these?' She dropped a box on the counter.

'What are they?'

'They're Mum's old photographs. They need sorting out, putting into albums, which are...' once again, she studied the boxes, 'in there. The one on the floor, next to the radiator.' She pointed. 'Mum had around seven or eight empty albums, was probably intent on sorting the pics out herself, but...' She paused, swallowed, reminded herself to breathe. 'Today, well, you have the perfect opportunity. You could build a fire, get the duvet down. Get all snug and organise all of those into albums.' She thought of how their mother would have planned to do this, of how she'd have arranged each photo into its own category. She'd have a pile of pictures she'd want to keep, and others that she wouldn't. The 'others' would normally end up in a photo box pushed under a bed, just in case.

Opening the back door and satisfied that Beth would be busy

for the whole day, Molly headed for the shed and began to pile logs precariously along one arm, picked up the coal bucket with the other and went to close the door behind her. But then stopped. Looked back in. The rusty old spade that had hung by the window was gone. She knew she hadn't moved it and knew that Beth would rather starve than do anything manual, which meant only one thing. Once again, someone else had been here. Turning, she scoured the garden, looked across the bay, took in the rugged coastline. The inaccessibility. The thought that someone had been in here continued to poke at her mind, like a finger, constantly prodding, reminding her of the way Charlie would hover over her as a child, the belt from his trousers held tightly in his hand, the spittle flying out of his mouth as he screamed and the way he'd angrily haul her from one room to the other, launching her against walls and banister rails. 'You need to learn to be good,' he'd scream. 'Bad things happen to naughty girls like you, really bad things.' The words would make her cower, do anything he'd asked as she'd imagine all the things he could do, all the ways he could hurt her.

But then, with a shake of her head, the doubt set in. Charlie was evil, but he wasn't stupid. By coming here, by sending messages, he'd be risking his parole, the risk of going back inside a definite possibility. No, she knew that taking spades wasn't Charlie's style and her eyes drifted to Niall's, to the men who were already busily working on his garden and while listening carefully, she scanned the garden, all the time searching for clues. Uneasily, she went back into the house, locked the door behind her. Checked it twice.

'She'll be fine,' she promised herself. 'She'll be all right... and... and he can't get in.'

28

The thick, depressing clouds that had circled around the sky all day had suddenly turned to darkness with the moon hidden behind them to make everything look and feel a little more eerie than normal. Keeping one eye on the sky, the other on the road, Molly tried to decide whether the torrents of rain would once again come down, just as they had during almost every day for the past week and, when they did, how difficult getting home along the lane would become.

Yawning, she caught her breath and frowned as a loud ping caused her to quickly glance down at the neon orange fuel light. Cursing, she turned the car around, went back towards town, to where she was sure she'd just driven past a supermarket, but couldn't remember if there had been a petrol station beside it or not. It was just another reminder that she needed to learn about the local area, and while adding it to her list of things to do, she tried to count just how many things had already gone wrong in a single day since getting up that morning.

Pulling into the fuel station, the sound of her ringtone began. Beth's name flashed up on the screen and immediately she felt the nerves bubble up in her throat. Instinct told her to answer, that something was wrong and, without thought, she immediately pulled straight through the forecourt, out of the other side, clicked to answer.

'Beth, what's wrong?'

'Moll, it's late, where are you?'

Feeling relieved at the sound of her sister's voice, Molly began to answer. 'It was a late one at the surgery, couldn't be helped. An unerupted molar, more difficult than normal. Had to practically dissect it to get it out. Suture it up after. Patient was a bit shaky and, in the end, she didn't want to drive and had to wait for a friend to come and collect her. Anyhow, I need to go for some fuel, so that's where I'm going right now, to the petrol station.'

'Moll, please. Please just shut up for a minute.' She paused, sobbed, her words came out broken, sporadic. 'I need you to come home – right now.'

Molly took short, sharp breaths. Her heart boomed audibly in her ears and she could feel the blood pulsating through her mind.

'Okay, I'm coming. Where's Gran?'

'She – had to – go home.'

'Beth.' Molly couldn't breathe, couldn't understand why their gran had left and images of their mum having been home alone flashed in front of her eyes. 'Beth, are you alone, is anyone with you?' Again, she waited for an answer that didn't come, just soft muffled sobs that came from her sister. 'Beth, listen to me, I'm on my way, lock the doors.'

She sped up. Aimed the car out of town, towards the main road. Narrowly missed a kerb and heard a car's horn blasted out to her right. Swallowing hard, she looked over her shoulder, saw the red light, the one she'd just driven straight through. 'Beth, are... are you okay? Tell me what's wrong.' Apart from another sob, Beth was silent. 'Beth... damn it, speak to me.'

'Moll, the police. They came, they were here,' she finally said, her words interspersed between a torrent of tears. 'You told me not to let anyone in, so I didn't.'

'Good girl. That's good.' Oblivious to anything else on the road, Molly looked over her shoulder, tried to work out where she was, which roundabout she was approaching. Realising all too late that she'd taken a wrong turn, she held her breath, quickly moved across the lanes, heard the blast of a horn, another driver she'd managed to annoy, and without waving or acknowledging, she went around the roundabout, headed back to the main road. 'Beth, Beth, keep talking to me. I'm not far away now.' She bit down on her lip, searched the road signs.

'Carol. She's missing. No one's seen her for days. The last place they say she went... was here, she went to this house. Last Friday.'

'What?' Slowing the car, an explosion of questions shot through Molly's mind as her thoughts went back to Friday. She could clearly see the back door, the keys swinging in the lock, the picture and then, there had been the milk, the cat... the missed appointment. Everything pointed to the fact that something had happened, something bad.

'Moll. They asked about the house, wanted to know if we'd seen her.'

'And what did you tell them?'

'I said we hadn't. That by the time we got here, she'd already gone.'

Molly nodded. 'Good, that's good, you didn't lie. It's true, we haven't seen her.'

'But, Moll, I told them about the door. I told them it was open, that she'd left the keys. That we'd thought it odd and that we'd tried to phone her. I told them you'd been to the house.' She paused. 'They asked why. Wanted to know why you'd been... and I had to tell them the truth, didn't I?'

'Hey. It's okay. You did the right thing.' Moll could hear the anxiety in Beth's voice. Felt the need to be there as a fist of nerves struck her in the gut, like a thunder ball, along with the sour taste of bile as it rose in her throat. Shaking her head, she pushed the questions to the back of her mind, spotted a road sign. 'Beth, sit tight, honey, I'm just turning out of town. I won't be long. I promise.'

Driving at speed, Molly felt her stomach tighten without pain, every part of her felt numb. Her eyes glossed over as she looked down and saw the orange neon light. It still flashed at her, she was still running out of fuel. The thought that she could run out at any second was one thing too many, too many things were going wrong, and it wasn't as though they'd only just started. If they had, if everything had simply begun on Friday, like Niall had said, she'd blame it on the house. But it hadn't. All the strange happenings had begun so long ago, she now considered them normal. They were simply her life, the way they'd lived. In truth, the moment her mum had met Charlie, an unpredictable whirlwind of events had begun, events that had followed them throughout their whole lives and she thought back to that day in the car, wished she'd rung the police, told them her suspicions. Only then could she have rationalised what had happened, while all the time knowing that each tiny piece of information alone added up to nothing, sounded ludicrous. But mixed together, they were a whole cauldron of problems that gave her just one conclusion... Charlie.

Driving as quickly as she could, Molly felt the car grunt and groan. It hit each and every pothole and for once she didn't care, she drove over them anyway, and then, as the house came into view, she felt relieved that the fuel had got her there. With her foot heavy on the brakes, she lurched forward, flung open the car door and ran along the cobbled path, towards the house.

'Beth, it's me, open the door.' Cupping her hand over her eyes, Molly peered through the side window, saw Beth sitting on the bottom step of the stairs. 'Come on, honey, let me in.' Stepping through the door, Molly immediately saw Beth's tear-stained face and pulled her into a hug. 'It's okay, I'm here.' Holding her as tightly as she could, Molly moved Beth back to sit on the step. 'Hey, come on. It's okay.' She scanned the lane. 'You said the police were here, where... where did they go?'

Wiping her eyes on the back of her hand, Beth held out a business card. 'They left this. Said we should call them. You know, if we saw Carol or if we thought of anything that might help them.'

Molly nodded, concentrated on the business card, read the policeman's name. 'Okay, that makes sense. After all, she didn't really live here, did she? The chances that this was the last place she'd been, well it's unlikely, isn't it?' She tried to reassure Beth, gave an uneasy smile, unsure who she was trying to convince. 'Where's Gran?'

Standing up, Beth moved to the living room, beckoned for Molly to follow. 'There's something else you need to see. We found this, when Gran saw it she got all funny, said she had things to do.' With a shaking hand, she passed Molly an old, tatty photograph. 'I know it upset her, but I don't know what it means?'

'Ah, the picture, you found it?' Molly whispered but felt her hand shaking as she looked down and with a gasp, she took note of the composition. It was a picture of Michael. Once again he was leaning against the door jamb and the child's bike lay on the path beside him, but that was where the similarities ended.

'It's taken on the same day, isn't it?' Beth added. 'But look...'

Her finger shakily pointed to the edge of the photograph and to the woman who sat on the grass, the white cotton shirt, the ripped jeans, her face plain to see. 'Moll, this picture, it's old. Looking at Mum's face, her age, it was probably taken before we were born, right?' She paused, shook her head. 'So, what was our mum doing, sitting on the grass of this house, right back then?' A sob left her throat. 'And if she'd known Michael before, why the hell didn't she tell us?'

29

Molly turned over in bed, punched at her pillow and cursed the lack of curtains. Shielding her eyes from the morning sun, she checked her watch. It was still too early to get up, far too early to go to work and she lay with her eyes closed, thinking about the picture, about the fact that their mother hadn't told them the whole truth and the fact that this house, in all its glory, had more answers to give than Molly had ever given it credit for.

Rolling her memory backwards, Molly thought of the comments her grandad had growled, wondered what he knew. 'You're breaking her heart, hasn't she lost enough, all those years of keeping everyone's business, your mother's secrets, pretending all is okay, when so much was wrong?' The words had invaded her dreams, her mind and her waking hours as she tried to understand what he'd meant. Turning over and opening her eyes, Molly remembered the look that had passed between her grandparents. The formidable glare that had made it more than obvious that her gran had known exactly what he'd meant. The strange exchange that had alerted Molly and set off the radar that had annoyingly spiralled around her mind like an old-fashioned film rapidly flicking past to show years of their lives, frame by frame. She'd wondered about the truth for half the night, about how many secrets their mother had kept and, even more, what her grandparents knew. Because whatever those secrets were, each and every one seemed to revolve around this house.

Pushing herself up against the pillows, Molly felt for her handbag and pulled out the picture she'd hidden there the night before. 'They'd known each other a long time, probably loved each other all that time. So why was it a secret?' Her finger gently traced the line of her mother's face, until it came to rest above her heart. 'Why pretend you'd only just met? What were you hiding?' She paused, took a deep breath, thought of the refuge they'd lived in. The years of hiding. 'Who were you scared of?'

Turning onto her back, she stared up at the old-fashioned coving that surrounded the room, knowing she'd soon have to decorate. Her mind flicked onto fast forward and she began wondering how many layers of décor there would be and, beneath them, how many new secrets would emerge.

'What trouble have you caused?' she asked the house. 'How many secrets have you kept?' She turned, heard the sound of the waves crash onto the rocks below. The tide was coming in, just as it had been that morning many years ago when she'd watched Beth run into the sea. She could still see it now, the wave, the tears that had followed and the man who'd scooped her up and into his arms. Had that been Michael? Had he been there all along, watching them play? Was that why Charlie had been so cross? Had he known Michael too? And if he had, if there had been animosity between them, could she be sure that Michael's death had been an accident? Had he really fallen from the roof and, if he had, what had he been doing up there? No one had known. They'd asked and now... Carol Cooper, the only link to Michael, had disappeared too. The thought that it was all connected was too much to take in and she stared at her mobile, the business card the police had left her. She wanted to phone them, wanted to air her thoughts, her worries. But didn't know what to say. Couldn't understand what was happening herself and just knew that by saying it all out loud, she'd verge on sounding crazy. After all, Charlie had been in prison, he'd been locked up when it had happened, which brought her thoughts full circle. What else did this house have in common, who else could be behind the happenings?

Beth's alarm clock cut into her thoughts. The piercing noise was quickly followed by footsteps trudging crossing the landing. The bathroom door opened and closed. Then, unusually, the sound of singing could be heard. It was a sound that made Molly close her eyes and smile. Ironically, she felt a sense of achievement. Beth hadn't begun to complain within seconds of waking up. It was a sound she'd hoped for, especially after the night before, when they'd taken delivery of her new double sleigh bed and spent half the night painting the walls and positioning the bed, a time when Jackson's name had been repeatedly mentioned. The thought that Beth had a boyfriend had sent Molly's emotions through the roof. She'd been thrilled for her sister, the idea that she might have a new and first love was exciting. But the thought of the intimacy, the possible sexual activity, all else that went with it, terrified her, and she hoped her sister was more sensible than she occasionally acted.

Jumping out of bed, Molly began working her way around the room, ran her fingers along the windowsill, across the wall and finally the wardrobe door. She stopped as a realisation suddenly hit her, and she began mentally kicking herself from one side of the room to the other.

'Of course they don't... No one leaves a house to someone they've only just met, do they? No one does that. Not when they have a niece, family, others they could leave it to. But Michael chose to leave it to Mum and why? Because they'd known each other for years. According to the picture, they'd been in love for years. Yet no one knew... they'd kept it a secret.' Angrily, she swished open the wardrobe door, caught sight of the tiny, white, wooden door within, the entrance to her very own Narnia. The place that now contained the majority of her mother's possessions, the answers to her secrets. Which made Molly wonder, had she kept anything at all, anything that would give them the truth? Would she want them to search through the boxes, to find what she'd hidden?

A loud and intrusive knocking made her glance back at the clock. She pushed her fluffy white sheep slippers onto her feet, peered out of the window. Thought of the police, of their visit the night before. Wondered if they were back. If Carol Cooper had been found.

The knocking continued. 'I'll be down in a minute. I'm not dressed.' Pulling a thin satin dressing gown out of the wardrobe, she slipped it on over her chemise, pulled open her bedroom door and immediately heard Beth's dulcet tones rocking out a song, the sound of the shower, followed by another round of knocking that echoed up the stairs.

'All right, all right, I'm coming.' She hesitated with her hand on the door handle, her fingers on the key. 'Who is it?'

'Look, it's Niall. I'm sorry it's early, I just...' His voice trailed off as she flung the door open.

'Niall, oh, hi, how are you?' Feeling embarrassed, she avoided his gaze. 'You do know it's seven-thirty in the morning, don't you?' Using the door as a shield, Molly felt the colour rush to her cheeks and secretly, from behind the door, she pulled the dressing gown tightly across herself, fully aware that beneath the gown was just a simple chemise, and that right now, she wholeheartedly wished she'd gone to bed wearing her thick fleecy, totally unflattering pyjamas that covered every inch of her and more.

'Well... what do we have here?' Crossing his arms, he stood back. A look of amusement flashed across his face. 'I'd say I'm sorry,' he said cheekily, 'you know, that I came over a bit early. But... well, right now I'm kind of pleased.' Uncrossing his arms, he pointed to the sheep slippers. "Cause they are just too cute.' He laughed, clasped his hands together, raised an eyebrow into an arch and gave an appreciative smile. 'In fact, I think they're almost the cutest things I've seen today.'

'Ah, okay. Well, now you've made fun of my slippers, maybe you could come back tonight, at a time when I'll be dressed and wearing proper boots or shoes.' She was deadly serious, but seeing the sparkle in his eyes, began to wonder if once again she had make-up smeared all down her face, or the world's best bed hair, and nervously she moved herself a little further behind the door.

'To be honest, I wouldn't normally call this early, but I kind of need my jacket. You know, the one you borrowed the other night?' He looked down, puffed up his cheeks, slowly blew out. 'And I'm sorry. I didn't mean to embarrass you. Just the sheep.' He pushed his tongue firmly in his cheek. Began to laugh.

'Oh my God. I'm so sorry.' Molly kicked off the slippers. 'I should have returned it and...' She felt the colour begin at her toes and rise upwards, knew he could see it too. 'Anyhow, I kind of owe you an apology. The other night, you didn't deserve the way I reacted. Not after you'd helped me. It was rude...' Looking down, she gave the slippers a final kick, launching them into the space behind the door.

Eventually, he shook his head. Nervously stepped from foot to foot. 'Look, it's fine. I was going to ask if you wanted to share a drink. But it wasn't compulsory and by the looks of it, you must have had your reasons for backing off, so...' He held his hands up, palms out. 'Hey, ladies' prerogative, think no more of it.'

Enchanted by his smile, Molly felt reassured, unconsciously stepped closer to the door, took in a deep breath and caught those same undertones of the musky aftershave she'd smelled before, the same ones that had played with her senses, had drove her crazy and left her wanting more.

Rolling her eyes, Molly heard the bathroom door open, Beth's footsteps padding across the landing and the excited sound of her voice hollering down the staircase. 'Moll, is that Dan? What's he stood at the doorway for? Ask him to come in, make us one of his big home cooked breakfasts. I'm starving. I'll be down in a minute.'

Realising that Beth would have been able to see the front door from where she stood, Molly knew she was causing mischief. 'No, Beth, it's not Dan,' she said, firmly. 'It's Niall... our new neighbour.'

Annoyed with Beth being so rude, she stepped back, pulled open the door. 'Beth's right, we don't normally leave people standing in the doorway. So, please, why don't you come in?' She felt the breath catch in her throat as she said the words. She swallowed, knew she could count the people on one hand who'd crossed her doorstep since her mum had died.

'If you give me a minute, I'll get dressed and make some coffee...' She laughed, tried to remember if they had any milk, whether there was coffee in the cannister and, after stacking the dishwasher the night before, whether she'd have any mugs left to drink from. 'The kitchen's that way.' She gave him a genuine smile, hoped her words sounded as open and welcoming as she intended. 'In fact, if you know how one of those works, you could make a start?' She pointed at her mother's all singing, all dancing coffee machine. The one that had turned up just a few months before she'd died and that no one, not even her, had known how to use. 'If not, we have instant in the cupboard, which might be preferable, 'cause if I'm honest, I don't know how to work the machine either, so please don't ask.'

Niall strode into the kitchen, studied the machine. Shook his head. 'Looks like we're having instant.' He pulled open a cupboard. 'Are the mugs in here?'

Indicating the dressing gown, she placed a foot on the bottom step and took in a deep breath. 'Sure, help yourself. I'll be back down in a minute.' Running up to her room, Molly stood looking at herself in the mirrored wardrobe, gave herself a telling off for answering the door barely dressed.

'Oh my gawd, look at the state of you.' She dragged a jumper out of the drawer, pulled it over her head, scanned the unpacked case, spied a pair of jeans and sat on the bed to drag them on. Finally, she pulled a brush through her hair, added a smudge of lip gloss and pressed her lips tightly together. 'You'll have to do.' She felt her stomach turn. 'Why are you nervous?' she asked herself. 'He's just a man.' Feeling ready, she turned as the door burst open.

'What is *he* doing here?' Beth growled. 'It's a bit early for visitors, isn't it? Or... or maybe he was hoping to catch you half naked, which by the looks of it, he did.' Cocking her head to one side, she viciously rubbed at her hair with a towel and huffed. 'Unless, of course, he was here all night and the big pretence of banging on the front door was for my benefit?' She looked Molly up and down. 'Because if that's what happened, it's disgusting. You shouldn't do that. Not here and certainly not with him. You barely know him, for God's sake.' Her towel was dropped to the floor and kicked to one side. 'Oh, and as for me having to introduce Jackson before he's allowed in, well... be good if you returned the favour, wouldn't it?'

'Beth, you really need to shut up. You're being very rude,' Molly snapped. 'Go and get dressed, because you're more than overstepping the mark.' She felt her anger rise, checked her face in the mirror and noticed the bright pink tinge to her skin, the way her lips were pressed angrily together, the smudge of lip gloss that had already disappeared.

Beth grabbed the towel from the floor, threw it across a radiator. 'It should be Dan, not him.'

Molly took one last look in the mirror. 'Beth. It's neither of them,' she snapped. 'Now seriously, go and get dressed. Go to school.'

'But...'

'Do you know any other words, because 'but' is all you ever say these days. Now. Go. To. School. You're going to be late.'

'Can you—'

'What, after that outburst? Don't even ask,' she snapped. 'I'm not taking you and what's more, I'm sick to death of the attitude.' Pausing, she lowered her voice. 'No matter how much I do for you, it's never enough. So today, you get to catch the bus, and while you're on it, you can think about the way you damn well speak to me. It isn't right and Beth...' Pressing her lips tightly together, she wondered if it was time to tell Beth about Dan, that he wasn't exactly the knight in shining armour she'd imagined. Sighing, she decided against it. 'We'll talk about this outburst tonight.'

Dropping her hand from the door, Beth flounced across the landing and into her room, slamming the door behind her, leaving Molly to take a moment at the top of the stairs. Holding onto the newel post, she paused, tried to calm her temper and slowly crept downwards, careful not to be heard as the smell of good coffee intrigued her. Hovering close to the bottom, she could hear the clanking of spoons, drawers opening and closing, the sound of something being moved and then the sound of her heart as it pounded audibly in her chest.

Taking another step downwards, Molly sat down, leaned on the banister and watched Niall through the railings as he made his way around the kitchen. Humming to himself, he picked up the box she'd been unpacking the night before, lifted something out, put it back, then visibly sighed. Whatever it was he'd wanted to find hadn't been there and, with a scowl, he placed the box back on the floor. Systematically, he went from cupboard to cupboard, opening and closing them, all the time searching. All the time making her wonder who he really was, why he was searching through her kitchen and whether Tasha's comments had been justified. The only thing she really did know about him was that he employed former convicts, spent all his days with them. His loyalty to them appeared to be unconditional and endless. What she didn't know was how far that loyalty went, what he'd do to protect them, to help them. She wondered how many of them he really knew and whether he, or any of the others, could be working for Charlie.

Puzzled, she held her breath, tipped her head to one side and stood up, wondering what he'd do next, but then jumped as he turned, his whole face lit up. The sparkle in his eyes quite easily matching the dazzle of his smile.

'Hey, hope you really do like the real stuff, 'cause I spotted a cafetière poking out of that box, and a bag of coffee. How lucky was that?' he said as he placed a hand on the plunger, pressed it down. 'I did have a bit of a dig, a look through the cupboards, somehow I couldn't find any mugs, so you might have to help me out. Unless of course you like it black and prefer to drink straight from the jug.' He flashed her another smile, gave a comical shrug of his shoulders.

Relieved, she pointed to one of the cupboard doors. 'That's because they're all in the dishwasher.' She squeezed past him, felt his body touch against hers as she pulled at the door, passed him the mugs. 'And I didn't even know we had a cafetière, it... must have belonged to Mum.' She stuttered over the words and padded across the kitchen, pulled out a stool and perched on it, to sit by the breakfast bar, smiling.

It had been a long time since she'd had the opportunity to watch a man making coffee, especially a man in her kitchen. Damn it, other than Dan, she couldn't remember the last time a man had even been in her kitchen. Most of the men she'd ever dated had been university dropouts, interested in one thing and one thing only. They certainly hadn't offered to cook, clean, or make the coffee. She tried to smile, as once again she thought of Dan, of how they'd met, fallen in love, how she'd easily got used to him making her pancakes or bacon sandwiches for breakfast. How he'd have his playlist on full blast and sing as he cooked. 'Alexis, Alexis... play some Rag'n'Bone Man. Alexis! Damn thing never listens to me,' he'd shout at the top of his voice, knowing that by using the wrong name for the device he'd have Beth rolling around, giggling for hours. It had been this Dan she loved, a love that could have lasted forever. But he'd changed. He'd become cold, secretive, and there had been hours and hours of silence where he'd done nothing apart from tap on a screen. He'd walk down the garden, make hushed, secretive calls, and disappear for hours. Suspicion had eaten away at her, until one day she'd spotted him in the city, a chance sighting. At first, she'd been excited, was going to run over, ask if he wanted to grab a coffee, or lunch. Could still feel the desperation that had passed through her as she'd walked towards him, then found herself backtracking, ducking in a doorway, and watching in disbelief as he'd walked up to a man, shook his hand, and accepted money in exchange for a small packet. At first, she'd tried to ignore what she'd seen, tried to make excuses. Gave him every opportunity to tell her what he'd been doing, where he'd been that day. Then watched as he'd ducked the questions, the way his eyes had lit up with fear.

'Dan, I know what I saw, and I won't be a part of it.' She'd paused as the nausea had threatened. 'You're a prison officer for God's sake, you could lose your job and me, well... if I were caught with drugs anywhere near me, I could be struck off. Do you know that? I could lose my job. Just by association.'

Molly had known the relationship would end. It had already broken down. Her bags had been packed and she'd been just about ready to move out when the news came of her mother's death and suddenly she had nowhere else to go. She had Beth to look after. Forensics had moved into what had been their mum's home. Dan had made all the right promises and, in the end, moving Beth to another refuge, to another safe house, another school, hadn't felt like an option. She'd already lost so much and, at the time, she needed to be there, needed to stay close to her friends, to people she trusted.

'Let me guess, milk, one sugar, am I right?' Niall's voice broke her thoughts and she watched as he turned, opened the fridge, pulled out the milk carton and gave it a shake. 'A little or lots?' Pouring the milk, he picked up the sugar cannister, spooned a teaspoon of granules into one of the mugs, then confidently and as though he'd done it a thousand times before, held the mug out to her with a satisfied smile.

Accepting the coffee, Molly blew at the contents, took a tentative sip. 'You look very comfortable in my kitchen,' she whispered. 'I'd say you look at home, but that, well, that'd be crazy, wouldn't it?' She held her breath, kept her eyes on his. Still felt a little wary, but she liked what she saw, had the sudden urge to smile uncontrollably.

'Well, I have been here before, came over once or twice for coffee. Had a drink with Michael last Christmas and I must admit, it is really homely and I always liked this kitchen.' Niall turned as he spoke, rested his hand on her shoulder. 'What's more, I'm told I make great coffee.' He bit down sensuously at his bottom lip, caught her gaze. 'Can't say I'm great at washing up, though.' With an easy laugh, he reached out, took her hand in his and with a sharpness in his attitude, and a firmness in the way he stood, he pulled her towards him. 'However, I would like to talk about the other night, about what happened.' He searched her eyes. 'We were getting along just fine. If I'm honest, I thought we'd started something good, something real and then...'

He was right. It had felt real. In fact, she couldn't remember a time when it had felt so real. Not for her. And now she felt embarrassed, didn't know what to say. 'It was kind of you to say that it was ladies' prerogative,' she finally said, 'you know, earlier. But...' She felt the need to explain. 'I feel really bad that I was so rude. You didn't deserve it...' She nervously searched his eyes, moved in closer. 'When I saw the wine, I freaked out, it was...'

'Urgh, don't mind me!' Beth's words were sudden and intrusive, making Molly jump backwards. Her hand flew to one side. The coffee mug rocked, and she watched in horror as the contents spilled over the side like a small tidal surge, where it slopped onto the counter and down the kitchen unit to form a small pool of coffee on the tiles below.

'Shit, sorry.' Molly pulled at the kitchen roll, threw it at the floor, pressed it with her bare foot, felt the warmth of the liquid seep through.

'If you two don't mind, I'd quite like to get some breakfast. It's almost time for the bus and I have to walk all the way down there – before it arrives. Not to mention having to clean my shoes of all the damn mud before I get on.' She pointed to the lane, rudely pushed past where Molly stood, now hugging the half empty coffee mug.

Once again, the dramatic Beth was back and Molly watched as she pulled open the fridge and with one hand holding the milk, rapidly moved the rest of the contents of the fridge around with the other. 'Actually, do you know what? I've changed my mind,' she shouted, thrust the carton back in the fridge and marched across the kitchen. 'I seem to have lost my appetite.'

'Beth, wait.' Molly closed her eyes. Counted to ten. Pressed her lips tightly together and hoped that by the time she looked up, Beth would have got over her tantrum. 'You need to eat.' She spoke firmly, tried to calm her heartbeat. Bit down on her lip. Tried to desperately avoid Niall's gaze. 'Beth, please, get some breakfast.'

Beth flicked her hair over her shoulder, looked back. 'As I said, I kind of lost my appetite. So, I'm gonna leave you two to do whatever it was you were about to do,' she growled. 'But don't forget about Dan, he's coming over later. I mean, you do remember Dan, don't you?' She stood, glared at Molly with a look that could have penetrated metal, yanked the door open and slammed it behind her.

Opening and closing her mouth like a hyperactive goldfish, Molly stared at the door, couldn't think of what to say. Finally, she just gave Niall an apologetic smile. 'I'm so sorry. I have no idea what's wrong with her.' Pausing, she pulled at another piece of kitchen roll, took the antibacterial spray and began to attack the cupboard doors with both. 'One thing you can count on is that if Beth is pissed at you, she doesn't normally leave it too long before she tells you about it.' She carried on wiping the counter. 'And as for Dan, he isn't coming over later. I'll be seeing him tomorrow. We're going into town. I owe him a drink or two.' She tried to explain, saw Niall's expression change, harden.

'Right... now it's a little clearer.' He spoke slowly, puffed up his cheeks, gave her a questioning look. 'I didn't know he was your boyfriend. I mean...' He looked thoughtful. 'I thought he was just a friend of the family.'

'What makes you say that?' Molly asked. For something to do with her hands, she turned to the kettle, filled it and set it back to boil.

Shaking his head, Niall stared at the floor. ''Cause I'd seen him around here, before you moved in. I'd like to say before Michael died, but I'm not a hundred per cent sure and then when you moved in, his car seemed to be here again at times when you were in and when you were out.'

Molly began to laugh. 'Who, Dan? No, you're mistaken. Michael was my mum's boyfriend, nothing to do with Dan. They'd never met.'

Stepping towards her, Niall placed a hand on her arm, furrowed his brow. 'Do you know what?' He pulled her towards him. 'You're probably right... but he is up here a lot now, so...' Pausing, he searched her eyes. 'Is he a boyfriend or not, 'cause...'

Feeling her stomach do an involuntary somersault, Molly took a sharp breath in, began to laugh with nerves. 'No, he isn't, and 'cause what?'

''Cause if he isn't a boyfriend, I'd really like to kiss you.' Slowly, his hand went to cup her chin, his lips were lowered to press firmly against hers. Then, as though she'd given all the permission he needed, he moved his mouth slowly, sensually over hers. His hands pulled her hips closer. She could feel his arousal, could feel his need. Felt herself gasp beneath his touch.

Lifting her hands up, Molly ran them over his shoulders, felt his muscles flex beneath her touch as she sank deeper into his arms.

'Oh, for God's sake. Do you two have to?' The front door had been flung open and Beth's voice broke the moment. 'It's ridiculous. I didn't even reach the gate before you were at it.'

'Beth, that's enough,' Molly snapped, feeling her temper rise.

'But—'

'No more buts. Just you wait till you're attracted to someone. My God, will I have fun reminding you of this moment.' She moved away from Niall, poured hot water into what was left of her coffee. Lifted it to her lips and took another sip.

'Well, for your information,' Beth chided, 'I'm going to Gran's after school; I'm gonna stay there tonight.' Leaning against the door, she crossed her arms. 'Should make you two happy. You know, if I'm not around and you get the whole house to yourself.'

Angrily, Molly stood her ground. 'Okay, Beth, that's fine. Go to Gran's.' She watched the smug look cross Beth's face. Tried to decide how to continue and felt her breathing quicken. She knew that whatever she did or said, it'd be wrong. But she also realised that allowing Beth to begin sleeping out whenever she liked was the first step to her moving out altogether. 'You have a perfectly good bedroom here. One that I've just finished decorating for you. So, I'll be there by nine to bring you home and you will be outside, ready and waiting.' Her words were firm. Her voice much calmer than she felt. All the time, refusing to look in Beth's direction until once again, the door was opened, slammed shut behind her.

'I am so sorry. I'd like to say that she isn't normally like that and that you caught her on a bad day, but I'd probably be lying.' Feeling embarrassed by Beth's actions, she pushed the bar stool under the counter, took a deliberate step backwards, kept a distance between her and Niall. 'It's… it's time I got ready for work.' She padded across to the front door, pushed her feet into the sheep slippers no longer caring if her feet looked stupid, all the time watching the front door, fully expecting Beth to burst back through it. 'Can't go in looking like this, can I?' She pulled at her jumper, glanced up to see his face change, the soft lines around his eyes grow stern, almost sad.

'Right.' Picking up the mug, he took a final slurp, moved close, until she could feel his breath drift across her face. 'So, you're attracted to me, are you?' He nodded, wrinkled his nose. 'I'll take that.'

Stunned, Molly stepped back. 'I didn't say that...' Feeling her cheeks flood with colour, she pulled open the cupboard under the stairs, unhooked his jacket from the peg, passed it to him.

'Oh yes you did, a few minutes ago and I quote, "Just you wait till you're attracted to someone. My God, will I have fun reminding you of this moment." You can't deny it, can you?' He used his hands to air quote the words, gave her a killer smile, took the jacket from her, opened the door and stood, looking out.

Molly felt herself blush and stepped into the doorway. The sound of Dillon howling broke the tension and she felt herself begin to laugh. 'Sounds like he wants you.'

He tipped his head to one side. 'Can't say I blame him, at least someone does.' He pressed his lips together, looked hopeful of a response. 'And Molly, I'd still love to get my hands to work on...' he paused mischievously wiggled in fingers around in the air, 'your garden?' he finally added.

30

Charlie O'Connor swerved the borrowed van into the gravel at the side of the road, climbed out, lifted the hood, and pretended to check the engine, while his gaze was firmly fixed on the farmhouse that stood in the distance.

Even though he'd been a regular visitor at the farm many years before, it was the first time he'd seen it since leaving prison. Yet the place still looked the same, as though time had stood still, and he stared open-mouthed at the bright red tractor that still stood by the gate, like an ornament that no one had moved from that day to this. It was surrounded by a brood of chickens and ducks that roamed freely around the yard. A yard that was full of outbuildings and stables. All overshadowed by a giant oak that he remembered so well. Laughing, he noticed the swing tyre that still hung from a long overhanging branch. It swung freely next to an old ornamental telephone box, its dulled red frame taking pride of place in the corner of the yard. It was the last thing Henry would see each day as he went through the gate and had become a long-standing joke within the family that Rose had had it placed there as a reminder to Henry that he should phone her, at least once a day, while out tending his sheep.

Surprisingly, he realised just how many memories this house held for him. It had been a time when he'd had a family, a wife, daughters. A time when he'd been welcome to sit for hours in front of that big, old inglenook. The humungous settees he'd happily lie on, a child sat on each side of him, cuddling in as he read them a book or sat on the veranda in the heat of the summer, drinking fresh lemonade, watching his girl swing back and forth on that very same tyre, her contagious giggle ringing out for all to hear.

Noticing the patio door swing open, he dipped his head to one side. While keeping himself out of view, he watched as a woman wearing a long skirt, apron and headscarf emerged.

'My God, Rose. Is that you?' He nodded appreciatively. 'You always were a good-looking, eccentric old bugger.' He laughed as he spoke, watched her move slowly around the yard, to pick up a basket of clothes, which she tucked neatly under one arm. It was an act he'd watched her do a hundred times before, but today she was hampered by a liver and white spaniel pup that ran in circles around her ankles, chased chickens and comically jumped up and over bales of straw. An older black and white sheepdog sat to the side of the yard, in the shade of the oak tree, calmly looking on.

'You always were surrounded by those damned animals, Rose.' He shook his head. 'Nothing's changed, has it?' Pulling the dipstick out from the engine, he pretended to check it. 'You're still laundering everyone's secrets. Making sure my girl thinks I'm a first class nobody.' He paused, cursed. 'I know you had a hand in keeping her away from me. Well, I've got news for you.' He gave a half smile, curled his lip. 'I'm back and it's been a long time coming, but this time, she's gonna hear the truth.'

Smirking, he cast his gaze beyond the farmyard. To a flat back truck that meandered across the field and the small flock of sheep that ran closely behind, with their noses in the air, following the food. As the van stopped, the old man climbed out, studied his surroundings, stared longingly back at the house and then down at another old sheepdog who moved slowly, following instructions and keeping a beady eye on its owner as a mixture of hay bales and silage were unloaded, spread loosely along the ground for the animals who eagerly followed. Standing back, Henry stood tall with one hand flat, held across his brow, shielding his eyes as he looked across the field, and towards the road.

Nodding, Charlie's eyes followed the line of Henry's gaze. 'Who are you looking for, old man? My girl?' He moved slowly around the van, checked his watch and hid his face from view as a vehicle drove past, slowed down and dropped its window, the driver leaning across the passenger seat to catch his attention.

'You okay there, buddy?'

'Sure, I'm fine. All fixed. Thanks.' Desperate not to be seen, Charlie pulled the collar of his old brown leather jacket up, lifted a hand, dropped the hood, hurriedly climbed back in the driver's seat and kept his gaze down. Waiting a few minutes, Charlie eventually looked back up, found himself searching the fields, looking for the flat back and eventually noticed it had pulled up in the yard. Henry had climbed out and was now shuffling across the yard, where he picked up a bucket and dipped his hand in and out to throw the contents across the gravel and into a coop, where the chickens obediently followed.

Putting the van into gear, Charlie reversed until he came to a stop further along the road. He knew Henry had been looking for something, which in itself wasn't unnatural. It was something he always did. But if his information today had been correct, Charlie knew he'd be looking for Beth and, with his phone in his hand, he checked his rear-view mirror.

'Where is she?' he growled down the phone. 'You said she'd be here.'

'I'm not her keeper Charlie, all I can tell you is what she tells me.' Jackson's voice was distant, barely a whisper, overpowered by the sound of the waves, the shouting of others on the beach beside him. 'Besides, if you'd wanted to talk to her so badly, why didn't you do it at the bungalow? You were right there, in the next room.'

Annoyed, Charlie checked his mirrors, watched every car that went by, just in case Beth had missed the bus and caught a lift. 'Don't be clever. I know I could have seen her at the house. But then they'd know, wouldn't they, they'd know how close I was, how easily I could see them come and go, how I knew their every move.' Smiling, he watched the school bus pull up to a stop. Four teenagers disembarked. One headed in the opposite direction, two walked closely together and the last headed across the road and straight towards the farm. 'Gotcha,' he whispered and he felt his chest swell with pride; his eyes grew wide. 'There she is. That's my girl.' He squinted, took a closer look. 'She's here. Now, I don't care how you do it, but you need to make sure she's outside the farmhouse, half past eight, tonight.'

Dropping the phone down heavily on the dashboard, he felt a pang of jealousy hit him in the gut like a punch as she walked straight to the old man, the look of love and happiness all over her face as she fell into his hug and kissed him on the cheek. The sheer act made Charlie's temper boil. 'It should be me,' he growled. 'It should be me you hug when you get home from school. Not him. Not the old man.' Again, he leaned forward, glared in her direction, watched every movement. Then, as his mood softened, he found himself smiling at the simple act of her placing her school bag on the ground while she ruffled the older dog's ears, and then knelt down to make a fuss of the puppy, which had launched itself at her school bag, grabbed the handle and had begun tugging and chewing, while its whole body bent back and forth with excitement.

Watching her laugh, Charlie laughed with her, felt his heart leap with pride. 'You look like her, do you know that?' he whispered. He could see her mother's eyes, the shape of her lips, even the colour of her hair. 'You're her bloody duplicate. You are.' It was a mixed emotion, a feeling he hated just about as much as he loved it and with the narrowing of his eyes, he tipped his head to one side. 'So, why do you look like him too?' he growled, felt his heart thump angrily in his chest as he took one last look at the farmhouse. 'If I find out...' He nodded, shook away the thought, knew there was a more important job in hand. 'There's something I need back, something I want and you... whether you like it or not, you're going to help me find it.'

31

'What the hell...' Molly thrust herself out of the car and didn't feel her feet touch the ground until she reached the gate, where she stared in disbelief at Dan who stood, shovel in hand, looking just a little more than pleased with himself. He leaned back against the house, pressed his tongue firmly between his lips and tried not to laugh.

'Sorry, but I kinda feel a bit busted,' he finally said, dropped the shovel, held his hands up as though in surrender.

Overwhelmed, Molly held onto the gate, tried to work out how much topsoil, timber and aggregate lay all over her garden. Why a section of her lawn had been divided up by small posts and ropes and where the shed had seemingly disappeared, along with the paving slabs it had stood on.

'Seriously, Dan. What the hell are you doing?' Her hand swept outwards as she tried to encompass the whole garden all at once. 'You're not a gardener. In fact, you hate gardening.' She thought of the small garden at his own house, the slabs he'd had delivered over a year before and his inability to find the drive or motivation to lay them.

Walking confidently towards her, he gave her a cheeky but apologetic look. 'Come on, you're not mad at me, are you?' Taking her arm in his, he spun her around, pressed his fingers into the flesh. 'I've worked really hard. Beth said you wanted the garden done and after the way you went on about it the other day, I kind of thought she was right. I did it to make you happy, I thought you'd be pleased. Or was that when you thought lover boy over the road was going to do it?' Flaring his nostrils, he looked her straight in the eye, tipped his head cockily.

Shaking her arm free, she squeezed her hand into a fist. 'Do you know what, Dan? I wouldn't call my mood either pleased or happy, I'd call it shocked, or, or... angry, yes, angry. I mean... happy... that might come later, but right now I'm pretty well pissed off, because not only have you done this without asking me, I've got absolutely no way of paying for it.' She took a step back, glanced across at Niall's garden where she could hear the normal banter of his workmen and closed her eyes for a second, considered his feelings. He had wanted the job, he'd mentioned it on more than one occasion, yet never would he have done what Dan did and started work without permission. And now, now he'd think she'd taken an alternative offer, paid someone else to do the work, hence turning his offer and expertise down.

Stamping past Dan at speed, she walked around the house, to where another man knelt, painting the shed. 'Oh my God.' She studied its new position. Hated herself for liking it. She took deep, measured breaths as she saw that the slabs had been re-laid. The shed's roof was now covered in new bitumen shingles, the broken window had been repaired with a new polycarbonate sheet in place of the old one. Its timber had been painted a soft sage green that blended perfectly with the existing trees and bushes, all of which had been pruned. 'Jesus Christ, Dan, you've hit an all-time low... doesn't he work for Niall?'

"Course he does, but he kind of owes me a favour or two... and it was time to pay me back.' He patted the man on the back, 'Wasn't it, Grant?'

Confused, Molly stepped back. She didn't like the bravado. Didn't understand why Dan would pull in favours, not from former convicts. The thought made her uneasy, suspicious. 'So...' She glanced across at Niall's house. Saw another van pull up outside. 'You stole his staff and brought them here, to work under his nose in my garden?'

Dan laughed, cocked his head from side to side. 'Well, if you put it like that. Yes. But come on, Moll, I only stole one of them. I could have pulled in favours from all the others too, but your neighbour... well, he didn't look too pleased.'

Keeping her face averted, Molly moved slowly around in a circle. Rolled her eyes upward. Saw Niall, wheelbarrow in hand, filling it with gravel, before stamping off down his drive. Only a few seconds later, the sound of the gravel being tipped filled the air.

'And Dan, what the hell are all the railway sleepers for?' She counted the sleepers, tried to calculate what they might have cost, didn't know where to start. She just knew that deliveries on this scale had been thought about, planned, didn't know or understand why Dan would do that. Not without asking her first.

Proudly, Dan pointed. 'It was you that mentioned them, the other day. Said you wanted them along the cliff edge to form raised beds.' He forcibly grabbed her hand, began walking towards the cliff. 'They'll be as good as a wall, when I get the chance to move them. What was it your friend over there suggested, a natural barrier between you and the cliff, to stop anyone going over the edge?' He began to laugh. 'You know what I'm like, Moll. I've never had a good idea in my life, but I've stolen plenty of them.'

Molly nodded. She felt her temper increase – all the suggestions had been Niall's. It had been him that had thought about moving the shed. That the greenhouse needed more shade. The raised beds to form barriers. They'd all been his ideas, ones that Dan had taken onboard, decided that it was his job to do them. Turning, she took in a deep breath, then walked away. She needed some space. Tried to decide whether Dan had genuinely been trying to help. Or just making sure that Niall couldn't? Wondered how much Beth had said to him. After all, she'd made it more than clear that she didn't want Niall around, that her allegiance was with solely with Dan. Well, it was about time Beth heard the truth, about time she knew that Dan wasn't quite the man she'd thought, that once again a grown up in her life had let her down and with that in mind, Molly wondered how on earth she was going to get Beth to trust or like Niall. For her, the attraction between them was real and for the first time in what felt like a very long time, she felt an emotion pass through her that wasn't grief. And if that morning had been anything to go by, Niall had felt it too.

Walking pitifully across the garden, Dan stopped in front of Grant. Shoulders slumped. His gesticulating hand signals told her he wasn't pleased, and she closed her eyes, wondering how ungrateful she looked. How nasty and cruel she was for throwing his good nature right back in his face.

'Dan, look. I'm sorry. I know you meant well, but you can't do this. You just can't turn up, do what you want, it isn't your house.' She gave him a genuine, almost apologetic smile. 'And now, now I have to make it right, you need to tell me what it cost, and I'll give you the money.' She looked down at the floor, avoided the look on his face, tried to work out what cost would be behind all the aggregate, the sleepers, could already feel her mum's money disappearing with the tide.

'How about we talk about it?' he asked with a huge grin. Pulled her into a hug. "'Cause I know you'll love it, just as soon as you get used to it.' He leaned back, caught her eye, and uneasily, Molly moved her gaze. She knew full well that in any other universe, she and Dan could have been happy, that everyone had thought them to be the perfect couple and that at one time him turning up and doing something on this scale really wouldn't have bothered her.

Feeling exasperated, she realised all too late that too much had happened and although the hug was welcome, the feeling had gone, the love had gone and now, only a tiny thread of friendship remained.

'I'm gonna put the kettle on,' she said, took a step backwards, rubbed her eyes. Didn't notice Niall, who once again stood by his gate, wheelbarrow in hand, carefully watching the interlude.

32

Taking her time and allowing herself one last look at each photograph, Beth began to put them back into the boxes. She'd sat for the whole evening looking through them, reminiscing, smiling at each before passing them on to her gran, who in turn would pass each one to her grandad. It was like a conveyor belt of pictures, being slowly transported from one hand to the other, before stopping abruptly as her grandad dropped them, upside down, into a pile on the settee beside him. The pile of pictures had messed up her mother's filing system, which had previously had all photos in categories defined by the year in which they were taken, and each year had its own small, unique, hand-crafted box, made to size depending on how many pictures belonged to that year. Laughing, Beth found amusement in her school photographs, which had been placed at the front of each year's box, the traditional 'first and last' days of school, each pair paperclipped together with the year and name of school written on the back in pencil. 'Do you see,' she asked her gran, 'how on the first photo of each year our uniforms drown us, but by the end we'd almost always grown out of them.'

Smiling, Beth had become aware that the boxes highlighted how her life had been – always split into two halves. The half before her dad went to prison, and the half that followed. Even though the half that followed had spanned a lot more years, it still felt as though the dividing line was clearly there. Marked by the day she lost him. Feeling her bottom lip begin to quiver, she flicked over a photograph, saw her mother's smiling face. It was one memory too many and quickly, she placed the picture back in the box, wondering if in future years she'd begin to segregate her life into three parts, rather than two, and have another dividing line – on the day their mother was killed. The day their lives had once again changed, never to be the same again.

Hearing her mobile bleep, she picked it up. Stared hopefully at the screen.

Hey beautiful, how u doing? Don't forget. Be alone at 8.30 p.m. I'll FaceTime you. XOXOXO 😊 J xx

'Oh my God, did you see the time?' She jumped up, retrieved her coat from the back of the settee, pulled it on. 'Moll said I had to walk to the gate. Save her coming in.' She rushed around the room, pushed her feet into her shoes, collected her school bag.

Giving a knowing nod, her Grandad looked up from his crossword and pulled his glasses down his nose until Beth saw him stare at her over the top of the frames. 'And Molly can't come in these days?' he questioned disapprovingly.

'Oh, you know she would. But then she'd sit down. She'd have a brew, Gran would forcibly make her eat some of that apple pie that's left over from tea and before we know it, it'd be gone eleven and, well... I'd be struggling to get up for school tomorrow and our Moll would moan at me if I came over on a school night again.' Beth comically tipped her head from side to side as she spoke at speed. 'So, to keep her sweet and because I'm coming back over here tomorrow night, I'll go wait at the gate, like she asked.' Laughing, she ran a hand over the pup who'd begun bouncing around the kitchen. 'And you, she'd want to play with you too, wouldn't she?'

Reluctant to leave the warmth of the farmhouse, but eager to have just a few minutes to herself, to speak to Jackson, Beth said her goodbyes. Heard the farmhouse door slam behind her and ran to the gate, before pulling the mobile from the depths of her school bag, to excitedly flick her finger across the screen and checked for more messages, knowing there'd be some.

Feeling herself blush with excitement, she quickly read the words on the screen, along with the trademark emoji and kisses, all from Jackson.

How was the evening with the oldies? 😊 J xx

While rolling her eyes at the use of emoji, Beth pulled her coat tightly around her. Used the tractor as a windshield from the breeze that without much encouragement had suddenly turned into a gale. Not wanting to appear too eager to answer, she waited, stared patiently at his words, reading them over and over and then, with a stomach full of knots, she finally allowed her fingers to bounce up and down on the screen, carefully typing her reply.

At Gran's, waiting for Moll. You said you'd want to FaceTime? Beth x

Give me a minute x ⏰

Lifting her gaze, Beth stared into the distance, spotted the headlights that had turned off the main road onto the lane. Cursed that Molly was early and, while holding her breath, she took one last look at the screen, all the time hoping for a response. She squealed as the three dancing dots appeared, a clear indicator that Jackson was there. With anticipation she willed for the message to appear. She moved towards the gate without looking up. It had only been three days since they'd met. Three days of constant FaceTiming, Snapchatting and messaging. She'd skipped school and they'd spent the whole of Tuesday hanging out on the beach and going in and out of his grandad's bungalow. Plans had been made and she'd already begun moving her clothes, bag by bag. Knowing how unbearable her life would be without him, she prayed that the phone would ring, that she'd be able to see his face, for just a minute.

Can't phone. Sorry. Will try later. 🖤 J x

Hitching her heavy school bag higher on her shoulder, Beth sulked, then bounced with excitement. 'He put a love heart, yay.' She held the phone to her chest. Heard the car pull to a stop beside her. Looked up.

'Hi, Beth.' The deep male voice trembled nervously from within the huge black van. 'Is that really you?'

Feeling her whole body begin to shake, a mixture of nerves and excitement spiralled around her mind, her stomach twisted, and she felt as though the breath in her lungs had left her body, making it difficult to speak. Taking a step backwards, she felt the tractor behind her, glanced anxiously towards the farmhouse. 'Daddy?' Shaking her head, she put a hand backward, began feeling her way along the vehicle's long, rusty metal frame. 'You... you're not supposed to be here. You know that, right?' Inquisitively, she raised herself up and onto her tiptoes, looked into the cab, at the man she'd once hugged as though her life depended on it, the man she used to run to, not away from. Felt his eyes search hers.

'Hey baby girl, you look scared... don't be scared.' He hurriedly shook his head from side to side. 'I'm not going to hurt you.' His voice was deep, low, surprisingly gentle. 'I know what they'll have told you. But on my life, I promise you, I'll never hurt you, not while you're my girl.' He turned away, looked through the windscreen all the time checking, watching. Making sure he wasn't seen.

Feeling her eyes flood with tears, Beth bit down on her lip, turned her attention to the floor, to the cracked, broken tarmac, and kicked out at the gate. She'd waited her whole life for this moment, to see this man, her dad. Yet, now he was here, all she could think of was the list of warnings Molly had issued, the way her mother had repeatedly moved to a new house, a new refuge, just to escape him.

'Our Moll, she says I'm not supposed to talk to you. Says you're dangerous,' she suddenly blurted out, then gave him an anxious smile as she looked back towards the road, wishing that Molly would appear. Tell her what to do.

Holding his hands up, palms out, Charlie gave her a half smile. 'Do I look dangerous?' He laughed. 'Actually, no, don't answer that. I know what you think of me, I... I know what you'll have been told, but I had to come.' His eyes searched hers. 'You're my girl, Beth. I've missed you.'

'Our Moll, she's coming to pick me up. She'll be here soon.' She checked the time on her phone, nervously looked past the truck and along the lane, fully expecting the car to turn up, for Molly to jump out and for the battle of wits to begin.

'Then we need to be quick. I've risked everything to come here, to see you.' He looked across at the farm. 'It could land me back inside. And I really don't want that to happen, so I need you to trust me, to help me – 'cause Beth, you're my girl.' He nodded hopefully. Patted the seat beside him, smiled as obediently, Beth climbed in.

* * *

'You been waiting long?' Molly pulled up beside the farm, pushed a hand through her hair, watched Beth step from foot to foot, her face flushed and anxious. 'Beth, what happened?' Molly's mind went into full alert, with panic spinning around, pressing every button her mind contained.

'Nothing,' Beth snapped. 'I've just been walking along the lane, chatting to Jackson. I went a bit too far, lost track of time. I had to run to get back to the gate.' Her hands went to her bag, where she pulled the zip back and forth repeatedly. It was something Beth had done before, something she normally did when lying.

Keeping calm and turning the car, Molly kept her eyes on the lane, all the time searching the laybys, looking for Charlie. It wasn't long until she spotted a truck, a man in it, who turned away as she drove past. With eyes fixed on his number plate Molly took note of the number, the colour, the make, then glanced across at her sister, carefully watched her mood, saw the tears flooding her eyes, felt grateful she hadn't gone with him.

Angrily, she looked back in the rear-view mirror, at the man who now stared in their direction and, nodding, she stared right back. 'And that was your second mistake, you bastard,' she spat under her breath. "Cause now I'm angry.'

33

After a long day at the surgery, Molly headed into Filey, jumped out of the taxi, took in a deep breath of sea air and smiled at the passers-by, the Friday night party goers, and nervously began to walk through the town, in search of the pub where Dan would hopefully be waiting.

Holding up a hand, she acknowledged a patient she'd met that morning. Took pleasure in the way the town had come to life with an atmosphere different to the city she'd known, but felt encouraged by the way everyone laughed, stood chatting in groups, and danced in doorways. It was a scene that made the whole town buzz with energy.

With trepidation, she tried to remember the instructions she'd been given. Knew that when she eventually found Dan, there would be a conversation to be had, words that kept going over in her mind. Words she dreaded. With her mind working overtime, she considered his reaction, hoped he'd understand her reasons for asking him to step back, to leave her and Beth alone. It was a conversation she never thought she'd have, but after the gardening incident, it was now a conversation she knew had to happen.

She walked past a bar; music blasted out from within and laughed at a man who stood in the doorway, a tray of sparkling wine precariously balanced in his hand. 'Opening night,' he shouted joyfully. 'Come on in, take a glass, it's free!' He held one out to her, gave her a welcoming smile that made Molly look over her shoulder, check behind her. A hand went up to her chest and then, once she realised he'd been speaking to her, she gratefully stepped forward and took the drink from him.

Sipping the fizz, she wrinkled her nose. Felt the bubbles slip easily down the back of her throat. It was sweet, not dry, and much too easily sipped. Taking pleasure in the drink, she leaned on the windowsill, stared outside, heard herself physically gasp, as her whole body froze with fear. 'What the hell?' She heard the words leave her mouth as she ducked, kept herself out of view of the window, practically hid behind the man who held onto the tray, and cowered in the corner. Placing her bag on the freshly mopped mosaic tiles, she pretended to search inside, peering suspiciously around until, once again, she focused on the lone figure of a man who paced along the road, mobile phone attached to his ear.

'You... you can't be here. You just can't be.' Her voice now a whisper, she looked over her shoulder, frantically pulled her mobile out of her bag, flicked at the screen, pressed Beth's number and immediately saw it go to voicemail. 'Beth... damn it, answer your phone!'

With her mind in a full spin, she thought of Beth, remembered the way she'd sat in the car the night before, the tears that had flooded her eyes. Then, as they'd arrived home, the way she'd smugly commented on how good her gran's pie had been for tea and how much she was looking forward to going back again tonight. It had been a comment that had irked Molly at the time, yet now she sighed a breath of relief, knowing that while Beth was with her grandparents, in their house, she was as safe as she could be. That even Charlie wouldn't mess with her grandad, not with his shotgun always at hand, almost certainly ready to use.

Focusing on where Charlie stood, Molly looked along the street, felt her temper rise as she read the sign over the pub door that stood just three doors away from where he hovered. The bar where Dan would be waiting. Sighing repeatedly, she felt the pressure begin to build. He'd asked her to come out, thought they were out to have fun, when in reality, she'd only come to thank him for what he'd done, but also and under no uncertain terms, to ask him to back off, to stay away.

Taking a second glass of bubbles, Molly felt the need for Dutch courage and downed it in one. She kept her eye on Charlie. She could see that he was older now, more rotund, but still looked as evil. His lip curled in an irritating manner. His phone was pressed to his ear. His dark, beady eyes constantly searched the street. Obviously looking for someone. She tried to think rationally. Thought about ringing Dan and telling him how she was running late, had things to do. Automatically dismissed the idea, felt worried he'd walk outside to answer his phone and straight into the former prisoner, who still hovered outside. She tapped out a text and bought herself some time.

'Would he even recognise you?' She pondered the thought, shook her head. 'Takes a real man to shoot a woman in the back, doesn't it?' Molly chided, her eyes fixed on the way he leaned on the railing, laughing and joking.

She wondered how he'd react if he knew she was watching him.

34

Closing my eyes, I lean against the wall, listen to the sound of the town and take in the jovialities that surround me. People naturally laugh, sway and dance, as soon as alcohol begins to flow, and the music is loud enough to cause a rhythm in the streets.

A mixture of seafood and takeaway food fills my senses and I raise my eyebrows in shock as I see a man walking towards me, the biggest battered fish I've ever seen held tightly in his hands, while all the time ducking and wafting his hands comically at the seagulls who constantly swoop at his food, determined to relieve him of it.

Staring at the gull, I notice how free it looks. How it doesn't seem to care about anything, apart from where the next mouthful will come from. For the gulls, there are no rules, their lives are led from day to day with no one telling them what they should do. Who they should love. How to live, and more importantly who they should kill, just to survive.

Moving forward, I lean against the railings. Throw you the briefest of glances. I see you hiding in the doorway, peering out, and I shake my head, roll my eyes and watch as you accept one free drink after another. An act that proves your stupidity, and in the knowledge that you're easy prey, I begin to laugh, realise that you don't have a clue what your fate will be, or that when it comes, how it will be no less than you deserve. Just like your mother. She was stupid, too. She invited her killer in, poured the wine, then begged for her life. It was a prize that came far too easily, a prize I didn't really deserve. Yet still, I see her eyes, wide, disbelieving, staring back at me. The tears that filled them when I told her my plan. They were eyes that reminded me of yours, even though I know that you won't beg, not for your own life... not unless I threaten to kill your sister.

Stepping forward, I watch the glass leave your lips, the way you place it back on the tray, thank the waiter in such a polite and proper way. Disappearing out of your sight, I laugh at the look on your face, you think you're safe. And for a split second, I consider waiting, following you home, knowing you'll be there alone. But I immediately dismiss the thought. It's a race I don't really want to begin. It would be far too easy and almost not worth winning.

Instead, I wait, watch, hope for the opportunity to commit the perfect murder.

35

Relieved to see Dan waiting for her by the roadside, Molly smiled nervously and so as not to get split up, she cautiously allowed him to take her hand and pull her through the swarm of people that had spilled out and onto the street.

Most of the Friday night drinkers were stood around in groups, while others, sitting alone on low walls or at tables, had their eyes fixed to handheld devices, their fingers flicking at screens. Even though it was late, dark and way past a baby's bedtime, one woman systematically pushed a baby's buggy back and forth at speed, the pram narrowly missing the ankles of anyone who dared to cross her path, causing both Molly and Dan to swerve, hop over the kerb and rush inside.

On reaching the door, a wall of music, voices and laughter met her, each person trying to desperately shout above the music, a battle they were never going to win. And although Molly felt some degree of safety in numbers, tonight the crowd was overwhelming. She couldn't see through the mass of people. Didn't know who she'd walk past next, and with a constant fear in the back of her mind, she kept looking over her shoulder. Looking for Charlie.

'Wow,' Molly giggled, felt herself wobble. 'Dan, the floor, it's moving all by itself!' She tried to sound happy, tightened her grip on his hand. 'Please don't let me fall on my arse – not in here. I'd die of embarrassment.' She slurred the words, could feel herself automatically sway to the music. The bubbles had begun numbing her thoughts, taking hold with a vengeance.

Feeling uncomfortable, she let go of Dan's hand. Stepped in front of him. Felt his arm hook itself around her waist, his body pressed against hers. Closing her eyes, Molly took a deep breath. 'Dan! Dan!' she shouted. 'Can we get out of here?' The crowd moved in, closer, more intense, her skin bristled. She scanned the room. Wished for air. Needed to leave. To go outside. The conversation she knew she had to have spiralled around her mind, a conversation they couldn't have, not in here and the thought of it was causing an overbearing weight on her shoulders she could barely lift. 'Dan...'

Spinning her round, he smiled, 'Come on, Moll. Dance with me.' With his arms in the air, his feet apart, his body moved slowly to the beat.

Gasping, she avoided his gaze. Felt his body press against hers, a feeling they both used to enjoy. This was the Dan she'd fallen in love with. The Dan who knew how to party, how to make her laugh and suddenly it occurred to her how long it had been since she'd seen him laugh. Since either of them had laughed.

'Hey, what's wrong?' His hands were at each side of her face. His eyes searching hers. 'You okay?' He'd stopped dancing and Molly gave herself a mental shake, smiled, began searching the crowd.

'Sorry, yes. Yes. I'm fine. I was just...' She froze, didn't know how to answer, began paying attention to the stage. Saw the woman, the long blonde hair, the slender figure, the dazzling smile.

'Oh my God. That... that's Tasha.' Her hand shot out, pointed. 'She works for me – she's – my assistant,' she finally managed to say. Catching her eye, she smiled, waved. Mouthed the words to the song. 'Hey, I'm gonna dance with Tasha.'

'Oh no you're not.' Kissing her protectively on the forehead, Dan steered her towards the bar. 'If we don't sober you up soon, you're gonna have one hell of a hangover in the morning.' He pushed his tongue firmly into his cheek. 'I love seeing you drunk. But if you do fall on your arse in here, you're not blaming me.'

Molly heard her words slur. 'Dan. You've been the best friend, ever. Do you know that?' She looked everywhere in the bar but at him. 'But... I can't... I...' She struggled with the words. Felt herself being manoeuvred across the room. 'Dan... you have to listen to me.' Rolling her eyes to the ceiling, she was momentarily blinded by the lights. Blinked repeatedly.

'What...?'

'What do you want, Dan?'

Dan stared deep into her eyes. 'What I want is to find you a chair before you really do fall over.' Pulling out a stool and with a hand on the top of each arm, he forcibly sat her down. 'Now, don't move while I get you some water.' Stepping in front of her, he lifted a hand, caught the eye of one of the more voluptuous, younger barmaids, who in a pair of bright red stilettos and low-cut top happily trotted towards him. With her eyes never leaving Dan's, she leaned forward to place her cleavage firmly in his eyeline, tipped her head to one side and pouted. 'What will it be?' she said, raising both eyebrows at once. 'Anything you want.'

Molly placed a hand on Dan's shoulder and so as to be heard over the music, she leaned in as close as she could. 'I'm gonna leave you and the barmaid to... you know.' She gave him what she considered to be a sarcastic smile, pointed to a table and slowly slid from the stool.

'Moll, seriously, you know she's not my type,' he whispered as he looked around. 'That's a pint of Stella, and—'

'Just water.' Knowing she needed to sober up, she walked closer to the door, took in a deep breath, thought of her car, where she'd parked outside the surgery. Felt the need to go home and wished she'd thought to stay sober.

'Molly... come dance with me.' From nowhere, Tasha appeared, grabbed at her hand. 'They're playing *Grease*, you can't beat a bit of *Grease*, can you?' With her arm around Tasha, she pulled off her jacket, threw it over her shoulder, walked across the dance floor, in true Sandy style and found herself giggling as Tasha did the same, kept up the play acting. Held out her hand, pretending it was a microphone. 'The one I need, oh yes indeed...'

Molly laughed. Tasha was fun, her innocent attitude to life was contagious. She constantly smiled, and now the continual barrage of questions had stopped, the day passed quickly. Yet above all else, she was professional, good at her job, didn't make mistakes.

Spinning around, Molly gasped as Dan suddenly jumped on the stage. He took hold of the microphone, sang along to the song with ease. He held her gaze, smiled, pointed and with hip swaying movements, he sang in a way that made her feel as though he were directing every word at her. Beleaguered, she moved to one side, realised the barmaid was standing directly behind her, leaning on the bar, her voluptuous breasts almost hanging out of her T-shirt. Her tongue seductively running across her teeth, seducing Dan from a distance.

With relief, Molly moved out of the way. Picked up the water he'd left on the bar, drank half, took a breath and gave him an approving smile. But then the smile quickly disappeared from her face as she spotted Charlie. He was standing by the bar, a pint held up, the words 'cheers' forming on his lips. Knowing he'd recognised her, she saw him sneer, before taking a long, meaningful slurp of the beer.

Hurriedly, she gave Tasha a wave, stepped away. 'Monday, I'll see you – Monday,' she mouthed. Smiled awkwardly. Placed a hand on Dan's shoulder. 'Dan, I'm gonna leave you to it.' She pointed to the bar, the waitress. 'Have some fun.' She swallowed hard, kept her eyes fixed on Charlie. Felt the room close in around her. Breathing out, she shook her head.

'Are you okay?' Dan was suddenly by her side, his eyes full of worry.

'I'm fine, just a bit drunk. That's all. It's not a good look,' she whispered, made for the door. Felt annoyed with herself for not having the nerve to tell him what she had on her mind, smiled, hoped wholeheartedly that the barmaid would take him in hand and make the conversation completely unnecessary.

36

Feeling the cold, dark night air before she stepped into it, Molly gave an involuntary shudder. Pulled her coat tightly around her and with one hand on the wall to steady herself, she began to slowly but purposely make her way through town and towards the taxi rank in an attempt to get home.

Sighing, she heard the sound of a train leaving the station, headed towards it, to where she'd been told the taxis stood. She saw the long queue of people. Most were singletons, who stood alone, and for one reason or another, were taking an early ride home.

Hoping the queue would miraculously diminish, she looked at her watch. Considered the wait. Tried to decide whether she should phone Beth. See if she fancied coming home, and whether she and Grandad might come into town, pick her up. Put her to bed.

Wearily, she propped her body against the wall in a half sitting, half lolling position. She felt distant, discombobulated, made an attempt to reorganise her thoughts. With one eye half closed, she pushed the breath out of her body, gingerly breathed back in. Immediately she gagged at the smell of the men's toilets, the distinct odour of urine wafting past her.

Lifting her arm up in the air, she once again made an attempt to study her watch. Closed one eye, tried to focus. Couldn't. Inching along the wall, she hoped the taxi would hurry, felt desperate to get home quickly, longed for a full night's sleep and couldn't remember a single night since her mum had died that she hadn't woken up multiple times, with hot sweats and panic torturing her mind. She'd lost count of the times she'd sat up, gasping for breath, reaching for water, initially believing her nightmare had just been a dream. Then, just a few seconds later, the reality would hit her, and once again, she'd feel the gut-wrenching pain tear through her. Once awake, getting back to sleep was rare and almost impossible. Real, deep, undisturbed sleep had become a thing of the past. Which was ironic because right now she felt as though she could happily fall asleep – perched on a very cold, very uncomfortable wall.

Raising both eyebrows, she listened to the sound of the queue. To people chatting. To the sound of mobile phones buzzing, bleeping. To the sound of Dan's voice as it cut through the darkness. 'Moll... don't... you can't go.'

With a mixture of emotions, she turned away. Pretended not to hear. Felt his hand run gently down her arm where it stopped, turned her towards him and drew her in. 'Where do you think you're going?' he questioned. Paused. Stepped back. Saw her wobble. Placing his arm protectively back around her, he tried to usher her away from the queue.

'Dan. Please. Don't. I'm going home,' Molly managed to say. 'Oh, wow. I'm so hot.' She began pulling at her coat, tugging at the zip. Wiping a hand across her brow.

'You really have had too much, haven't you?' He forced a

laugh. 'Come on, let me take you home. Put you to bed.' He paused. 'Stay with you.'

Grabbing at the wall, Molly felt the pavement move beneath her feet like a boat, bobbing around on the water. She couldn't focus, nothing felt real.

'Moll.' His hands went to the top of her arms. His eyes frantically searched hers. Ran a hand indecisively across his face, through his hair. Looked around as though looking for help. 'It's okay, she's fine, we're together...'

The whole scene played out in slow motion. The noise of the queue seemed to drown out his words. There were voices of concern, mixed with giggles. Molly tried to concentrate on Dan's lips. Watched them move. Only heard every other word. Felt the tears flood her eyes. 'Dan, I... I think.' Shaking her head, realisation hit her, she thought of the last drink she'd had, of the water. The way Charlie had stood there, smirking. Tried to remember how much of it she actually drank, the glass, the sips, the half she'd left on the bar. She didn't want it to be true, couldn't think of any other reason why she'd feel so spaced out, so inebriated. 'I think... I feel – spaced – out.'

'You'll be fine. I'm taking you home, I'll look after you.' She saw him give her a half smile, a half look of concern, felt his hands press against each side of her face. Then, without warning, his lips began to move slowly, passionately over hers.

Protectively, her hands went upwards. Pushed out as hard as she could. 'Dan... stop. This... no... no. We... we can't.' Closing her eyes, she felt Dan continue. His lips seared a path down her neck, his hands roamed across her body. She was aware of the people watching and wanted him to stop, wanted to take the kiss back, didn't know how. Feeling overwhelmed, the thought of drugs crossed her mind and she felt anger bubble in her chest. 'Was it you... did you – do this to me?'

His arms surrounded her. 'Do what?'

'Dr... drug me.'

'Don't be daft. Why would I do that? You're the last person I'd ever want to hurt, Moll. You do know that. Right?' His face swam in front of hers. 'I love you. I've always loved you...' He paused, looked away, closed his eyes, inched her away from the crowd. Then, in a final attempt, his mouth once again moved towards her. She could feel his breath on her face as he spoke. 'And I'm so sorry things went wrong. I wish it hadn't happened. If only we could turn back the time.' He cupped her chin with his hand, lifted her face to his. 'I'd do things so differently, Moll. I'd make different choices and – and I'd love you more.' Moving her to one side, his hands went back to each side of her face, his mouth firmly on hers.

Unsure of what else she could do, she found an energy she didn't know she possessed. Lunged her hands upwards, pushed him away. 'Get off me...' She thrust her elbows out and with her arms and fists flaying, she quickly forced her way to the front of the queue. Heard the shouts, curses and comments from behind. Didn't stop until her hand landed on the taxi's door. 'Sorry. So sorry... taxi. It's...' She took a breath, felt her stomach churn repeatedly. 'Medical emergency – someone – could die,' she lied, prayed that after only being in town for a week, no one would recognise her as being the local dentist.

'Molly. Don't do this. You can't go back there alone. It isn't safe.' He grabbed her hand, held it to his chest, stared into her eyes. 'Please, don't end up like the rest.'

'What... do you mean, the rest – that it isn't safe?' Her whole life suddenly flashed through her mind. Her mother, Michael. The picture. The spade. The missing niece.

He almost crumbled before her. 'Moll. Please...'

'Please what?' she asked. Tried to understand what he was

saying. Tried to focus. 'Because do you know what? I don't want you to kiss me. I don't want you to protect me. I don't want – any of this.' She bit down on her lip, tried to think, tried to make sense of what just happened. 'Why – don't you – leave me alone – go back in there.' She made an attempt to point at the pub. Watched her hand sway in front of her eyes. 'Go – sing – to the bloody barmaid – she's more your type.' The moment the words left her mouth, she regretted them. She saw the hurt in his eyes. Couldn't stop the words haemorrhaging from her. 'Now, for the last time – let go of me. I'm going – home. Without you.'

37

Leaning back with her eyes closed, Molly could still make out the yellow sodium streetlights that flashed intermittently through the taxi windows. Fast and rhythmic at first, but then slower and more hypnotic, as the vehicle headed south and made its way out of town.

After what seemed like an age, the lights stopped flashing. The vehicle took a sharp left and Molly squeezed her eyes more tightly together, took pleasure in the darkness until suddenly, acid burned her throat and anxiously she rummaged in her bag, pulled a plastic carrier from its depths and purposely took in deep, deliberate breaths, held the bag close to her chin.

Concentrating on the monotonous drone of the engine, she worked out that they'd already left the main road and were heading towards the coastline. It was a thought that made her relax, and she felt herself drift, her mind slipping in and out of a half-conscious state and then, without warning she felt herself sinking, being pushed deeper and deeper down a hole. The earth landing on top of her, burying her. Until all the daylight had disappeared. Yet instead of panic, she watched the darkness close in. Felt calm as her whole body surrendered to whatever fate was about to follow.

A sudden jolt, followed by the tightening of the vehicle's brakes brought her back to the present. She grabbed hold of the seat, squinted through painful eyes. Slouched forward and peered out to recognise the turning circle, the place where the school bus normally pulled up. Realised that the taxi was about to turn into the lane.

'Err, excuse me,' she shouted a little too loudly. 'Stop. Stop here. You might...' She couldn't manage the words, felt the exhaustion take over. Forced herself awake. 'There are – a lot of potholes... If I didn't live down there – I wouldn't drive over them either – so if it's all right by you... I'll walk – from here.' Her words were sporadic, spaced, her eyes difficult to open. Closing her eyes tightly, she puffed out her cheeks and blew out as the sour taste of bile continued to flush the back of her throat. 'Oh, boy, I need to get out,' she shouted, grabbed at the door handle and began to panic. 'Please... oh my God, open the door. I'm trapped. I can't open it. Please, you have to let me out. I... I need some air.'

'Okay, okay, lady, calm down.' The window dropped. 'Don't you dare throw up, not in my cab or you'll be cleaning it.'

Cold night air flooded in and Molly leaned forward. Almost pushed her whole upper body out of the window. Sucked in the sea air, with long heavy gulps. Refused to open her eyes and she took immense pleasure in the wind hitting her sharply in the face until the nausea began to dissipate and eventually she slumped back into her seat to feel the cold leather against her skin, making her shiver.

With one hand reaching out. She continued to rattle the door. 'It's still locked,' she sobbed. 'Please. Please. I can't open it.' Her stomach tightened with fear and confusion. She couldn't get out, didn't understand why. Wished she hadn't had the last drink, tried to remember exactly what she'd had, whether at any point she'd lost sight of her drink. Knew she must have.

'You don't get out. Not till you've paid.' The taxi driver's stern voice pierced through her thoughts, making her reach for her bag, for her purse. Staring at it, she willed it to open. For the driver to be paid. Her hands felt bigger than normal, like giant balloons. She couldn't work the zip, the clasp, couldn't feel the coins in her fingers. Watched as her small change dropped from her hand, it rolled across the floor, to rattle around by her feet.

Allowing herself to glance at the driver, she watched him tapping at the meter's buttons, the bright orange glow blurring in front of her eyes, a look of concern crossing his face.

'Look, lady. You really need to leave the damn door alone,' he grunted. 'And, if I'm honest, I can't say I'm happy about dropping you here. We're in the middle of nowhere. It's not safe. And I'm not sure you're capable of looking after yourself.' He pursed his lips. Gave her a look that reminded her of her grandad, the many times he'd looked at her in an annoyed and disapproving way. 'Do you have a phone, is there someone you could call? Someone at home?'

Taking on the warning about the door, Molly let go. Sulking, she looked into the darkness. Could just about make out the lane. Thought about the potholes. The amount of jolting she'd have to go through if she stayed in the cab and of the nausea that would no doubt make a dramatic appearance by the time she reached the house. 'It's fine.' She pointed. 'My house – it's just – just down there.' She handed him a twenty-pound note through the Perspex screen, tried to smile, gave a dramatic wave. 'Keep – the change.'

'Thank you – but you know – you should call someone,' he shouted as the door clicked open and she scrambled out of the taxi, her feet slipping on the step, fearful of the door locking again, of being trapped in the taxi forever.

As her feet hit the lane, cold, sludgy water seeped into her ridiculously high-heeled shoes, making her curse as she looked down and into the puddle. Not for the first time that night, she wished she'd worn a pair of trainers, something more sensible. She stared miserably at the lane ahead, felt her shoulders slump. It looked longer and darker than it ever had before. She knew she had no choice but to walk along it and for the first time since moving there, she realised why Beth had been so annoyed about having to do it on a daily basis.

Taking a deep breath, she tried to concentrate on just one of the two parallel tyre shaped paths. Pulling her phone from her jeans pocket, she eyed the screen with much deliberation. With one eye closed, she tried to focus with the other. Flicked and stabbed at the screen repeatedly with a long, pointed finger. Then finally, she smiled triumphantly as a narrow shaft of light appeared, lighting up the area before her. 'That's right – now we – now we have a torch.'

Feeling satisfied that between the phone's torchlight and the full moon she could just about see her route, she focused on a puddle. It was just a few feet away and she stumbled towards it. Standing with her feet wide apart, Molly leaned forward, wobbled and looked down at her reflection in the water.

'He shouldn't – he, no, he shouldn't have done that – should he?' she slurred, still didn't understand what he'd meant, what danger he thought she'd be in. A sob left her throat and tears of frustration filled her eyes. She felt scared, alone, as far from home as she could be. Staring down and into the puddle, she could see Charlie's face. The way he'd looked at her across the bar, the way he'd smiled, lifted his glass, watched as she'd drank what was left of the water. Her mind continued to swim, to sway in all directions. Feeling sure she'd been drugged, she struggled to stand, didn't like being out of control and she cursed outwardly as she leaned to one side and felt the firmness of a gate beneath her hand.

Looking up, she saw the first of the bungalows. It was a property, old and derelict, hidden amongst the trees. It was hard to work out where the property stopped, where the undergrowth began and which of the two was more prominent than the other. Holding her phone up in the air, Molly could just about make out the old sash windows, with ivy that grew up and around them like an unwanted blanket covering everything it touched, giving the house a look of being forgotten, abandoned and unloved. It was a feeling that resonated, a feeling she'd slowly become accustomed to. Everyone she'd ever loved had hurt her, left her or had been cruelly taken away without sense or reason.

Rolling her eyes towards the sky, she picked out a distant star. The memory of the evening flashed through her mind, and although hazy, she could still see Dan's face staring down at hers, along with the way he'd kissed her gently, but forcibly held her. Most women would have welcomed his advances, after all, she had loved him and possibly she could have forgiven him. So why hadn't she? It had been more than obvious he'd wanted her.

'He isn't Niall, is he?' she whispered, stunned by her own emotions. She saw Niall's face, his smile, the kiss they'd shared, the warmth, the sensitivity, but most of all the passion. The way his fingers had felt like mini electric shocks on her skin and now, how she desperately wanted him to kiss her again. She laughed as the realisation hit home. Her eyes flooded with tears.

'What if it's too late? What if I totally cocked it up?' She pushed the phone into her pocket. Leaned against the gate, felt droplets of water fall like a shower from the tree beside it, making her cringe and laugh, but she didn't move. Didn't want to move. 'Life shouldn't be this difficult, should it?' she managed to say, gasped as the light was swallowed. And darkness surrounded her. 'It just shouldn't.'

Closing her eyes, she listened to the noise of waves. Took pleasure in the way they crashed on the rocks below. The sound was slow, repetitive, yet in their own way, explosive. It was a sound that was strangely reassuring. A noise she'd fast become used to. Then, the noise of a taxi slowing, stopping, made her turn. The lights blinded her and like a rabbit, she stared at them, unable to move, until she heard a voice cut through the darkness.

'Moll!' Dan shouted as a door slammed. 'Yeah, keep the change and no, don't wait,' His footsteps moved quickly but didn't quite equate to a run, although it was more than obvious that he was jumping the puddles, and dodging the quagmire.

Panic prickled her skin. She didn't want to see him, not tonight, and anxiously she looked over her shoulder, pushed at the gate, stepped beyond it and crouched down to curl her body around the trunk of the tree. Heard the footsteps go past within just a few feet of where she cowered, her whole body physically shaking. The sound of Dan's voice continued to echo along the lane, grew more and more distant until she heard Dillon bounce against the metal of Niall's gate and bark. Swallowing, she tried to decide what to do, which way to go, and with trembling hands, she pulled herself up, inched her way through randomly planted trees, a mini woodland with fallen leaves that had been left to rot exactly where they'd landed. A rough path had been cut through the middle of them, a distinct indication that someone else had recently been there, someone else had taken this same route.

'Damn it, no, she isn't here. What do I do?' Once again Dan's voice cut through the darkness, and without knowing why, she shrank behind the house, where she pressed her back flat against the wall. For a moment she listened to the conversation, thought he might be talking to Beth, but then her mind flipped over and over as his tone became harsh and aggressive. 'Not a fucking chance, it's not happening.' He paused, his voice shaking with temper. 'I don't care what you want. Not this time.'

Furrowing her brow, she shrank close to the floor and with only the moonlight to guide her, she crawled through the undergrowth where an old car stood, the grass so long, so dense that the vehicle could barely be seen from the road. Hiding behind it, she waited until his voice grew distant, his footsteps disappeared and once she felt sure he'd gone, she pulled her phone from her pocket. Flicked at the screen.

Staring down at the luminous screen, she felt the brightness scorch her eyes, a painful reminder of where she was, how dark it had become. Squinting, she knew she needed to send a message, to let Beth and Gran know she was okay, she needed to tell them she loved them but could barely focus on the screen. She tapped away, hoped she made sense, then gasped and held her breath as the message went and her phone beeped, loudly.

Waiting, she listened. Couldn't hear anything but the sea and slowly she crept back to the house and with the solidity of brick beneath her fingertips she inched her way around it. Internally, every part of her wanted to scream. Something deep inside told her to run, to never come back, and she felt an overwhelming need to disappear, to jump down a rabbit hole or to simply open the tiny wooden door that led to the eaves of her house, her very own Narnia, the perfect escape. But she knew she couldn't. This time there was no escape. No running away.

With her anxiety building, she followed the side of the house with her fingers, grazed the wall, the door, the window, felt the way the wooden frame suddenly crumbled beneath her fingertips. Then, a sharpness that made her yelp, and cautiously she stepped away. Rubbed her fingers down her jeans, leaned forward to look more closely at the window, couldn't see, and with trembling, clumsy fingers she once again used her phone as a torch. Saw the nail sticking up. Felt the sudden need to peer into the house, around what was left of the torn, threadbare curtain.

Two copper taps hung from a wall. A plastic bowl stood beneath it. An array of dirty, unwashed pots were randomly piled inside. A loaf of bread had been cut into, a slice left on the table untouched as though someone had been about to make a sandwich and forgot. Curling her lip, she took in the littered windowsill and wondered who would want to eat amongst so much dirt. Then, inquisitively, she tipped her head to one side and through clouded eyes, she took in the small wheelie case, the denim shoes that looked much too similar to the ones Beth had worn just a couple of days before. A rush of concern was met with disbelief. 'What are the chances...' She didn't want to think, didn't want to believe that the pumps were Beth's. But knew that the likelihood of two people on a lane of three houses owning the same pair of shoes had to be remote.

Moving around the house, Molly hooked her handbag across her body, shone the torch through another window. Furrowed her brow as she saw a carpet. All rolled up. Thrown in a corner. Its pattern distinctive, unmistakable and even in her drunken state, she recognised it.

'Molly, I know you're there.' Dan's voice suddenly came from the side of the property, making her heart boom audibly in her chest. Swallowing hard, she heard his footsteps, which squelched as they moved through the leaves, then stamped angrily as he reached the path.

Taking in a deep breath, she felt her head swim. She didn't feel in control. The voice no longer sounded like the gentle, caring Dan she knew, the person she'd loved, relied on, lived with. Now, she felt herself shaking with fear. The nausea turned in her stomach and fearfully, she curled herself into a ball behind the wheelie bin. Every breath was magnified. Every beat of her heart louder. Harder. Stronger than she'd ever known it before.

Suddenly the gate clanked. She didn't know if Dan had walked away or if someone else had entered the garden and, in her panic, she began to scramble through the undergrowth, towards the sound of the sea. She wondered if there was a way to inch along the edge of the cliff, the narrow ledge between this house and Niall's, a place where she knew the two gardens met, where Dillon might still be patrolling.

Crawling on hands and knees, she ducked behind trees, bushes, and kept one eye on the moon, the other on the sea, listened to the waves crashing against the rocks below. With her fingers reaching out, her hand suddenly shot forward, the sandstone crumbled, she lost her grip on the phone and suddenly, it dropped over the edge. Unable to see where it had gone, and too afraid to make a noise, she carefully lay down on her belly, reached out. Felt nothing.

With her mind spinning, Molly closed her eyes. Tried to imagine what she'd have said to Beth if she'd gone into a stranger's garden in the night, crawled through undergrowth and along the edge of a cliff in the darkness. Hearing a noise, she turned, listened, as hot, scalding tears roll down her cheeks. She could no longer work out what to do. The old, derelict bungalow suddenly blurred before her eyes. The gate and garden had become shrouded in darkness and she could no longer hear the sound of Dan's voice, or his footsteps. Feeling lost, alone, she didn't even know why she was hiding. It wasn't as though she'd ever been fearful of Dan and now, feeling full of her own stupidity, she sat on the cliff edge, allowed her legs to dangle over the side. Pulled her coat tightly around her and stared at a sea that reflected back at her in the moonlight.

38

Shivering relentlessly, Molly realised that sleep had taken over. Her hands felt numb, awkward, making her stretch them out and wiggle them around anxiously until the feeling began to return. Confused, she tried to understand where she was, why she was so very cold and why small spots of water were hitting her in the face, making her waft her spongy hand angrily outwards. 'Don't...'

Grimacing, she imagined Beth to be standing there, playfully splashing water at her face, doing all she could to wake her up. With annoyance, Molly rubbed her eyes, felt the pain behind them.

Reaching out, her hand curled around wet, rotten leaves. Panicking, she began to breathe fast. Realised that she was still outside, that daylight had just about broken, raindrops had begun to fall, that she hadn't made it home and that she was still precariously close to the edge of a cliff. Crawling into a space behind a tree, she used it as an anchor and while silently chastising herself, she took in a breath of fetid rotten compost, which hit the back of her throat with force, making her sit up and retch.

Desperate to get home, her hand pulled at her bag. It was still hooked across her body and she flicked it out of her way until it landed over her shoulder and then, unable to stand, she scurried on her hands and knees towards the bungalow. She felt for the path and with her knees scraping on the gravel, she tried to stand and then, one foot at a time, made her way along it until she could see the gate and the lane beyond.

Hearing a noise, she stopped. Listened. Looked back at the hiding place she'd occupied during the night, tried to decide if she could get back to it quickly, but froze as the gentle rustling grew louder. It was a rustling that was quickly followed by a familiar, welcome panting, and a wet, friendly nose. Nestling up to her, and as though sensing her mood, Dillon gave her a loving lick, before lying down as close as he could to give off a soft but sorrowful howl.

'Hey, boy.' She threw her arms around him. 'Where's Niall? Go on. Go fetch Niall.'

A few seconds later, she heard his voice. The sound of the gate. The footsteps as they grew close, then his hands as they reached out and took hers. 'Jesus Christ, Moll, what are you doing? You're freezing.' He scooped her up into his arms. 'Come on, I've got you.'

With relief that hit her like an oncoming wave, she sank unresisting into his arms. 'I didn't know where to go.' Her voice began to quiver. 'I was...' Her fingers gripped onto his jumper. Held on. 'I got all lost,' she whispered, and, with her mind still spinning, she began to feel the warmth of his hold.

'How did you get here?' Niall's arms held her tightly to him. She could hear Dillon walking by his side, the slam of the gate as they went through it, and down the lane, towards home.

'I was in town, I think I...' She paused, shook her head. Twisted in his arms, looked over his shoulder. 'My car. It isn't here. I... I must have got a taxi.' Images of the taxi came back, the door that wouldn't open, the money dropping on the floor. 'Yes, a taxi. I remember coming home in a taxi and...' She looked back at the gate, the bungalow. 'I must have fallen asleep – in the garden...' She tried to remember what had happened, why she'd been there. Crazily, she thought she remembered Dan, the sound of his voice. Feeling scared and disillusioned, she shook her head, and the thought of drugs came into her mind. A sob left her throat, as she felt sure she'd been hallucinating, imagining the voices, the words. After all, why would she hide from Dan? 'I'm so cold.'

'Don't worry. I've got you. We'll get you warm.' He pulled her in closer. 'Why didn't you go home?' His voice cut deep, his words stern. 'That garden, Moll, there's no fence, just a sheer drop, you could have—'

Shaking her head, she held tightly to him, felt his body heat through her clothes. 'I don't know, but I don't think anyone lives there... I was looking through the window, I think I was imagining things, I thought I saw some shoes.' She gazed wistfully back at the house. 'Beth's shoes. Why would I think I saw her shoes in that house?' Turning back to meet his gaze, she felt the soft graze of his lips on hers. The kiss was soft, welcoming and within a second, Molly had pulled him closer. Then as though afraid to touch him, her hand went up to his face and for a single moment all she could feel was his breath on her face. Wanting more, she pulled him towards her. 'Niall...'

He paused, purposely thoughtful. Gave a sharp shake of his head, turned his mouth away from hers. 'You have no idea how much I want to kiss you, Moll... but this – this isn't quite how I planned it, so...' He paused, fixed his eyes on hers. 'Let's get you home.'

39

With flashbacks of the night coming and going, Molly sat in the bath. Swished the bubble-filled water around her, lathered shampoo through her hair and sighed with relief as the warmth finally began to penetrate her skin, and the shivering stopped.

'You all right in there, Moll?' Niall's voice came protectively from the other side of the door, where she could imagine him pacing, waiting for her to come out. 'I've just nipped Dillon home. Given him some treats for finding you.' He paused, laughed. 'And obviously I came straight back. Wanted to make sure you were okay. I...' He paused nervously. 'I hope that's all right?'

Barely able to breathe with excitement, she rinsed the water from her hair, took pleasure in the way it trickled down her back, felt every single beat of her heart as it pounded within her. 'I'm almost done,' she shouted as she stood up, wrapped a bath sheet around her body, and another smaller towel around her head like a turban. 'The water was lush, I could have stayed in there all day, it feels so good to get warm.' Closing her eyes for a beat, she knew she was rambling, tried to think about what she should say, what thanks she should give, how she should give it. Decided that Dillon deserved more than a treat.

Looking in the mirror, she could see the blush of her skin. Every part of her pink with warmth. She pulled the towel free of her hair, watched as it dropped roughly onto her shoulders. The make-up she'd worn the night before had washed away, leaving her to look fresh and awake, all seen through eyes that were now clear and focused.

'Shall I make some coffee?' Niall shouted up the stairs, his voice now distant, and Molly imagined him back in the kitchen, looking for mugs, for coffee. Laughing, she thought of the first time he'd been in her kitchen and wondered which he'd go for today, the instant or the real.

After quickly throwing clean clothes on, she purposely pushed her feet into her big, fluffy white sheep slippers, tiptoed down the stairs, and smiled as he passed her a mug.

'Ah, hot chocolate.' She slurped at the drink. 'Good choice.'

Moving towards him, she lifted a hand to his face, allowed her eyes to lock with his and then slowly, she lifted herself up and onto her toes and smiled seductively, as Niall's arms went around her. Taking his time, his lips lowered to hers and began to move sensually, possessively, making every touch explosive. Every kiss became deeper, more passionate, more ardent. The feel of his hands, firm, strangely familiar. Gasping, she felt his fingertips move up and over her shoulders. Her whole body tingled with excitement. Each touch became faster, more deliberate, more spine tingling than the one before, as his hands began to roam slowly and possessively over her body. Then, as his lips left hers, he stopped abruptly. The sound of his breathing accelerated.

Hovering, his eyes searched hers. His voice broke as he spoke. 'You have no idea how many times I've wanted to do this.' He hesitated with his forehead touching hers. 'If you want me to stop

– if you want me to wait...' he said, with his mouth just millimetres from hers, 'I will.'

Leaning into him and wide awake with adrenaline, Molly smiled. 'Niall, I...' She felt the colour rise to her cheeks, knew she wanted him, didn't know how to say it.

'Say it,' he teased, his hand gently touching her face, cupping her chin, pulling her towards him. It was as though the waiting was almost too much, and suddenly an immediate passion had taken its place. 'Say it, Moll.' Lifting her into his arms, she felt herself melt in and out of his kisses. Every movement of his lips, every beat of his heart, every touch of his fingertips made her feel as though she'd never been touched before. Yet, deep down, his firm, powerful touch was exactly as she'd imagined.

Time stood still. Nothing mattered. Every second felt like an hour as her clothes were systematically removed, item by item, until just her underwear remained to leave her partially naked body crushed beneath his, every contour of his body pressed sensually against her, his arousal fully apparent.

Step by step, they inched their way back up the stairs. Until finally Niall pulled her towards him. The movement was so quick she felt her breath catch in her throat.

'Moll, you have no idea how much I want you, this... but...' he whispered between kisses, blew out a breath, searched hers with his. Then he purposely distanced himself, took deep intakes of breath, stood with his back against the wall, her bedroom door just millimetres from his side.

'But what?' Confused, Molly grabbed at the balustrade, pulled herself along the landing, her arms automatically hugging herself with a sudden need to cover her body.

'You had a drink, I – Moll, you were practically unconscious.' He closed his eyes, squeezed them tightly together. 'I... damn it, you have no idea how hard it is for me to stop. I want you so much, but the last thing I want to do is take advantage and... Moll, for the love of God, please go to bed.' He kept his eyes averted, took a step down the stairs. 'I'm gonna catch an hour's sleep on the settee, just in case... you know, in case you need anything.'

Feeling stunned, Molly felt a tidal wave of embarrassment. For the past few months, since being single, she'd wondered what it would be like to meet someone new, to end up in a passionate embrace, to feel something other than grief. The last thing she'd ever dreamed or imagined was that she'd be standing on her own landing, without her clothes and being told to go to bed, for her own sake. Wishing for the floor to open up, to swallow her whole, she pulled open the airing cupboard door and angrily grabbed at a bath towel, wrapped it around herself. 'I – I'm fine. I'd barely had anything to drink... I wasn't drunk,' she insisted. Again, the sight of Charlie raising his glass was like a punch to the gut, her hand went to her throat, gently caressed her neck, wondered what she'd drunk, what he could have possibly fed her. The thought that he'd got so close, so easily, terrified her. She felt the urge to tell Niall what had happened, what she'd suspected. But now in the cold light of day if she hadn't known how bad she'd felt, how disorientated she'd quickly become, the accusation would seem almost ludicrous.

Looking at anything but Niall, she felt her temper rise, hated the thought that Charlie could once again dominate her life, her thoughts, her mind. A sob left her throat. 'Look... maybe you should go, I really don't need a babysitter and... I really need to sleep...' Cuddling into the towel, she felt the heat rise to her cheeks, the tears threaten to flood her eyes. Tears she knew would scald without falling.

Standing on the top step, Niall ran a hand through his hair, across his well-trimmed beard and finally, he pulled at his jeans, made himself more comfortable. Then, with a measured breath, he took the step that separated them, pulled her into his arms, held her close. 'Please don't get upset. I don't want to hurt you. I want to protect you.' He then gave a gentle sigh of relief. 'I just wanted to know you're sure...' He held out a hand to hers, pulled her into his arms, held her close. 'When we wake up... I want you to be happy, not full of regrets.'

With a sudden understanding of the situation, she tipped her head to one side and cheekily laughed. 'If you prefer, I'll get dressed. We can go downstairs. We can drink coffee, we can even be polite and, what's more, we could both pretend it'd make a difference.' She seductively moved out of his arms, towards the bedroom, dropped the towel onto the floor as she went. 'Or, we can take ourselves to bed, get warm and make love.'

Within a second his body was pressed hard against hers. 'You're sure?' His eyes questioned, seductively. His lips playfully and gently grazed hers. Then, he sensually slid his hands down her body to skim her hips, her thighs and then the base of her spine. Shock waves spiralled through her and then, with no effort at all, he scooped her up, and within seconds, the bed was beneath her. With gentle, tender movements, Niall's fingers began grazing her naked skin, his mouth moved down to her neck, over her collarbone, down her stomach and onto her thighs where, instinctively, her body arched toward him. Without saying a word, Molly felt herself surrender to his touch, knowing that each kiss was being carefully placed and that maximum explosive pleasure would follow.

'Wait... just one minute.' She gave him a cheeky wink, rolled out of bed and clumsily onto the floor, pulled a condom from a wicker basket and passed it to him. 'See, I do know what I'm doing.' She smiled. 'You might need this,' she whispered, taking in the sight of his firm, naked body before moving back to the bed. 'I haven't taken birth control for... well, forever. So...'

Falling back into his arms, she relaxed into the gentle, unrushed lovemaking he offered. The tenderness he showed, and finally, after all the days she'd hoped for this moment, she felt him drive himself deep inside her. The world sped up, their bodies moved in unison, one scream followed the other, and a crescendo of explosions escalated between them.

40

Using her arm as a shield, Molly covered her eyes. Made an attempt to protect them from the autumn sunshine that had annoyingly burst in through the curtainless window, making her turn away from the light and into Niall's naked body as he peacefully slept beside her. Catching her breath, she snuggled in closer, playfully began to touch him, move her hands over him, felt a rush of adrenaline flow through her as she did. Being here, in this house, with Niall, feeling so content, was all so new and surreal, like a bubble waiting to burst, and not wanting that to happen, she took pleasure in watching the steady rise and fall of his chest as he slept, took in every moment, making each one a memory.

'Hey...' she whispered. 'Are you really here?' Moving closer, she threw a leg over his, pushed the sheet down to uncover his body and began to move her fingertips up and down his chest, through the thick dark hairs, seductively administering each touch, until his mouth passionately caught hers.

'I want you again and again,' he whispered between kisses. 'And I don't just want you once, I want you today, tomorrow, I want you the day after that.' His hands moved over her, tentatively hovering just below the sheets until she arched her back, threw back the duvet and laughed as it fell unceremoniously from the bed to land in a heap on the floor.

Staring longingly at him, she took in the shape of his body, the curvature of his muscles, the deep volcanic sparkle of his eyes, and then at his mouth that now smiled with new meaning. It was an image she wanted to hold onto. A life she'd dreamed of.

Gasping, she felt him move into position above her, enjoyed the way his hands and mouth worked fervently to please her, until once again, he drove himself deep inside her, his movements slow, deliberate, rhythmic. The rushed desire of earlier had gone, and in its place was now an act of discovery, a slow, more restrained lovemaking in which, cautiously and patiently, they matched each other, both in pace and tempo until a soft scream of ecstasy left Molly's lips.

41

'Moll, urgh... for God's sake, what the hell's going on? Your clothes are all over the bloody floor.' The sound of Beth's voice suddenly vibrated up the stairs, making Molly grab at Niall's watch, throw her legs over the edge of the bed, jump up. In seconds she felt her heart accelerate from what had been a peaceful resting tempo to one similar to that of a sprinter moments after finishing a race.

'Niall. Get up. Beth's home.' She went to grab at the door but laughed as Niall's hand grabbed at her leg. 'Don't, she'll hear.' She moved out of his way, grabbed at her dressing gown and stared at her reflection in the mirrored wardrobes with horror. Her mind and body began to spin in opposite directions and with her head bowed, she waited for the feeling to pass. 'Oh, wow. I have the hangover from hell.' She waved her finger up and down in the air, pointing at him like a wand. 'And what the hell is Beth gonna say to this?' She tugged at the duvet until Niall leaned towards her. Pulled her back to the bed, where she melted into a slow, sensual kiss.

'Moll, you up there?' Beth yelled. 'Urgh. Whose shoes are

those? Don't tell me you've got that bloody man-mountain up there with you,' she snapped. 'I just knew this'd happen the moment I wasn't here. You went out with Dan. You were supposed to be bringing him home with you, not some random stranger you picked up on the damn street.'

Pulling at the door, Molly stood, listened to the sound of Beth opening and closing the fridge, boiling the kettle, the relentless shouting. 'Moll, are you coming down? You do know Grandad's waiting, don't you? He won't come in, he's outside, in the car, which is probably a good job in my opinion. I messaged you an hour ago, I told you to be ready.'

Molly suddenly remembered the rushed text she'd sent to Beth the night before.

Stay at Gran's. I've left the car at the surgery. Bit drunk, taking taxi home. x

Realising now that those few simple words would have been shared around the farmhouse and, with her grandparents being the way they were, an instant recovery mission would have been instigated. A plan put in place. And today, here he was ensuring her car was retrieved at the crack of dawn, before anyone could notice she'd left it behind.

Looking around the room for her phone, she took in a deep breath. 'Niall... where's my... oh my God, my phone, I dropped it. It's...' She pointed through the window, down the lane. 'It's in that garden, I was near the cliff. I couldn't see. I think... it might have fallen into the sea.' She shook her head in disbelief, furrowed her brow. 'Why the hell do I think I saw Beth's shoes in that house?'

Lying back against the pillows, Niall stared at her. Laughed. Shook his head. 'Moll, do you always speak in tangents?' He paused, sat up. 'That house has been empty for a good couple of years and, as far as I know, no one has been in it since the old lady who lived there. She died at least two years ago, didn't have any family, so, I really doubt anyone's been in there since.' He paused, raised an eyebrow. 'I guess you'd had more to drink than you imagined.'

With thoughts spiralling around her mind, she saw flashbacks of the carpet, the way it was rolled up, thrown on the floor. 'And my hallway carpet. That was there too, in that house. I swear, I saw it through the window.' The anger built inside her. 'If I find out that Beth moved it, that she's trying to scare me, I'll kill her.' She rolled her eyes. 'Metaphorically, of course.'

Pulling her into a hold, Niall allowed his fingers to cup her chin, his lips repeatedly teasing hers. 'Tell me exactly where you were when you lost the phone. I'll go see if I can spot it, take a look through the windows, see if I can make any sense of what you may or may not have seen.'

Molly picked up his jeans, threw them at him, peered out of the window through the sea fret and could just about make out her grandfather's car where it was parked in front of the gate. His fingers visibly drumming against the steering wheel, the engine still revving.

'Go on, your grandad's waiting, go get your car and drink some coffee before you drive.' He pressed his lips firmly to hers. 'I'll meet you back here.' He headed towards the door. Gave her a half smile. 'What's wrong?'

Molly's shoulders physically dropped. She already felt like a teenager caught in the act. She had no choice but to face her grandfather, who would now witness her walk of shame. And as though the day couldn't get any worse, she watched Dan's car pull to a halt, right beside her grandad's. 'For fuck's sake, that's the last thing I need. What the hell is he doing here?' she whispered under her breath. Began to pull her clothes out of the wardrobe.

Hurriedly dressed as memories of the night before flashed into her mind. The drugged feeling, the taxi rank, the awkward kiss. The thought that he'd run past, that he'd been stomping around in the undergrowth, shouting. And her, cowering fearfully in a garden that didn't belong to her. Had any of it been real?

Standing at the top of the stairs, she inquisitively peered around the corner, past the newel post and into the hallway.

'Morning, kiddo. Where's Moll?' The cheerful sound of Dan walking into the kitchen vibrated up the stairs. 'Give us a bite.'

'Hey, that's mine,' Beth shouted. 'Give it back.'

'What? Mmm, that tastes so good.' He paused and Molly could imagine him stealing Beth's food. She'd always previously seen the amusement in the way they quarrelled; nothing seemed to have changed, another reason for her to think she'd imagined it, that whatever she'd swallowed had been affecting her mind. 'Okay, here you go. Have it back.'

'Urgh, Dan...' Beth began to giggle. 'Don't... Why the hell would I want it back now? You just sucked it.'

Molly saw the toast fly through the door, land in the hallway. On the new carpet. Butter side down. 'Hey, you two, enough. You're gonna ruin the damned carpet and I only just paid for it.'

Suddenly, Beth was standing at the bottom of the stairs, fury in her eyes and hands on hips, looking up, Dan by her side. 'Oh, so now you care about the damned carpet, do you? Doesn't look like you cared too much about it last night, while you and him were stripping off in the hallway.' She pointed to the shoes, to the dried-on mud, the marks on the carpet beneath them. Bending over, Beth picked up the toast and then launched herself back into the kitchen, slamming the door behind her to leave Dan standing at the bottom of the stairs, grunting as both Molly and Niall sheepishly made their way down the stairs.

'I shouldn't have come. But crazily...' He paused, bit down on his bottom lip, considered his options. 'After what happened between us last night, I kind of thought we'd have something to talk about.' He stood with his hand on the door. 'I'll call you later.' His eyes flicked angrily from Molly to Niall. 'When you're alone.'

'Dan, wait.' The door slammed, Molly closed her eyes, hung onto the banister, heard a brief exchange between Dan and her grandad. Then the noise of his car, the engine kicking into gear, skidding in the mud.

Feeling shocked, she stared at the door, leaned against the newel post, took a deep breath, then rolled her eyes at Niall who'd picked up his shoes. 'Okay, well that certainly wasn't what it sounded like, but if I were you, I'd take my chances and make a run for it now.' She looked up, gave him an apologetic smile and felt her stomach twist. The happiness of their early morning lovemaking session had quickly disappeared, as their perfect morning came to what felt like a sudden and unexpected end.

Stepping away, Niall blew out a breath, and silently he yanked his shoes on, his frustration obvious. Pulling open the front door, he paused, carefully considered his words. 'Yeah, I think you're right. I kinda,' he looked her up and down, 'I kinda need to process what just happened, take it all in.' Hesitating, he leaned forward, kissed her firmly on the lips. 'I'll go look for your phone, and Dillon, I need to take him out, I'll... I'll catch you later.'

'Niall, I promise you. It's not how it looks, nothing happened. Dan came onto me, I pushed him off, made it very clear that he was out of order and well... it doesn't look like he appreciated it,' Molly shouted after him as he lifted a hand to wave at her grandad and then, with his hands pushed deep into his pockets, quickly disappeared into the sea fret and out of sight.

'Moll.' The kitchen door flew open. 'You haven't forgotten Grandad, have you? 'Cause when you've finished with the boyfriend, he's waiting for you...' Beth pushed another piece of toast into her mouth, chewed and looked nervously over her shoulder as her grandfather's horn blasted out. 'He's getting annoyed. You know what he's like, he won't wait.' She scowled, pointed a finger at Molly. 'But you might wanna finish getting dressed before you go collect the car, cause what you're wearing right now wouldn't be a great look if you broke down. Oh, and...' She continued to wave her finger, this time at the stairs, at the clothing that still lay there. Embarrassed, Molly scooped up the clothes, marched them into the utility room, threw them in the basket. 'Can I ask? Is he coming back? 'Cause if he is, I'll be in my room. I really don't feel like making small talk over breakfast.'

Flopping onto her knees with a cloth, Molly attacked the mud that had dried on the new hallway carpet, watched Beth flounce up the stairs, across the landing and into her room, where she disappeared, slamming the door loudly behind her. Exasperated, she leaned against the wall, threw the cloth at the step, heard Grandad's horn as once again it blasted out. Every day she seemed to do everything for everyone. The demands constantly grew, the expectations became more. Everyone wanted a piece of her, a piece she couldn't always give. Yet the appreciation had become so much less. No one was ever happy, she couldn't do right for doing wrong and on top of all that, her stress levels had grown to the point that she was imagining things, seeing Charlie everywhere she went.

Molly pulled herself up, picked up the clothes that were still scattered all around her and began to get herself ready for the onslaught with her grandad, who she just knew would have an opinion, too.

42

'Grandad... I...' Molly slouched in the passenger seat and pulled her seat belt across. She felt her mind spin and her stomach lurch as they drove through every pothole, and after the night she'd just had, she felt sure he was doing it on purpose. In the hope she could quell the nausea, she dropped the window and took in huge gulps of air.

With a sideward glance, she saw Niall walking down the lane and into the garden of the derelict property, the one where she'd unnervingly slept on a cliff edge just a few hours before. Sitting up in her seat, she watched for as long as she could, until the car had driven past. The last she'd seen had been Niall disappearing out of sight and around the back of the property. Her instincts were to jump out of the car, run to his side, look for the phone with him, but knew that her grandad was already in a mood, that he'd want to get back to the farm and to the sheep, who'd be waiting to be fed.

'I appreciate you coming over. I mean, it was a long way to come to help me, not sure what I'd have done, apart from get a taxi, which after last night might not have been the greatest idea.'

She rambled on, gave him a sidewards glance and grimaced at the way his eyes were fixed firmly on the road, the way his brow was furrowed. His lips had formed a tight, straight line, as though he'd superglued them together. It was a sight she wasn't used to. Not from her grandad. He'd always been a man who spoke his mind. Made his opinions known. Yet recently, since her mum, his daughter, had died, he'd become withdrawn beyond recognition and for a moment Molly wished he'd shout, tell her his thoughts, give her back a piece of him that seemed to have become lost.

'Your gran asked me to come, wants me to pop to the chemist, pick up her prescription while I'm out.' He nodded firmly, turned the car towards town. 'There's a chemist near that new surgery you're working at, so I thought I'd call there.' He lifted a hand to rub his unshaven chin. 'And when I get back, there's plenty to do, so I won't hang around,' he threw at her with a defensive tone.

Feeling that the conversation was at an end, Molly stared out of the window, tapped her pockets, feeling for a phone that wasn't there. Wished she'd asked Beth about the shoes, and just like the photograph and the spade, she wondered if they were another item that had disappeared from the house and, if so, who had been in to take them and why.

Jumping out at the surgery, Molly felt relieved to escape the confines of the car and smiled inwardly as her grandad's car disappeared along the road and out of sight. Breathing a sigh of relief, and with her keys in hand, she let herself into the building, headed for the kitchen, switched on the kettle. Niall had been right about one thing, she really did need to drink some coffee and probably lots of it before she drove. While waiting for the kettle to boil, she switched on the staff television, flicked the channel onto the news and gasped at the red banner that filled the screen. *A body found in a remote field close to the cliff tops of Filey is believed to be that of missing woman, Carol Cooper.*

Stumbling across the kitchen, her legs became weak. Her mind went over the happenings of the past couple of weeks, of all the signs she'd seen and ignored. Fearful that she was about to faint, Molly reached for a chair, sat down and leaned forward. Placed an elbow on each knee and positioned her head firmly between her legs.

'No, no, no... this can't be happening, she can't be dead.' Feeling the panic rise within her, Molly jumped up, leaned over the sink and with the cold tap running, she splashed water onto her face, cupped her hand and took huge gulps of water between gasps of breath.

'Thought I'd find you here.' Dan's voice suddenly came from behind. 'You should be more careful and lock the door. You don't know who's lurking around, do you?' He jangled a set of keys in his hand. 'Don't worry, I've locked it now.'

Molly turned with caution, wiped her chin on her sleeve, looked Dan up and down. 'I came for my car, thought it a good idea to drink some coffee while I was here.' She paused, heard the kettle click, tried to stay calm. 'Do you want some coffee? I hadn't made it yet,' she asked cautiously while watching him pace around the room. Picking up the kettle, she filled two mugs. 'Here... you look like you need this as much as I do.'

Sitting down, Molly held the mug close to her chest, breathed in the steam that rose from it, took a sip and nervously watched Dan who paced up and down the room with his hands bunching in and out of fists. He was pale, looked angry, distant and as she turned down the television, she could clearly hear him grinding his teeth and fought the urge to tell him not to.

'What are you doing here, Dan?' she asked, realised without a doubt that he was more than angry, probably very hurt. 'I mean... you could have come to the house later. We could have talked there.' She rolled her eyes around the room. 'It's not really appropriate to meet up here, it's where I work, not somewhere to meet socially.'

'Socially,' he spat. 'Is that what you call it, is that what we do now?' His hand slammed down on the work surface, the mugs jumped, almost toppled, making Molly grab at them, pour the content down the sink.

'Dan, I have no idea what's got into you, but you need to leave. Right now.' She felt the air being sucked out of the room, tried to pull oxygen into lungs that refused to fill, placed a hand on the back of the chair and held onto it tightly.

With a single step, he was standing in front of her, nose to nose. 'You don't know what's wrong, do you?'

With his breath in her face, she could see the perspiration gathering on his forehead, on his top lip, the anger in his eyes. 'Dan, I'm sorry I hurt you... and I'm grateful for all you did for us... but I don't know what else to say. I can't take us back in time, because if I could, I would.' Immediately realising she'd said the wrong thing, she tried to step backwards, and arched her whole body over the worktop as his face moved even closer to hers. 'Dan, you're hurting me, please...'

'You'd take us back in time, would you?' he growled. 'When would that take us back to, Moll? What point in time would that be?' His hand touched her cheek, gently, but firmly. 'Would that be to a time when we were together, when we were happy, or to a time when you spied on me... thought you knew what I was doing, when you thought I was selling drugs?' He curled his lip, pressed his body against hers.

'I... I saw you, you were passing drugs, in exchange for money. I saw him pay you.' A violent trembling surged through her body, her eyes never leaving his as she twisted out of his grasp, headed for the door. 'I didn't want it to be true, but I saw... I was in Scarborough and I saw.'

'You saw nothing,' he screamed violently, launched himself towards her. Saliva sprayed her face, his hand gripped her wrist, held it tight. 'What you saw was me protecting you. You fucking idiot.' Turning away, he leaned over, struggled to breathe. 'While I paid him, you were safe. Beth was safe.' With one hand he reached out, scooped it across the worktop, knocked the contents across the side, onto the floor and then, with an animalistic howl, he dropped down onto his haunches. 'While we were together, I could help you. But now, now you're with him...' He rolled his eyes to meet hers. 'So now, I don't see why I should do it, not now.'

Closing her eyes for the briefest moment, Molly tried to understand what he was saying, but shook her head. 'Who...?' she finally asked, almost too terrified to know the answer. 'Who were you paying?'

Now sitting on the floor with his back against the unit, his legs stretched out before him, Dan's eyes filled with tears. He stared at the floor, barely moving, even to breathe. 'It wasn't always in money,' he whispered. 'I paid him in kind and when you know what I did, you'll hate me, you'll never forgive me.' Dan's hands went up to his face, rubbed viciously at his head, ran fingers through his hair until he gripped it tightly, pulling at it with anger.

Apprehensively, Molly knelt beside him. She was terrified of the truth, but wanted to know it, needed to understand what he was saying, knew she'd only ever get this one chance to get him to ask. 'Who did you pay, Dan?' she whispered. 'Who did you work for?'

His words were simple, his eyes full of self-pity, of sadness. 'Charlie. I had no choice.'

Nodding, Molly inched her way to the door, suddenly terrified of the man she'd once loved. 'What did you do, Dan?' Her whole body shook with fear. Her hand, almost numb of feeling, went to the door handle, clumsily pressed it down and while Dan's eyes were closed, while tears were dropping down his face, she didn't wait for the answer.

Running down the corridor, she went through reception, into her surgery and out through the fire door. She had to get home, had to get to Beth and cursed as the door slammed behind her, realising all too late that the keys to her car were now locked inside.

43

Running into the house, Molly watched the taxi turn on the lane and unlike the night before, she hadn't felt guilty that he'd driven her to the door, down the lane or through the many puddles, even though he'd chuntered the whole way there about having to wash the taxi down and make it clean again before he'd be allowed back on the road.

Locking the doors behind her, she headed straight up the stairs, found Beth fast asleep on her bed and for a moment she sat beside her, ran a hand over her hair, down her cheek, remembered the promise she'd made to her mum, the promise to keep her sister safe. With the intention of phoning the police, she prised the mobile out of Beth's hand, puffed up her cheeks and blew out a long, meaningful breath. Quivering with emotion, she stared at the screen, allowed her finger to hover over the number nine, tried to work out what she'd say, how she'd explain. She couldn't quite comprehend what he'd meant and played his words over and over in her mind, like a video on continual loop.

He'd said she'd hate him for what he'd done, but for the life of her she couldn't imagine what that would be. Every thought went through her mind, every conversation they'd ever had. With the need to rid herself of his touch and without making the call, she placed the phone back on the bed and headed into the shower. She stood with her eyes closed and allowed the water to hit her directly in the face. A continual stream of questions ran through her mind and while she stood under the flow, she tried to make sense of the past two years. She tried to decipher what he'd been saying, at what point Charlie must have come into his life. And like the pieces of a jigsaw, she tried to piece their time together, the way they'd met, the way he had fallen into her life, infiltrated it on a daily basis, and then how she came to depend on him. She'd turned to him, loved him, and relied on him, especially after her mum had died.

Leaning back against the tiles, she allowed the tears to fall down her cheeks. Had those two years been a lie, had he always worked for Charlie? Then, like a thunderbolt, the words the policewoman had used hit her. 'It doesn't add up. The front door wasn't forced. The wine was poured.' Wasn't red wine both her mum's and Dan's favourite drink? Hadn't they often shared a bottle? She shook her head, couldn't believe it was true. Not Dan, he wouldn't – couldn't. She stepped out of the shower, sank to the floor, wrapped a towel around herself and stared at the tiles as she remembered the hours after her mum had died. She'd tried to message him, tried to phone, tried to get him to come and had only managed to track him down after the police had left. She'd climbed into the car with Beth, driven to his house and, without invitation, she'd moved them both in. Now Carol Cooper was dead. It was all over the news and, undoubtedly, Charlie would know what that was about too. She just had no way of proving it or explaining her suspicions to the police without sounding a little bit crazy.

'Moll.' Beth suddenly banged on the door. 'I'm going out!'

Footsteps immediately thundered on the staircase. Jumping up, Molly tried to shout, yanked open the door, wafted a hand through the steam that hung in the air, thick and heavy, and stepped onto the landing. 'Beth, please... don't... I think you should stay here. Beth, do you hear me?' she shouted down the stairs, as the front door slammed to a close. 'Beth?' Running to the top of the stairs, she stood on her tiptoes, and watched Beth disappearing down the lane, running at speed.

44

The earlier sea fret had gone and, because it was the weekend, the noise of whooping and laughter came from the beach, from children playing in the sand, making sandcastles, or splashing in the water, just as she and Molly had done so many years before. Standing on her tiptoes, Beth stood at the top of the wooden steps, nervously looked along the shoreline, checking for Jackson.

In the distance, she could see Niall walking towards her. His dog Dillon ran in and out of waves that for once seemed full of surfers, all taking advantage of the previous night's stormy weather, today's high tide and the early morning sunshine that had suddenly burst out from behind thick, threatening clouds.

Trying to calm herself, she looked up and down excitedly, waiting for Jackson. Thought about learning to surf. About Jackson teaching her. Then shook her head. 'Who are you kidding?' She laughed, thought of the story Molly had told her. The way she must have loved the sea as a toddler. How she'd run straight in, been thrown back up and onto the beach and how the man had scooped her up and into his arms.

'Hey, you all right?' Jackson waved from the water's edge, gave her a wide, disarming smile. 'I'll be up in a minute.' He held his phone in the air. 'Just need to check in with Dad,' he shouted, before turning with the phone to his ear and walking the waterline.

Kneeling down, Beth kept one eye on Jackson, watched as he swung a towel around the shoulders of his wetsuit, kicked at the sand while he made the call. Checking the time, Beth pulled a make-up bag from her rucksack, began to brush a light powder over her face. Heard the sound of his neoprene pumps on the wooden steps. 'Give me a sec, I just need to finish this.' She laughed. 'Our Moll isn't fond of me wearing make-up, so I waited till I got here.'

'I don't know why you bother putting it on.' He turned, gave her an appreciative smile. 'It's not like you need it, is it?' He shrugged his shoulders, rubbed vigorously at his hair with the towel, threw it at the floor and stood on it while he pulled the pumps from his feet, shook them free of the sand.

Feeling herself blush, Beth thought about her answer. She didn't want to mention the morning she'd already had and hastily she applied a light brown eyeliner, a smudge of nude lip gloss, and smiled back at her reflection.

'There, that'll have to do.' Standing up, she leaned back against the cliff and with one foot crossed over the other, she preened herself, tried her best to look cool. 'So, what are we doing today, are we going to the house?' She held up the bag. 'I've brought more of my things. Not much left to bring, so... as soon as you give the word,' she said cockily, 'I'll be ready to go. Anywhere you choose.'

Sighing, Jackson anxiously stepped forward, began to pace back and forth. 'Beth...' He ran a hand through his hair. 'We're not going anywhere. You do know that don't you?' He caught her eye, gave her an awkward smile. 'I like you, Beth, I really do. But you're fifteen and if they thought I'd touched you or anything, I'd get locked up.'

Beth rolled her eyes, laughed. 'Ha, you're so funny. Now stop joking around, you promised. You said we'd do your grandad's house up, live there or... or you said we could run away, that we'd be happy and...' Stepping backwards, her voice trailed off. 'And I'm sixteen soon, so it'll all be okay, won't it?' she whispered hopefully.

Looking up at the clouds, Jackson's face became contorted with pain as he struggled with the words. 'Beth... on that day... I should have never taken you to the bungalow.' He paused, stared aimlessly out to sea, to the waves. 'And to be honest, I'd have said just about anything to stop you running.' He took deep breaths, in and out, his shoulders heaving with emotion. 'If I hadn't stopped you, you'd have been on a bus to York and I couldn't let you do that. It wasn't part of the plan.'

Shaking her head, she timidly pressed her lips together. Most of what they'd said to each other over the past few days had been done on Messenger or Snapchat and now all of those messages came flooding back, every single word, every innuendo. All of them with two meanings. All of them taken in the exactly the wrong context.

She pretended to squint. 'Plan, what plan?'

He held out a hand, took hers in his, pulled her around the corner, searched her eyes with his. The excitement and fear of the moment hit her all at once and her anger with him was momentarily forgotten as she waited, hoped he'd kiss her. It was something she'd waited for. Thought about. Dreamed of. And now she held her breath, didn't know what to do, how to react and finally, with an awkward smile, she looked up and caught his eye. 'See, you were joking. Weren't you?' She slapped his arm, giggled. 'You had me going for a minute.'

'Beth.' Jackson looked over his shoulder, his smile gone. There was a stern look crossing his face. 'I'm not joking. I really like you.' He spun around, pressed his lips firmly against hers. 'And... you do trust me. Don't you?' Once again, he looked nervously over his shoulder, ran a hand through his hair.

'Yes, of course I trust you,' she finally managed to say, smiled as he moved back to her side, leaned against the cliff face, held her hand in his.

'Then tell me about your dad, Beth. Who he is? What he's like?'

'My dad? What do you want to know about him for?'

'Beth,' he questioned, 'please, just answer the question.'

'I... well, I don't really know him, not yet...' She took in a deep breath, rolled her eyes, thought about the question. Molly had told her over and over again how dangerous he was, how much trouble he'd caused, how terrified of him their mum had been and of how she should be terrified too. But deep down, she remembered the man he'd been, the daddy she'd had and the little girl who'd craved his attention. 'If I'm honest, I've only seen him once since he got out of prison and that was only for a few minutes, I haven't been allowed to see him for years, my Mum wouldn't let me, but he is my dad and... well, I was only little and I remember all the good things.'

'Are you scared of him? Do you think he'd ever hurt you?' Jackson's voice was becoming more and more urgent. His arms flaying up and down in the air. 'You have to tell me, Beth. And quickly.'

'Why would you even ask that? Right now, it's you that's scaring me.'

Shrugging his shoulders, Jackson turned, punched out at the

cliff. Screamed, rubbed his knuckles down his wetsuit. 'Look. I have to go. But trust me, it'll all be for the best, you'll see.' Leaning quickly forward, Jackson once again pressed his lips firmly against hers, then stepped away, grabbed at his surfboard. 'Just remember it wasn't all a game.' He held her gaze. 'Honest, it wasn't.'

Watching him disappear down the wooden steps, Beth was about to follow him, to ask him what he meant, but as she ran across the road, she heard a noise, someone calling her name in almost a whisper. Stopping in her tracks, she spun around, searched the trees, the undergrowth, spotted Charlie stood within, felt her stomach do a nervous somersault.

'Quick, over here.' He was standing hidden behind a tree that stood by the bungalow's gate. Holding it open, he beckoned her across, anxiously kept one eye on the lane, making sure he wasn't seen.

Hesitating, Beth held her breath, stared in disbelief that Charlie, that her dad, was standing there, on the lane where she lived. Repeatedly, she spun around, tried to work out where he'd come from, how he'd got there and then she remembered Jackson's question, how he'd said he shouldn't have taken her to the bungalow. Shocked, she picked up her rucksack, took a step towards where her dad stood. Knew that if she saw her, Molly would be furious, especially after all the lectures she'd been given. Every single one came rushing back, leaving Beth feeling torn between doing what was right for her sister and getting the chance to see her dad, to speak to him, to ask him all the questions she'd wanted to ask for as many years as she could remember.

Taking in a deep breath, she swallowed hard, thought about how Molly and the neighbour had brazenly walked down the stairs just that morning. The look of hurt on Dan's face and her overwhelming annoyance that Molly hadn't done what was right, what Beth had repeatedly asked her to do. It wasn't as though it was someone new, she'd loved Dan once, so surely she could have loved him again. The simple fact was that she'd chosen not to and in doing so, she'd taken away any dream Beth had had about them all living together, happily as one family unit. 'She let you down...' Beth whispered. 'She chose her own path, one that had not a thought for you, and now, now you get to choose your own path too.'

In a half run, she headed across the lane, gave her dad a quizzical smile. Wondered how he'd known she'd be there and then sighed as even to her, it was more than obvious what had happened and with images of Jackson in her mind, she could see the constant messages, the unscheduled, impromptu meetings, the rambled words, followed by the unexpected kiss. 'Well, I'd ask how you knew I'd be here, but I'm guessing Jackson did your dirty work for you?' With an anger she didn't know she possessed, she spat the words, didn't really want to know the answer and looked across the sand to see the boyfriend she'd thought she'd had run into the waves, his body flat on the board, his arms and hands paddling masterfully against the tide.

'Wanting to see my daughter isn't dirty work, is it? He's a good lad, been keeping an eye on you for me, that's all.' Charlie grinned sarcastically. 'Didn't know how else to get hold of you; my parole has restrictions. I can hardly come knock on the door, can I? And the boy, well, he kind of owed me. So, I pulled in a favour or two.'

'You forced him to be friends with me?' she asked in disbelief, and with her heart lurching in her chest, she threw an arm outward, saw Charlie's hand immediately shoot out and grab at her wrist. Then, as quickly as he'd reacted, he released her, and she watched as he slowly blew out through his teeth. Stunned,

Beth stared at the floor, rubbed at her wrist, felt her bottom lip begin to quiver. 'I need to get home.'

'Hey, come on, I'm sorry. It was a reaction, that's all,' he scoffed. 'When you've been in prison for a while, you make sure that anything flying towards you gets deflected.' He lowered his head apologetically, tipped it to one side, caught her eye. 'Now, are you gonna give your old dad a hug, let him say hello properly?' He held his arms out and dutifully, she stepped into his hold, hugged him back until over his shoulder, she spotted Niall jogging along the beach, towards the steps.

'I should probably go, our Molly's boyfriend is about to run this way.' She raised her eyebrows, pointed to the beach. 'And I've already had one run in with him this morning. I really don't fancy another.'

Quickly, Charlie moved through the gate of the derelict bungalow, pushed it open. 'Come on, let's go inside. You don't want him seeing me and telling your Molly.' He took hold of her hand, began to plough a route through the leaves. 'She'd phone the police and if she does, I'll end up back inside, and I really don't want that, do you?'

Obligingly, Beth followed him to stand in the makeshift kitchen. Watched him move around it with ease and noticed that since the last time she'd been there, the kitchen had been tidied, the windowsill wiped, the ashtrays emptied and a wooden plank had been erected across one side of the room, where the camping stove now stood, along with two mugs, one plate, a bowl, and a knife and fork, all carefully stacked.

'Come on in, come in.' He held out a chair, dusted it off, poured water into a pan, and placed it on top of the camping stove. 'I'll make us a drink. Won't take me a minute and then we can go sit down, have a chat.' He pressed the button on the stove, rolled his eyes as the constant, click, click, click echoed around the house, as he tried to ignite it.

She studied his face, tried to remember how he had looked, compared to now. Realised that his crooked smile was the same, as were the dark bushy eyebrows that had always amused her as a child. His dark floppy hair had gone and in its place was a shorter, more cropped style that was peppered throughout with grey flecks. He looked more distinguished, she decided, until he looked up, caught her eye and she noticed that the vividly sparkling eyes she remembered from her childhood had been replaced with a deep, overcast and sullen look that reminded her of a bad-tempered gorilla.

'I've waited years to see you.' He flashed her a look, a sidewards smile. 'Do you know that?' He hovered over the pan, watched it boil, took two mugs from the pile of crockery and spooned Bovril into each. 'Sorry, I'd have made coffee but there's no milk and no damned shop around here for miles... so.' He tapped the side of the mug with the spoon, watched the last of the brown sticky fluid drop into them. 'Bovril it is.'

Amused by his terminology, with the fact that he'd used the exact same phrase that she had, she stood up. She leaned against the door and could hear a distant yell. The sound of Molly on the lane, shouting her name. 'I should go, that's Molly, she'll be worried, she's shouting me.'

He slammed his fist down on the table. 'I've been worried about you. Every day for ten years I worried about you and it's my damn turn. Not Molly's.' He moved himself in front of the door, turned the key in the lock. 'So as far as I'm concerned, Molly can damn well wait.' His voice came out as a growl. He looked nervously around the kitchen, pushed the key into his pocket, poured hot water on the drinks.

'Come on, down here.' He ushered her down the corridor and

into a room in the middle of the house. It was the same room that Beth had almost pushed the door open to just a few days before, the one Jackson had stopped her from entering. A room with no windows, just a two-seater leather settee, an oversized bean bag, a pile of boxes and randomly placed candles that gave the room an eerie amber glow.

'You've been here the whole time, haven't you? You were listening to every word we said, I...' She thought of the time she'd sat with Jackson, the way she'd poured her heart out, with her dad in this very room, listening. 'What did you do, sit in the dark?'

'I had to be near you, to watch you. What's more, once and for all, I had to work out what the damned truth was, all by myself.'

'What damned truth? And you hardly worked anything out by yourself if you had a sixteen-year-old boy doing your dirty work for you, did you?' Angrily, she sat down on the bean bag, pulled at a thread on her jeans, felt her mouth go dry to the point she could no longer swallow. The thought that Molly was out there looking for her made her stomach twist uncomfortably, while her mind screamed at her to leave. Keeping her eyes on his face, she saw a stern, unforgiving look. Suddenly, it was a look Beth remembered only too well. The one he'd often used when she'd been small, misbehaving, and in need of a lesson. The one she'd been terrified of as a toddler, and the one that had haunted her for all of the early years while she'd lived at the refuge. It had been a side of him she'd chosen to forget.

'I need to call Molly, tell her I'm okay.' With her eyes fixed on him, she pulled her mobile from her bag, began to flick at the screen. Then jumped backwards as he launched himself forward.

'You're phoning no one.' As he grabbed the phone from her hand, Beth screamed, watched as the phone flew through the air and violently hit the wall. The screen imploded on impact and the phone fell to the floor with a loud, explosive bang.

'That's mine, you can't do that.' She stared in disbelief, her eyes fixed on the phone. 'Our Molly, she'll be furious, she'll...'

The sound of the door slamming made her jump, the candlelight wavered with the sudden gust of wind, and Beth closed her eyes as she heard the click of a key turning in a lock.

45

Seeing Niall emerge around the corner of the lane, Molly smiled and shouted to Dillon, who happily ran to her side, dropped his ball by her feet and eagerly waited for her to throw it. Whereas Niall stood at a distance, awkwardly looking on.

'Did you see Beth down there?' She nervously bit down on her bottom lip, walked to the edge of the lawn, to look at the beach where she studied the waves, the surfers, the people watching. 'She ran off while I was in the shower and I can't see her.'

Niall slowly shook his head, walked to the cliff edge and stood beside her. 'Well, I don't think I saw her, or at least I should say that I got to walk along the beach without anyone hurling abuse or toast at me.' He gave a confident nod. 'So, I'd say you should definitely look for her somewhere else.'

Pacing, she took in deep, unhurried breaths. 'Carol Cooper, they found her. It was on the news.' She pointed to the cliff tops. 'Somewhere along there.'

Niall nodded. 'Yes, you can see the police activity from the beach. A big white tent's been erected, although...' he held a hand to his forehead, used it as a sun shield, 'not sure a tent will hold if another storm blows in.' Pensively, he picked up the ball, threw it along the lane, gave a wry smile as Dillon took up chase and stormed through every puddle.

'Maybe you were right.' She rolled her eyes up the house, to the roof, to where Michael had been, another tragedy, another accident, another death. 'Maybe it does have supernatural powers.'

Crossing her arms protectively, Molly took a step back from the cliff, ran a finger across the sleepers, the ones Dan had ordered, had been going to lay. 'He did this to stop me being with you, do you know that?' She could still see the venom in Dan's eyes, the way he'd thrown every word across the room. 'And last night, nothing consensual happened, he forced himself on me outside the taxi rank. He was trying to make you jealous and, by the looks of it, he succeeded.' She tried to stay calm, lifted her fingers to her lips. 'When Grandad took me back to the surgery, to collect my car, I did what you said, went inside, made some coffee, and Dan was there. He said things I didn't understand.'

Her bottom lip began to tremble, and she caught Niall's eye, watched as he stepped towards her, took her in his arms. 'He was my friend. He said horrible things. Said he'd been working for Charlie.' She began to tell Niall what had been said, tried her best not to sob. 'I don't know what any of it meant. All I can think is that he knows something about Michael, about my mum, about what happened to them and now they've found Carol Cooper. I'm terrified he might have had something to do with her death too?' She took a breath, felt the panic rise in her voice. 'Am I next on the list? Is that what he meant? And if so, why? What did I ever do wrong to Dan? He was supposed to be my friend.' She held onto Niall. Nuzzled into his neck, felt the anger run through him.

'I hope for his sake he never shows himself around here again.' Niall pulled her tightly into his body. Held her close. 'We need to phone the police.' His fingers lifted to her face. He tipped her chin slowly upwards, gently kissed her.

'I don't know what to say, it's just hearsay, isn't it?'

'I don't know, but we have to find out and that's their job, not ours.' Taking a step backwards, Niall caught her eye, gave her a reassuring smile. Shook his head. 'He'll never hurt you again. Not if I can help it.'

Tears rolled down Molly's face. 'You can't say that though, can you? You're not my babysitter and look how much has happened already. Look how many have already died.' She stared at the house. It was her home, the one place she was supposed to feel safe. 'It just can't be a coincidence, can it?'

Taking a swift step back towards her, Niall's hands went to each side of her face, held her in position, gave her no option but to look directly into his eyes. 'I'll make you a promise. Whatever it takes, I will look after you. All you have to do is ask and I'll take care of things.' Carefully he kissed her mouth, ran a finger tentatively across her lips. 'Do something for me?'

'Anything.' She nodded, knew it was true.

'Pack a couple of bags for you and for Beth. Go to your gran's.' He held a finger to his lips, urged her not to speak. 'Stay there. Just for a day or two. Let me deal with this. My way.'

'I will... just as soon as I find Beth.'

46

Shivering relentlessly, Beth moved carefully around the room, squeezed her body between cardboard boxes. All were stacked on top of each other, all leaning against the wall.

'Charlie, Dad, whatever the hell I'm supposed to call you. This isn't funny. I want to go home,' she demanded. 'Are you listening?' She continued to knock and kick at the door. Felt the pain in her knuckles. Felt her frustration rise. A sob left her throat, and she felt the hot scalding tears fall down her cheeks. 'He can't keep you here,' she whispered to herself, shook her head, shrugged. 'He just can't. And... and... they'll come looking. Won't they?' She thought of her sister. Of Molly. Of all the times she'd told her how dangerous Charlie was. How their mother had hidden in the refuge, night after night, knowing he'd find ways of getting to them if he could. 'She'll come, Molly will come, she... she was looking for me, shouting me,' she sobbed. 'She won't stop, not till she finds me. I just know it.'

With her eyes fixed on the door, she slid down the wall to sit on the floor as the candlelight began to fade and, quickly, she dug around in a small plastic bag. Pulled more of the tea light candles out, lit them and stood them on the small table next to the now cold and congealed mug of Bovril.

Wishing she'd worn a watch, she tried to work out the time, wondered whether Jackson would have finished surfing, whether he'd realise what Charlie had done, come to the bungalow and unlock the door. She lifted a finger to her lips, thought of the kiss.

'Were you really working for Charlie?' She shook her head in disbelief, went over all the things she'd said to him. All the things Charlie could have heard. The thought made her kick out violently. She felt her foot connect with the door, then she kicked out again, harder.

Opening her rucksack, Beth dug around inside. She pulled out her books. Her make-up bag. Hoped for a random chocolate bar to be buried inside. When she found nothing, she began pulling open the boxes that were scattered around the room, searched inside. The contents were things that had been hurriedly packed and poorly sealed, the layer of dust that covered each and every object made it obvious the items had been stored and Beth wondered if they'd been Charlie's things, things her mum would have packed, and item by item, she pulled each one out, sat on the floor, studied it, tried to pull back a relevant memory.

A small silver box caught her attention. It was a box she remembered, a box she'd seen many times in her parents' room, a box that as a youngster she hadn't been allowed to touch. Now that same box intrigued her and she placed it on the table, stared at it for a while. Took note of the markings, the image of a phoenix carved into the precious metal. Swallowing hard, she dared herself to open it, kept one eye on the door, sure that the moment she did, Charlie would come in, catch her in the act, look at her with those big silverback eyebrows.

Tentatively, she stroked the box with one finger. She moved a candle closer, then timidly she prised it open and stared disbelievingly at the gun that must have always been in there, in her house, when she'd been a child. 'Why, why would anyone have a gun?' She backed away from the box, felt the air leave her lungs, knew that her dad, Charlie, had gone to prison for murder, for shooting someone. 'Was this the gun?' She shook her head, tried to rationalise what she'd found, why he'd have it and the fact that after he'd gone to prison, the house had been searched. 'The police didn't find it.' Doubt crossed her mind. She tried to focus, to think about the box, about whether she could ever remember seeing it after he'd gone to prison and clearly remembered it being something their mum had kept. Which meant that Charlie must have been in their house, digging around in their mother's things. Her eyes immediately dropped on the picture, the one that had been in their hallway, the one taken while she and Molly had slept.

'Dad. Where are you?' With her back to the wall, she used the side of her foot to kick repeatedly at the door. It connected with the panel like a bass drum, constantly beating to the rhythm of a tune. 'So, you broke into our house, did you?' She spat the words. 'Well, if you want the gun, you need to come and get it.' She laughed, tutted. 'That's right, I found your gun and if you don't come and let me out soon, I might just shoot out the lock, the door, and hope to God you're standing behind it.'

After what seemed like an age, the door shot open, making her scramble backwards, and with a look that could have shattered glass, Charlie stood glaring at her. One hand was gripping tightly to the door jamb, the other was held out, palm up, and without saying a word, his piercing eyes demanded the weapon.

'Oh, so now you want the gun, do you?' she asked cockily.

'It's not my gun, it's your mother's, and I'm gonna prove what she did, what they both did, show her to be the cold-blooded murderer she really was.' The words drove through her like a thunderbolt.

'How can you say that? She did nothing wrong, apart from love you.' She looked him directly in the eye, saw the way he looked right through her. It was a look that told her all she needed to know, and quickly she grabbed the gun from its box. She kept her eyes firmly on him, nervously pacing.

'Oh, you think you can shoot me, do you?' he mocked. 'Come on then. Be a big girl. Give it your best shot.' He laughed, a slow, guttural laugh. 'You get one chance to pull the damn trigger.' He pursed his lips, shook his head. 'But don't forget,' he smiled smugly, 'that gun's been stored for years. So you must know that the second you pull that trigger that little beauty'll backfire so fast that you, young lady, will be dead – in – seconds.' He slowed his words, enjoyed saying them.

Beth felt herself sway with fear. Tried to concentrate on the gun. The way the gun's barrel moved around so much in her trembling hands, her chances of her hitting anything was more than remote. But still, she couldn't move. Her breathing slowed. She took a step towards the door. Watched Charlie match her, step for step, making her wish the room was bigger. That there was more space between her and Charlie. That she could leave without the confrontation. Knowing that if she could just get to the door, she'd have a chance of outrunning him. A chance of getting away, of alerting Molly, or Jackson.

'You – you need to get out of my way. I – I'm going home.' She tried to swallow but couldn't. Her mouth had gone dry, her mind pounded and wouldn't stop. 'You can't keep me here. I... I will shoot you.'

'No, you won't.' Pushing his lips out in a pout, he rolled his eyes. Grabbed a small cardboard box. Threw it and its contents at her, then laughed hysterically as she screamed, dropped the gun to the floor, saw it land just inches from his feet. 'See, I told you,' he said smugly. 'You don't even know how to fire the fucking thing, do you?' He reached forward, picked it up. Turned it over and over in his hand. 'You were too stupid to kill me, just like your father was.'

Beth felt the floor move beneath her feet. Her legs became weak. She couldn't stand. Held onto the wall and tried to balance. 'But... but... you're my dad, you—'

'No, I'm not.' He tapped the barrel of the gun against his temple. 'That might be what she told you. When she died, she took the damn truth with her. Didn't she?' He slowly and distastefully looked her up and down. 'I tried to convince myself she'd been faithful, and for years, I did. But the minute I saw you leaning against that tractor, I knew the truth. I could see that bastard, Michael, in you. You're his fucking double.'

'What? Why would you say this?' Lifting a hand, she dragged it across her face, wiped away her tears, remembered the photograph similar to the one he'd stole, the one of their mother years before, sitting on the lawn, looking up lovingly at Michael. Sniffing, she felt her whole world collapse around her like shards of broken glass, shattering around her ankles. 'She loved me. She'd have told me the truth. I just know she would.' Her voice wobbled and her mind spun until she felt as though she'd climbed onto a fairground ride that was spinning faster and faster and wouldn't stop.

'Really, did she ever mention how she set me up, how they set me up? How I ended up inside? While they walked free, leading separate lives? Did they ever tell you how Michael's first wife died, how she was shot in the back?'

Shaking her head, Beth furrowed her brow. She didn't understand, didn't want to understand.

'He stood in the witness box. Swore on the damned Bible.

Said he saw me shoot her. Robbed the house, took her jewellery and miraculously, her necklace was found hidden in our loft, right next to where your mother had told me to hide.' Turning, he punched the wall, cursed.

'So, if you were innocent…' She stuttered the words, remembered the day the police had burst through the door, dragged him out of the house. 'Why did you hide?' She barely dared ask the question. Her eyes constantly stared at the gun. At his eyes. At the madness behind them.

'I never said I was an angel. I knew they'd come after me one day, but I didn't shoot anyone. Stupid. It was the two of them, concocting a plan. Wanted both me and Michael's wife out of the way.' He began nervously tapping his foot against the skirting board. 'I'm amazed you never went on the internet, looked it all up.' He paused, swallowed. 'I warned her. I told her I'd be watching. Waiting. That I'd have my revenge, and I did.'

Shaking inside, Beth inched ever closer to the door. 'I didn't look at the internet because I didn't want to remember. That day, the day you left. I thought you were going on a holiday, that you'd be back and when you didn't, I wanted to forget. But now you're innocent?' she questioned, childlike. Tried to smile. 'I can help you. We can go to the police. We can tell them what we know, give them the gun, clear your name.'

Sweeping another box to the floor, he began to laugh as the contents shattered. Large pieces of crockery spilled out. 'God. You really are naïve, aren't you?' He fixed his jaw, ran a hand through his peppered hair. 'I'm not stupid, I'd never get to clear my name. Not now. Not after what I've done,' he hissed. 'I had them both killed. I took my revenge, made sure they knew why they had to die, why it was their turn.' He shook his head, waved the gun around in the air. 'If that came out, I'd go to prison, stay there for the rest of my life, and I can't let that happen, can I? Not again. Not now.'

Holding onto the wall, Beth made a conscious effort to breathe, each breath was pulled in as though it were her last. Every part of her wanted to leave, to go home, to learn how to surf. She even wanted to get to know Niall, to stop arguing with Molly and to go to the school she'd initially hated. A school that right now, right at this moment, didn't seem as bad as it had.

'Fucking masterplan, wasn't it? To get me out of the picture and with the gun gone, there was nothing I could do to prove my innocence. Not with a witness who swore I'd done it.' He paused, tapped the wall with the gun. 'You see, they'd been childhood sweethearts, much too young to cope and Molly, she was born before they left school. They didn't stand a chance, not really, and went their separate ways. Michael went off to university and your mother, well, she was disgraced, left to bring Molly up alone, and when she married me, she pretended none of it had happened. And I thought, I really thought we were happy.'

He paused, stared at the gun. 'But then, after a visit to the beach, she started to see him again, mostly from a distance, an odd wave, a friendly stroll. Sometimes with Molly. Sometimes alone. Told me she wanted to go walking, wanted to take time for herself, blow the damned cobwebs away.' Another low guttural sound left his body. 'They said I'd been engulfed with jealousy, that I'd aimed for him, and missed, hitting his wife with the bullet. Do you know how much I lost that day?' He looked up, screamed. 'I lost everything. And do you know what she did – she laughed. She made a big thing of telling me how she'd never forgotten him. How he'd been her first. Her only love. How you were his too, how both her girls had the same fucking daddy.' He paced back and forth to the top of the stairs. Looked down. Walked back. 'I didn't want to believe it. Couldn't believe it and I didn't. Not till I saw you.' He looked into her eyes as he spoke, but the emotion was gone. Now there was nothing but resentment, nothing but hatred.

'She'd have told me. She'd have told Molly. I mean, why keep it a secret?' Beth thought of the years that Molly had wished for a father, of her mother's stories, of how he'd left, gone off to university and was suddenly killed in a tragic, meaningless accident.

'Well, she didn't, did she? For whatever reason they had, she kept it a secret, paid for what she did, and I warned her. I told her she'd pay, and she did. They both did.'

He pressed his lips tightly together. 'And now you're the final link and you – you have to pay too.'

Beth heard the noise before she felt the pain. Her whole body shuddered violently. Heat burned through her. Like a poker, hot and red from the fire. Her hands went up and then, in slow motion, she dropped to her knees, doubled up in pain and saw the floor rush up to meet her. Lying with her cheek pressed to the floorboards, she gasped for breath, saw Charlie drop to his knees, lie on the floor beside her.

'I want to see you die.' He stared into her eyes. 'I want to see your pain. And then I'll dump your body. Like rubbish. Where no one will find you.'

Falling in and out of consciousness, Beth felt the life draining from her. She couldn't move. Could barely breathe. Rolled her eyes to give Charlie a cold, hard, stare. 'You... promised,' she managed to say, 'you... promised... you'd never... hurt me.'

'No... what I said was that I'd never hurt you while you were my girl, well you're not my girl, Beth, are you?' he said, with a twisted, deceitful smile. Then, with a final look into Charlie's deep, evil eyes, Beth sank deeper and deeper, as the darkness descended around her.

47

As the sky began turning dark with black, moody clouds, Molly stared at the luminous digits of the clock, realised that it was still relatively early, and that the darkness made it feel much later. But with Beth still missing and the police now hunting for Dan, she couldn't rest, and only the pounding of her own heart in her chest filled her mind, as she watched each minute disappear, only to be replaced by the next.

Walking to the window at the back of the house, she ran a hand across the bags she'd packed earlier and stared at the beach, at the sea that now rolled in, with a tide so volatile, so choppy that even the surfers had given up and gone home. Only Niall could be seen. He'd taken Dillon for a last-minute dash. But he constantly returned his gaze to hers, to the window where he knew she stood. Each time he caught her eye, they'd share a wave, a connection joined by an invisible thread. Since her phone had been smashed on the rocks, it was the only way of keeping contact, of him knowing she was there, that she was safe, and constantly watching.

Hearing the sound of the front door springing open, Molly

jumped up. Felt a relief flood through her that was quickly followed by terror as she heard footsteps stamp on the hallway mat, footsteps much too loud to be Beth's. Knowing that Niall was still on the beach, she crept around the edge of the room, stood behind the door and with her heart pounding louder, stronger, and more viciously than it had before, she held her breath. Felt as though with every beat her heart was trying to escape, along with a small artery in her temple that throbbed uncontrollably. Terrified of making noise, she tried to scour the room through the darkness, tried to find a weapon, anything she could use to protect herself but felt unable to move, and she placed a hand on the door handle, held onto it tightly and while looking between the small crack between the door and the jamb, she kept one eye on the hallway. She saw Charlie creeping towards her.

'Where the hell's my sister?' she screamed, used the door as a weapon, launched it as hard and as quickly as she could, felt the resistance as the door slammed into Charlie and propelled him backwards, to land heavily against the balustrade, gasping for air.

'You bitch,' he attempted to shout. His hands went to his face and even though the house stood in semi-darkness, she could see his wide eyes, his face contorted with anger.

Regaining his composure, Charlie threw himself towards her, immediately grabbing at her throat, squeezing tightly. The pressure grew tighter and with eyes that locked onto hers, she felt the blood pound through her veins. She couldn't scream. Couldn't breathe. The pain increased. Everything turned into a dark, terrifying blur.

'I'm gonna fucking kill you.' His words were venomous, came through gritted, yellowing teeth. The tip of his nose pressed violently against hers, the look in his eyes one of pure hatred and without warning his head went backward, thrust forward. Her mind exploded with an instantaneous pain that tore through every millimetre of her face. She fell to the floor and while gasping for breath, she saw the blood that covered her hands and even though he'd let go, she felt the pain accelerate. She grabbed at anything she could. Anything within reach. Tried to claw her way along the hallway, gain momentum, saw the blood splattered handprints that now covered the once cream carpet.

'P-p-please,' she begged, sobbed. 'Don't kill me.'

He hovered over her, his hands raking through his hair. His eyes, deep, dark, seething. 'You're just like your mother. Do you know that?' He turned, swept a crystal vase off the hallway shelf, laughed as it dropped to the floor, caught the skirting board and made a loud and unexpected noise, then laughed as Molly curled herself into a tight and terrified ball. 'I hear that she begged for her life, too.'

'She didn't deserve to die, she... she was a good mother. She loved us.'

'She loved no one.' Charlie's voice hit a new range. A strangled scream that came from deep within. 'No one, except for him, for that bastard. Well,' he laughed, a blood-curdling hideous laugh, 'he got his comeuppance, too. He got what he deserved, all planned to perfection, all happened before my release. All done in a way they couldn't blame me.'

Crawling backwards, Molly closed her eyes, felt the pain within. 'Where's my sister?' she screamed as fear sped through her body. She scrambled to the door, her eyes searching for Beth, all the time praying she'd stay away, that she wouldn't come home, not at this moment, not until Charlie was gone.

'Who, Beth?' He laughed, a long, shrill laugh that came from his boots. 'Silly girl held a gun on me, tried to shoot me.' He stopped laughing, lowered himself to the floor, to where he could look Molly straight in the eye. 'She should never have done that. Should she?'

A long, shrill, internal scream took over her mind, a surge of adrenaline quickly coincided with a fury she didn't know she had. 'And that... that was your final mistake, you bastard,' she screamed as she launched herself forward, clawed at Charlie's eyes, felt his fist once again connect with her face.

'Get away from her, you fucking animal...' Dan's voice came from nowhere. 'You promised... if I did what you said, you promised... you said you'd keep them safe. You said you wouldn't allow them to come to any harm... yet you... you killed her anyway.' The scream was low and guttural, full of pain, interspersed with sobs. 'Beth did nothing wrong to you, nothing and I... I did everything you asked. I tried to keep her and Molly safe and now... it was all for nothing. I killed them for nothing.'

His hands were suddenly on Charlie's neck. The two of them fell through the doorway, until they landed heavily on the grass in a ball of fists and fury. Jumping to his feet, Dan gave Molly a final look, his eyes connected momentarily with hers, the look of sorrow clear to see. 'Run... get out of here, get out of here now,' Dan screamed as he rushed at Charlie with a series of rugby tackles that were attempted and failed. Each man a good match for the other.

Sobbing, Molly dragged herself through the door on her belly. She couldn't stand up, could barely see through the swelling that surrounded her eyes and face. She knew that Beth was hurt, that she had to find her, had to get to her. 'Where is she?' she screamed and then held her breath as both Charlie and Dan neared the cliff, each throwing a punch. One at a time, moving backwards. Then, with a blood-curdling scream, she saw Dan disappear over the edge. One minute he was there and then he was gone, and now Charlie stood, looking over, the hideous sound of his laughter bellowing above the sound of the waves.

With a determination she didn't know she had, Molly pulled

herself up, took deep, inward breaths, and with her arms outstretched and the passion of a raging bull, she made a vehement dash at Charlie. She wanted to push him over the edge, to put an end to the now, to the past. But her mind spun, her energy failed, she fell to her knees, and as a cry left her throat, she clawed at the grass, pulled herself closer and closer to the edge of the cliff. Until she saw him. Dan. All twisted and broken on the rocks below, blood seeping into the sand. The sight made her retch with emotion, and once again she threw herself forward, grabbed at Charlie's leg. 'You bastard…' A sob left her throat as he spun towards her, physically lifted her from the floor to look her directly in the eye.

'You thought you were real fucking clever, didn't you?' His voice hissed through his teeth as he threw her back down. 'Well, we'll see who's so clever now, won't we?'

Screaming, she felt his boot connect with her ribs. Unsure what part of her to protect next and without knowing where his boot would land, she frantically made an attempt to protect every single part of her body, all at once. Thoughts flew through her mind at speed. Her eyes were fixed on his feet, on the edge of the cliff, on all the things that lay around the garden, the railway sleepers that ironically stood, stacked by the gate and much too heavy for her to use as a weapon. 'Where's my sister? I want to know where she is!'

He gave her a sideward glance, curled his lip. 'She's down there, at the house. Was making herself a nice little nest with young Jackson, she was. Well, now… she's gone, dead, just like she deserved.'

A violent trembling began at her toes and worked its way upwards, until every part of her body shook with terror. But the fear was no longer for herself. It was for Beth. For her sister. 'She's just a child, a baby.' Consumed with anger, she tried to stand. Felt a short sharp scream leave her throat, as the barrel of a gun was pulled from his coat. It glinted in the moonlight. Pointed at her.

'Take him down.' Niall's voice cut through the darkness. Dillon launched himself through the air and over the railway sleepers, making Molly fall to the floor and cover her ears as she tried to muffle the loud, sickening screams, all coming from Charlie, as Dillon took hold.

48

EIGHT MONTHS LATER

Carrying her trainers, Molly took advantage of the morning sun, inched her jeans up her legs and carefully pressed her toes into the wet sand, allowing the rolling waves to gently lap up and over them with the incoming tide.

'Here you go, boy.' She picked up the ball and tossed it pathetically across the sand. She laughed at her effort, then tipped her head to one side, arched her brow and gave Dillon a look as he turned his nose up at the ball, ran past it and straight into the sea, where he bit at the water and shook his head violently, obviously disgusted by the taste.

'Moll,' Niall shouted from the edge of the cliff, 'the guys have almost finished packing, do you want to come and check things?'

Looking up, she slowly shook her head. Allowed herself to look past him with the same wishful eyes she'd had as a child. Felt the nostalgia sweep around her as she could still imagine her mother sitting there on the beach beside her, next to the sandcastles. Pointing to the house. Saying how much she loved it. How much she'd love to live there. Her enthusiasm had been more than addictive and had Molly not been a child, she would have realised that those visits had never really been a simple trip to the seaside. She just wished she'd known how much a part of their lives Michael should have been, and the truth behind her parentage. It was just another secret their mother had taken to the grave. Although no one could understand why their mum and Michael had lived separate lives or how over the years, they'd managed to keep in touch. The only obvious answer they had was that their mother had known how things would turn out. She'd known all along what Charlie was capable of and, after they'd put him away, what revenge he'd want to take.

Yet, even with the impending danger, their mother had finally chosen to live the life she'd always wanted. A life with the man she had loved since childhood. Even though, by doing so, they probably knew they were sealing their own fate.

Stepping out of the water, Molly felt the roughness of the sand beneath her feet and walked towards the steps. She turned. Took in a deep breath. Closed her eyes and traced the sand with her toe. 'It's my beach now,' she whispered into the air, but where on this beach she'd previously felt her mother's arms wrap themselves around her, now she just felt a calmness, a deep longing for what should have been, what they could have had and for what was to come.

Jumping down the last of the steps, Niall wrapped his arms tightly around her, lifted a hand gently to her face, cupped her chin and grazed her lips with his. 'Once we've got your furniture into mine, I'll send the guys over to your grandparents', start moving them out of the farm and into the house.' He laughed, rolled his eyes. 'Which reminds me, I'd best get one of the guys to start building that run, otherwise we'll have Dillon chasing the damn chickens all over the beach.'

Molly nodded, kissed him gently on the neck, nuzzled in and took in the deep, earthy aroma of his aftershave. 'What would I do without you?' It was a question that needed no answer as she lifted her face to his, slowly kissed him.

Taking his hand in hers, she followed him back up the steps. 'I'm amazed we convinced our gran and grandad to move here at all. Grandad hated the place, just like Beth, who never did want to live here.' Her arm swept outwards. Pointed to the sea. To the rolling waves and to the way they splashed up and over the rocks. 'She never saw the beauty, not the way we do.' Reaching the top of the cobbled path, she turned in his arms, looked out to sea. 'Even though she got to meet Jackson here, she'd have much rather lived in town, with the unlimited Wi-Fi, shops and all of her friends, living right on her doorstep.'

'And now?'

Molly heard the giggle. She could hear Beth's voice over the sound of the waves. Caught sight of her bikini-clad sister as she ran past her and down the steps, the gunshot scar on her stomach clear to see. 'It's my survival scar,' she'd said on so many occasions but had never again spoken of either Dan or of Charlie. Only of the night when a bullet had torn through her, leaving her to fight for life, and the way Jackson had found her, close to death. He'd raised the alarm, stayed by her side, promised he wouldn't leave her. While all the time he'd gripped her hand, given her three consecutive squeezes, and meant them. Then, as her life had slipped from her, she'd seen Niall rushing in, her very own hero, who'd maintained her airway, stopped her bleeding and kept her alive until the paramedics had got there.

Kissing Niall's cheek on the way past, Beth bounced down the steps in bare feet. Her love of shoes had gone, and with a surfboard under her arm and Jackson close behind her, she headed straight for the sea, leaving Molly to watch in horror as a large wave hit them both, tossed them back up and onto the sand, where Beth squealed and lay laughing in Jackson's arms.

Finally, she'd taken on the look of the carefree and independent young woman Molly had always hoped she'd become. And with her heart bursting with pride, Molly turned in Niall's arms, looked up and into his eyes, saw the love that shone within them.

Without hesitation, she squeezed his hand three times and pressed her lips firmly to his. 'And now?' She repeated his question. 'Well, now... I'd say that there's no place like home. Wouldn't you?'

ACKNOWLEDGMENTS

As a teenager I used to stay at one of the houses at Hunmanby Gap. I used to love looking out over the bay and watching the fishing boats early in the morning as they returned to the bay of Filey and although my novel is loosely based upon this area, in reality the lane is much shorter, the houses much more beautiful and not at all run down or derelict and of course, like all my other stories this is one of fiction and in no way reflects the lives of the owners or their history.

Now, onto those I would like to thank. Firstly, I'd like to thank the people this book was dedicated to. To the hundreds of people who were key workers and, like myself, worked every single day of the pandemic and put themselves at risk, for the sake of others. In my eyes, you're all heroes. Thank you.

Thank you also to my husband, to Haydn. He's supported me in everything I've ever done and puts up with the rollercoaster that I constantly seem to be on. The last thirty years have been quite a ride, but I'm so pleased we've taken it together. As always, I love you loads.

For friends: Annemarie Brear, who shares her friendship and advice on a daily basis. And for Jenny Woodall, who is like another mother, a wonderful friend who keeps me on the straight and narrow, the amazing Jean Fullerton who always seems to know when I need a chat and for Kathy Kilner, who has been a great friend for over thirty years. I have no idea what I'd do without any of you.

Additionally, I'd like to thank amazing friends, Chrissie, Milly, Amanda, Rachel, Sadie and Jane. You keep me going every single day. You rock and I love you all.

After a year of uncertainty, I'd like to thank my new publisher, Boldwood Books, and my lovely editor, Emily Ruston, who has been an absolute pleasure to work with. Thank you for offering me this opportunity, for loving my stories as much as I do and for believing in me. You've been a great support to me this year. And, after a lot of hard work, we finally have a great book to be proud of. Thank you.

And finally, to you, to my dear reader. Thank you so much for buying and reading The Sisters Next Door. I really loved writing this book and hope you enjoyed following the story of Molly and Beth, following them through the smiles and the heartache, along with the trauma they went through and, eventually, the happiness they found. I'm sure you'll agree that they both really deserved it.

Like all other authors, I've been on quite a writing journey and I still find it surreal that my novels are 'out there' and that you, the readers, are buying them. With that in mind, I'd love to know your thoughts and I'd be delighted if you'd take just a few moments to leave me a review on whichever platform you bought it from.

Please feel free to contact me anytime. On Twitter I am @Lyndastacey and on Facebook I am Lynda Stacey Author. I'm always happy to hear from you.

If you'd like to receive my quarterly newsletter, please contact me giving permission (because of data protection), and please include your full name on the contact form that you can find on my website: www.lyndastacey.co.uk

Once again, thank you for reading my sixth novel, it was a pleasure to write it for you!

With much love,
Lynda x

MORE FROM L.H. STACEY

We hope you enjoyed reading *The Sisters Next Door*. If you did, please leave a review.

If you'd like to gift a copy, this book is also available as an ebook, digital audio download and audiobook CD.

Sign up to L.H. Stacey's mailing list for news, competitions and updates on future books.

https://bit.ly/LyndaStaceyNewsletter

The Serial Killer's Girl, another gripping thriller from L.H. Stacey, is available now.

ABOUT THE AUTHOR

L.H. Stacey is the bestselling psychological suspense author of over five novels. Alongside her writing she is a fulltime sales director for an office furniture company and has been a nurse, an emer-gency first response instructor and a PADI Staff Instructor. She lives near Doncaster with her husband.

Visit L.H. Stacey's website: http://www.lyndastacey.co.uk/

Follow L.H. Stacey on social media:

- facebook.com/Lyndastaceyauthor
- twitter.com/Lyndastacey
- instagram.com/lynda.stacey
- bookbub.com/authors/lynda-stacey

ABOUT BOLDWOOD BOOKS

Boldwood Books is a fiction publishing company seeking out the best stories from around the world.

Find out more at www.boldwoodbooks.com

Sign up to the Book and Tonic newsletter for news, offers and competitions from Boldwood Books!

http://www.bit.ly/bookandtonic

We'd love to hear from you, follow us on social media:

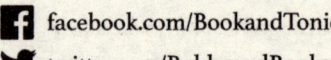
facebook.com/BookandTonic
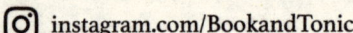
twitter.com/BoldwoodBooks
instagram.com/BookandTonic